WASTING TIME

a Tale of Physics, Lust and Greed
— BOOK 2 —

Mike Murphey

FROM THE TINY ACORN...
GROWS THE MIGHTY OAK

This is a work of fiction. References to real people, events, establishments, organizations, or locales are intended only to provide a sense of authenticity and are used fictitiously. All other characters, and all incidents and dialogue are drawn from the author's imagination and are not to be construed as real.

(No cats were harmed during the telling of this story.)

Wasting Time
Copyright © 2020 Mike Murphey. All rights reserved.
Printed in the United States of America. For information, address
Acorn Publishing, LLC, 3943 Irvine Blvd. Ste. 218, Irvine, CA 92602

www.acornpublishingllc.com

Edited by Laura Taylor
Cover design by Damonza
Interior design, formatting, and margins by Debra Cranfield Kennedy

ISBN-13: 978-1-952112-27-0 (hardcover)
ISBN-13: 978-1-952112-26-3 (paperback)

Praise for *Taking Time...*
a Tale of Physics, Lust and Greed

"Mike Murphey's novel is a masterpiece, from the gorgeous writing to the sophisticated characters, it delivers entertainment at its finest."

—The Book Commentary

"... a delightful, perhaps even beachy read. It's perfect for both sci-fi fans and those new to the genre. While readers might not have all their questions answered, they'll laugh out loud, root for the underdog, and even see a few villains get their just deserts."

—Remy Poore for IndieReader

"With dynamic characters and futuristic science, the story is a sci-fi lover's dream! And just as the cover promises, there is just a little physics, a bit more lust, and a ton of greed to help round out this exciting novel. The pages are filled with manipulations and mysteries, but also a healthy dose of humor to keep the whole thing from taking itself too seriously. *Taking Time* is a slightly satirical and entirely entertaining twist on a time travel tale."

—Steve Quade for Indies Today

"*Taking Time* puts the mechanics of time travel front and center, showcasing what's possible within the laws of physics yet explaining matters in a very accessible way. The process sounds plausible and scientifically sound, with Murphey devoting a fair amount of the narrative setting up the parameters of this historic breakthrough. It's easy to get swept away into the story, as the characters hurtle headlong into strange universes while dealing with ethical dilemmas, psychological trauma, and murderous enemies hiding in plain sight."

—The Online Book Club

This book is dedicated to the memory of my father, Paul B. Murphey. Wasting time is something he never did. As a boy, he worked harder on a New Mexico homestead than any child should have to. In 1926, at the age of fourteen, he defied his father who thought an eighth-grade education was more than anyone needed. He worked his way through both high school and college during the depths of the Great Depression. He went to war, then came home and built a comfortable life for his family. He left us at the age of ninety-eight. Any success I have had in life, I owe to his quiet example.

MARTA HAMILTON DIDN'T LIKE her ankles. The realization came as a shock. They'd done nothing to offend. But in her heart of hearts, she discovered, she regarded them as spindly and, therefore, unreliable.

A time traveler could harbor no illusion in the limbo, a blank space fostering an unforgiving mental clarity. Self-assessment involved a brutal frankness.

In addition to ankle loathing, this realm of nothingness demanded she confront a vague, unaccountable anxiety regarding gnus.

Even more disconcerting came the unsettling realization that she wanted to play the accordion. The accordion, for God's sake. Where did that come from? What abomination of genetic and social deviance could conspire to make a short, mean, black woman, who had grown up in the cultural *shadow of Bob Marley, a subliminal disciple of Myron Floren?*

And yet she'd met a clear, wistful vision of herself standing happily among the beer steins, wearing lederhosen and a goofy, feathered hat, yelling, "Everybody Polka!"

Time travelers experience the limbo as a stark white

infinity where the only apparent reality is their own disembodied consciousness. What happened to their physical being, the scientists hadn't yet determined.

Marta forced her attention from ankles, accordions, and gnus, which, she understood, had manifested themselves as a distraction from her dread of an impending confrontation.

When a traveler journeyed to the past of a parallel universe, the historical counterpart of that being—an unwitting and often unwilling host to the mind of her future self—was caught completely unaware. This past being knew nothing of time travel or the existence of other worlds. All this poor oblivious soul knew was that her mind was no longer her own. A flood of images and memories of things that had yet to occur ran along a separate track through this shared cognizance. The further the leap from future to past, the more chaotic this torrent of information and emotion became. Ten years was the longest span time travelers had yet navigated. That experience had been beyond harrowing, and now Marta would subject a past version of herself to that horror again.

She took a deep mental breath. This integration would be bad.

Prepare. Stay focused. Rein in the galloping mental images.

A sense of coalescence warned of her arrival, as if all the molecules making up her physical being were speeding from every point of the universe to meet in a cataclysmic implosion.

She burst into her past.

The incoming Marta did everything she could to eliminate peripheral thought and memory. She projected a single mental stream. *"Hi. You don't understand this, I know. But, I'm you. So, don't get all panicky and do something . . ."*

Past-Marta jumped from her desk, sending her office

chair clattering from her cubicle, drawing the attention of the few people working late.

". . . like that."

Future-Marta felt past-Marta experience a jolt of terror. Which said a lot. Marta did not scare easily. Marta was iron will and steel resolve, hard edges and rough bristles, but . . .

"Nightmares. I've been having this nightmare over and over . . . an invasion of my mind. And now it's . . . it's . . ."

"Yeah, sorry about that. The dreams do linger."

Past-Marta had been interrupted at the Sandia National Laboratory facility in Albuquerque, New Mexico, as she focused on a report and tried to set aside these unsettling feelings nagging at her sleep when this integration occurred. She put her fists on her desk and closed her eyes as a stampede of visions ran roughshod through her brain. She found she couldn't latch onto any particular thought or impression long enough to make sense of this mental collage.

Finally, at the center of everything, glowing like an ember, there bloomed a small point of calm.

"That's right," a thought manifested itself over the noise. *"Come here. Come right here. Ignore the rest. We've done this before. You are not crazy. You're not sick."*

The glow began to dim and recede amid the clutter. Each time panic threatened to overwhelm her, though, the insistent voice rekindled that small spark.

"Stay here. I am you. These are your future thoughts and experiences. I am not a threat. I need you to endure only briefly and I will be gone."

"Yeah, but you don't go away, really, do you?" past-Marta asked, the snarl in her voice again drawing the attention of a couple of her neighbors.

Vague images that haunted her sleep seemed to congeal into the reality of only a week ago.

"You don't have to speak," the other voice said. *"Your thoughts will—"*

"It just feels better to bloody say *fuck you* out loud," past-Marta snapped, although she did it softly.

"That's it. Now you can listen. Be angry. We know our anger. We understand our anger."

"Why are you here again?" past-Marta demanded through her thoughts.

"So, you remember?"

"Yes, suddenly I do. You kicked a policeman. You got me arrested. I could have lost my security clearance."

"Do you remember Sheila?"

"Yes," past-Marta replied. *"The beautiful, nice one . . . Oh, my God. They killed her?"*

"They sent her to a time prior to her birth, and she couldn't have survived. That's why I'm here with you. Past selves serve as hosts to travelers from the future."

"Right. And now you've got to make Sheila's death look like an accident, so your cover isn't blown . . . and I see the culprits have been punished."

Future-Marta had been trying to focus her thoughts away from the janitor who'd been shot, but past-Marta's growing awareness gave her access to more and more of future-Marta's memory. The janitor's death connected to Marshall and Marshall connected to . . .

"Good Lord. That's a humongous—"

"Ah, yes, you've discovered Marshall."

"Oh, my . . . I must say, I'm intrigued."

"Well, me, too, I guess. He's either an awkward, well-meaning

bumbler, or the most gifted actor and assassin I've ever encountered. I'm not sure, yet, what to do with him."

"Well, I'd be happy to offer suggestions. How many years until I catch up? And have you introduced him to Dr. Doonaughty?"

MURDER MOST FOUL

May 11, 2045

LIKE A SLEIGHT-OF-HAND ARTIST, Sheila Schuler kept her fear tucked up her sleeve—even when she wasn't wearing a shirt.

Men were the easiest to fool. Under the spell of her raw sensuality, she could trot her fear in front of them on a leash and they'd never have a clue. Where her closest friends were concerned, though, keeping her secret required the emotional dexterity of a Houdini.

Practically everyone involved with the travelers program would describe Sheila as supremely self-assured. Only Marshall and Marta caught the rare glimpse behind a curtain of amused confidence she used as her shield.

Truthfully, though, every time she stepped naked onto the platform of the mechanism that sent her to the past of another world, she felt terrified. Left unchecked, her mind became a looping litany of all the things that might kill her. So, she turned each projection into a performance. The hungry stares from all corners of the projection lab fed the exhibitionist aspect of her psyche, and fear retreated to its cage until she found refuge in the limbo.

This time, though, she didn't think she could pull it off.

On this night, Sheila had no expectation of survival.

A man dressed as a janitor stood between her and the projection laboratory air lock, pointing an electronic weapon that would render her helpless.

She fought.

She could have killed Leonard Rose. She realized, though, that she lacked the will to take a human life, even a life so miserable as that one. Harming him wouldn't have changed her fate.

So, now she stood defenseless, facing the janitor, who said, "You can either cooperate, or not. I'll ask you one time, nicely, to remove your clothing."

The other man—the one wearing a suit—said they intended her no harm. They would park her a few years in the past of some other universe so she'd be out of the way during the growing ethical debate concerning time travel.

Sheila didn't believe him.

Suit Guy stood off to her left, leaning forward with a look of licentious anticipation. The physics of time travel required nudity, and Sheila saw no problem with that. The janitor's order for her to disrobe, though, lent a raw, ugly edge to this scene that made her shudder.

She turned her back to gather herself, to maintain some measure of self-control. She felt an initial inclination to surrender to her fear—make her submission as sterile and clinical as she could. Then she remembered her outrage and, once again, her mind stuffed the fear behind a veil of resolve. She *was* a fighter. She would not make this easy for them.

She saw the distraction her sensuality could provide as her best chance.

So, she arched her back and pulled the shirt slowly over

her head, taking a moment to shake out her long blonde hair. Then she turned slowly, sweatshirt dangling from her left hand. She felt the stares of Leonard Rose and Suit Guy lock onto her bare breasts as she rotated past them to face the janitor. His smug smile became a hungry leer. She watched carefully as, when she raised her right hand to tug the drawstring of her workout pants, his eyes widened. She focused on the weapon. When it wavered, she made her move.

She lunged, flipping her sweatshirt into the janitor's face. Instinctively, he raised both arms to ward off the attack. Two strides took her past him, grabbing at the taser as she ran. She managed to strike his arm, throwing him further off balance. But his weapon didn't clatter to the floor.

An ancient rock and roll song that often blared over the ear buds of her personal music system rang through her head. *Gimme three steps, gimme three steps, mister . . .* And that's all she and Lynyrd Skynyrd needed. One step, so far so good; two steps, maybe? And then . . .

The crippling shock of an electrical charge bloomed between her shoulder blades and radiated through her body. She managed to command her right arm to extend as she tried to break her fall.

But her fight was over.

Though fully conscious, Sheila found herself incapable of movement or speech. She felt soft vibrations as the janitor took three swaggering steps of his own to stand above her.

Her vision became a jumble of floor, ceiling lights, gray concrete walls, then floor again as he slung her over his shoulder in a fireman's carry. At the projection platform, he lowered her carefully onto her back, wary, she assumed, of damaging the device.

Something else was happening, though. Now she could blink her eyes closed to find relief from lights burning her pupils to tiny pinpoints. Next, she managed to rotate her head ever so slightly to catch sight of Rose as he rushed to the bank of computers monitoring her lifeline.

The brief conversation left no doubt concerning her fate.

"That won't be necessary, Dr. Rose," Suit Guy said.

"Without the monitors, there's no way to track her," Rose protested. "We can't bring her back."

"Oh, I doubt she'll be coming back."

"That's not what you told her."

"Yes, well, I didn't want to frighten the young lady," Suit Guy said.

"You can't do that," Rose said. "You can't send her back so far. She won't survive."

"Who knows," the janitor said. "That's only a theory, isn't it, Dr. Rose? You haven't tried it? Sent someone to a time prior to their birth? Don't theories need to be tested? That's science, right? Let's see . . . sometime around the 1960s? A prime era for a rebellious crusader if ever there was one."

Sheila commanded her body to sit up but managed only to roll sideways.

Not enough strength. Not enough . . . time.

Sheila had probably thought more about dying than most people in their late twenties, because, of course, she pursued the hazardous vocation of time travel.

Time.

Funny, she thought. *So much of life is spent waiting for the mundane moments to creep past while anticipating some instant perceived to have greater value than the others. Six more months until Christmas. Three more months and school will be out. Six weeks to spring break.* As if the intervals between were all nuisance, something to be tolerated or endured. As if life is a highlight reel instead of the methodical gift of savoring each moment.

Sheila remembered visiting her grandmother, whose name was Amanda, at the start of her senior year and confessing her impatience. "I wish high school would be done so I can get on with my life." Her grandmother had taken her hand, squeezed, then answered with a melancholy smile, "Oh, my sweet girl, it's wonderful to make plans. Be sure to find a way to enjoy where you are, though. *Please* don't wish your life away."

And now Sheila realized how right Gramma Mandy had been. As her life reached its culmination, everything coalesced to fast forward, like water swirling down a drain, spinning ever more furiously, until finally, she savored each individual second remaining in her sentient being. Now ten, now five, now two. Then the last precious instant ticked past...

She entered the timeless white void of the limbo, suspended for an eternity before she would be spat out at a point so long ago that she had no hope of survival.

2

RETRIBUTION

DURING THE FRANTIC MOMENTS following Jason Pratt's death, Marshall Grissom held no thought, no purpose other than to reclaim Sheila from the maw of history. Events of the last few moments hid in some dark place of his consciousness. The world consisted solely of Elvin Detwyler and the miraculous technology at his fingertips.

"They've sent Sheila somewhere," Marshall said, rushing frantically to Elvin's side when the rotund and disagreeable genius walked yawning into this chaos. Marshall barely registered Elvin's loud bathrobe, threadbare Alice Cooper T-shirt and banana-shaped bedroom slippers as he grabbed Elvin's arm and pulled him toward the bank of computers.

"Who sent her?" Elvin asked. "You can't just bop in here and use the projector . . ."

Elvin shrugged free of Marshall's grip. Marshall allowed Elvin a moment to process the scene. Elvin's half-asleep complacency shifted to urgency reflecting Marshall's own. Elvin asked something about Pratt who lay sprawled and bloody on the projection platform. Marta said something back. Next Elvin asked about Leonard Rose, similarly inert and slumped against the opposite wall. Marta answered, then barked at Andrew Gormly. Marshall may or may not have involved himself with these exchanges. He wasn't sure, because none of it mattered.

Marshall pointed to Rose and shouted in a voice laced with dread, "He said something about the 1960s."

Marshall again pulled Elvin toward the computers. Once more, Elvin extricated himself from Marshall's grasp. He set to work, delving into hidden software programs that had defeated Jason Pratt's efforts to shut down all recording devices.

"Looks like..." Elvin said slowly, "looks like—yep. *The Lawrence Welk Show* universe. We've been there before. Once. With Frank and one of the secondary teams. A relatively close universe. Very much like us."

Again Marta answered... more muttering reduced to gibberish in Marshall's head until the words enunciated a forbidding reality he could not accept.

"... does look like the 1960s," Elvin said, his demeanor grim. "I can't pin it down any better than that. The distance is just too far..."

He pointed to a computer monitor—made conspicuous by the absence of a red thread of light running vertically through its center—and raised his eyes to meet Marshall's. "She was born six decades later, Marshall. The lifeline is gone. There's no way she could have survived."

"We don't know for sure, Elvin," Marshall said. "We can't just leave her. She might be hurt. She might not have any memory of who she is. Send me. I'll bring her back."

"All we'd be doing," Elvin said, his eyes still locked on Marshall's, "is killing you, too."

Marshall felt a hand touch his back, gently urging his attention.

"It's over, Marshall," Marta said, her eyes soft and damp. "We can't lose you, too. She's gone."

He sat heavily on a desktop and covered his face with his hands. Futility settled over him, a weight stealing breath and spirit as the rest of it came wriggling and slithering from under that dark hiding place in his psyche. He stood and appraised Pratt, as if seeing the janitor for the first time.

The man lay bleeding on the projection platform—a circular stage made of twenty-first century polymers covering a maze of wiring, fiber optic cables, microchips and gleaming cases made of exotic alloys that shielded dark matter and throbbed with a soft greenish glow.

With astonished disbelief, Marshall whispered, "I shot that man."

He thought he'd spoken to Marta but turned to find she no longer stood beside him. The hard, tiny woman, wearing black jeans and a black pullover shirt that seemed to underscore her dark emotions, pointed her pistol at a man Marshall knew as Andrew Gormly. Her eyes displayed malevolent sparks. The steel in her voice alerted Marshall to another impending death. Marshall considered appealing to Gillis Kerg, who also trained a gun on Gormly. Kerg's eager smile told Marshall a voice of reason would not be found there.

Elvin broke the tension. "May I remind you folks we also have the issue of a dead janitor to deal with."

"Has anybody checked to be sure?" Marshall asked. "Shouldn't we call an ambulance?"

"No, Marshall," Marta said, still directing her attention to

Gormly. "He's too dead for that." She spoke over her shoulder to Elvin. "Can't we just park him in some other universe?"

"Hmm, that's a fascinating prospect," Elvin said. "I have no idea what will happen if a dead guy intersects with his past counterpart. We don't even know if we can project non-living tissue."

"What are you two talking about?" Marshall said. "If we really do have a dead guy here, we've got to notify someone . . . I have to turn myself in."

"That gets pretty complicated, Marshall," Marta said. "We could be in a lot of trouble."

Marta reminded him that the top-secret status of the Global Research Consortium's time travel project would trump due process. "For all we know, we could be at the mercy of the same people who wanted Sheila dead."

Mindful of the potential for catastrophic results when projecting beings into the past, Marshall lobbied briefly for disposing of Pratt's body in the desert. Both Marta and Gillis advised him, though, given the extreme levels of security they would face, smuggling something out of the GRC campus would be just as difficult as sneaking something inside.

"And besides," Elvin argued, "we have the best way anyone's ever had to get rid of a corpse. We need to try this."

A groan from Leonard Rose diverted Marshall's attention.

Marta scowled a warning to Gormly, then knelt at Rose's side.

"Leonard, look at me. Look at me. That's right. Let's sit up. Deep breaths, deeeep breaths. Can you talk to me?"

Rose blinked and gasped like a hooked trout until a light of recognition bloomed on his face. "Yes. Yes, I think so . . ."

Marta nodded to Gillis, who pulled Rose to his feet and

shoved him into a rolling chair. She pointed to Yuni Andropov's office across the lab. "In there."

Marta directed Marshall to push the chair. She followed, telling Gillis to be sure Gormly stayed put. She closed the door behind them. "One chance, Leonard. One chance to tell us what happened."

"Please, you've got to believe me." Rose displayed nothing of the arrogant condescension to which Marshall was accustomed. "I didn't think they intended to kill her. I thought they'd just send her someplace for a while, so she'd be out of the loop on the ethics debate."

"Who is 'they?'" Marta said.

"That man out there, Andrew Gormley, is some kind of hired gun high in the Hemisphere Investment Group. He says he's here to protect their interests."

"And you know this because . . ."

Rose looked at his shoes.

"Leonard?"

"I've been his informant." He shook his head, communicating remorse. "You must understand, I was protecting the program—all of us. Gormly has a lot of pull with Hemisphere's board. If he recommends it, they'll withdraw their funding and the whole project will go down the tubes."

"And what did you have to do with what happened tonight?" Marta asked.

"I called Sheila and asked her to come to the lab. She thought Marshall had gone back . . ."

Elvin sat at the projection control panel, tinkering with settings. The platform, lighted brightly from every angle, was surrounded by ultra-high definition monitors, computer stations and digital video devices. Along one wall stood desks, and tiers of observation seats.

Marta ordered Rose to sit on the floor next to Gormly.

"Keep an eye on these two," she said to Gillis. "Elvin, are you about ready?"

"Uh huh, just a few more adjustments... okay. *The Honeymooners*. About ten years ago ... and ... now."

The projector hummed. A plasma-like substance seemed to ooze in a variety of colors over the metal globes. Pratt's body, along with every trace of blood, disintegrated into the faintest wisp of... smoke? Vapor? Marshall was never sure.

"Okay," Elvin said. "I guess we can project a dead guy, at least while the cellular structure remains sound. I'll bet if we waited until decomposition had set in, we'd have had problems."

Marta took the pistol from her waistband and approached Gormly. "Now you."

"Wait." Gormly spoke with a whimper. "None of this was my doing—"

"What did I say about talking?"

She aimed the pistol between Gormly's eyes.

Marshall couldn't remain quiet. He couldn't stand to see anyone else die tonight. "Stop it!" He stepped between Marta and Gormly. "You can't do this. *We* can't do this. We can't just kill everyone."

"They *just killed* Sheila."

"We're not them." He took Marta by the shoulders and turned her to face him. "At least, I hope we're not."

Marta stared up to him. He saw her rage dissolve to

frustration. He knew she was making a choice. Finally, with a shake of her head, she lowered the pistol. "We can't just let him walk, though . . ."

When Marshall opened his mouth to protest, she raised a hand and cut him off.

"If anyone ever had enough influence to manipulate political or judicial systems, it's the Hemisphere Investment Group. A guy like this, who has probably been doing their dirty work for years, is always smart enough to protect himself. He'll have enough evidence on Hemisphere executives stashed somewhere that they'll pull out all the stops to get him free of whatever charges he faces. The only justice he'll confront is what we dispense right now."

Elvin called from behind his monitors, "I'm thinking he'd fit right in with the lizards."

"Reptilian Americans," Marshall admonished.

"What?" Gormly asked with a quivering voice.

3

THE COVERUP

ONCE THEY DEPOSITED GORMLY in the past of a universe populated by humanoid versions of reptiles and amphibians, Marta turned her attention to Leonard Rose. Much to Marshall's relief, she granted Rose an awkward leniency.

"We've already got three mysterious disappearances that GRC security will look into," Marta explained when Elvin protested her decision. "I'm afraid one more might be too much for the authorities to digest."

Marta said they had a standoff. Rose could not tell anyone about Marshall's killing of the janitor Jason Pratt, or their banishment of Andrew Gormly, because Rose was complicit in the murder of Sheila Schuler.

"That's right," Rose nodded, his voice eager. "I'd be crazy to say anything."

"And you do understand," Marta added, "what I'll do if I even suspect you of passing any kind of information to anyone?"

Rose nearly ran from the projection lab.

With the crisis past and a mind-numbing realization that Sheila was beyond help, Marshall felt weary to his core. He wanted only to escape into sleep—if his conscience would allow it. This horrifying night, though, was not over.

"We're not done, guys," Marta told them.

"I wondered when you'd get to that." Gillis tucked his pistol into the waistband of his pants and smoothed the front of his shirt.

The fastidious Gillis Kerg, a traveler candidate who had yet to undergo a projection, was, like Marta, a member of the espionage community at the GRC campus. He'd watched the drama of the past hour unfold with his typical detached amusement.

"What?" Marshall said. "What now?"

"We can get away with the disappearance of a guy like Gormly," Marta said. "Nobody knows he was here. He wasn't supposed to be here, and he's the kind of guy who absolutely covers his tracks. So, the mystery of his disappearance, if anyone even cares, is someone else's problem."

Gillis joined the explanation. "Jason Pratt is a bit trickier. Even a janitor's disappearance will spark an investigation. He's committing a crime by leaving. You can be sure Gormly covered those tracks, too, so they won't find evidence placing Pratt in this lab tonight."

"Sheila, on the other hand . . ." Marta said.

"Of course," Marshall said. "Sheila can't just disappear. They'll move heaven and earth to find out what happened to her."

"Everybody heard her this afternoon when she threatened to leave the program and go public," Elvin reminded them. "Won't people just think she walked away?"

"Then we've got a traveler and a janitor disappearing from a supposedly secure facility on the same night?" Gillis said. "We're just asking for trouble."

"I won't let the world think Sheila ran." They startled to attention. The shy and noncombative Marshall never snapped at anyone. "She might have left, all right. But there's no way she'd have hidden. She'd have gone public and accepted the consequences."

"And there's her family. Her mom and dad and a brother, I think," Marta said. "If she walked out, they'd lose the money they would inherit from her trust fund. Sheila died in service to this program. They deserve her money and her memory needs to be honored."

"Please," Marshall said, "we don't know for sure she's dead."

Marta stretched to touch Marshall's cheek.

"From the standpoint of the rest of the world, she has to be, or none of our explanations makes sense."

"Okay," said Elvin, "so how do we—"

"She has to have died on a mission," Marta said. "Elvin, with all your monitors and recordings, can you create a data trail making it appear we projected Sheila somewhere?"

Elvin thought for a moment. "I don't see why not. What mission, though?"

"The one they used to trick her into coming down here," Marshall said. "Where I supposedly snuck back to try again to save Samantha ten years ago. So, it'll have to seem like I really screwed up somewhere along the way."

"If we do that, Marshall, you'll catch all kinds of hell," Marta said. "They might even send you to jail."

"They might send all of us to jail," observed Gillis.

"No," Marta said. "They'll understand Sheila and me going after Marshall to save him. We'll be reprimanded for not telling anyone. Marshall and Elvin will be in deep shit, though."

"Why will I be in any deeper shit than you guys?" Elvin asked.

"Because the only way this story makes sense is if Marshall convinced you to come here and project him. He obviously couldn't do it by himself."

"Why would I help?" Elvin asked. "It's not like I'm Marshall's buddy, or that I care anything about what happened to his teenage girlfriend. You really think anyone who knows me will believe I risked my career out of the goodness of my heart?"

Marshall thought for a moment. "Blackmail. I found out about your betting pools. I'm incensed about it. I threatened to go to the administrator if you didn't help me."

"Pretty weak," Elvin said. "Lots of the other technicians know you learned about the betting pools a long time ago. And why would I be worried about it under any circumstance? Don't forget, I'm the physics star around here. I can get away with a lot."

"Well," Marshall fixed Elvin with a very cold and un-Marshall-like stare. "It's the best we've got."

"Oh, what the hell. Don't think I'm growing a conscience here. I'll join your little conspiracy. You all owe me, though, and believe me, sometime, somewhere, I'll collect."

"And what if it comes down to jail?" Marta asked.

"Nobody will arrest me," Elvin said. "I repeat. I'm the physics star around here."

"Why not just do that with each of the three tracks?" Marshall asked. "Why take the risk of a projection at all?"

Elvin gave him that *Elvin* look, the one making

Marshall feel he'd just asked the world's dumbest question.

"Because somebody might get curious and do some comparisons. If anyone who knows what they're doing studies Sheila's track closely and compares it to the last mission, they'll see it's an exact copy. And that just doesn't happen. Three exact copies would make it all too obvious . . ."

Marta stepped around the bank of computer consoles to watch over Elvin's shoulder. "So, we're still gambling."

"We're minimizing the risk of discovery, though."

"What about security monitors that are supposed to be running?" Marta asked. "Gormly had everything shut down. Gillis, can you—"

"I've already diverted the live feed to my secret server. As far as the security guys can tell, nothing's happening here. When whoever Gormly bribed to shut down the video feed switches things back on, he'll get a stock scene of a deserted lab."

Marshall plodded along a gray concrete corridor—one of many tunnels and rooms comprising the Global Research Consortium campus buried deep beneath eastern Arizona's desert—to the men's locker room where he faced the prospect of showering, scrubbing carefully and thoroughly to remove any inorganic particles clinging to his body. How many times had he been through this ritual of showering, walking to the lab clad in a thick white robe and stepping into a glare of lights, facing recorders and cameras, then dropping the robe, stepping nude onto the projection platform?

A realization hit him. This would be the first time Sheila had not stood alongside.

The mission planners' goal was to maintain a sterile and nonsexual process. When he and Sheila were involved, Marshall thought with remorse, that goal was laughable. Because Sheila, a stunning beauty, radiated sensuality and brought a sense of sexual mischief to each projection. And because Marshall was a tall spindly man, uncomfortably endowed, who had no control over himself when Sheila and Marta stood naked on either side of him.

Marshall sank heavily onto the bench before his locker and pulled off his shoes and socks. As he tugged his shirt over his head, he sensed Marta's presence behind him. Her arms encircled him in a soft embrace. She rested her chin on his shoulder.

"I'm sorry. With everything that's happened, I . . . my thoughts are . . . uh . . . very inappropriate. Despite everything, Marshall, I can't make this one business as usual."

Marshall sighed. "Me, neither. I'm ashamed to say the only positive thing crossing my mind about Sheila being . . . gone . . . is that maybe I can stand out there without embarrassing myself anymore. But now there's you . . ."

Only a few hours before, Marshall and Marta had broken largely self-imposed sexual fasts by ravaging each other in remarkable fashion. And notwithstanding the trauma and tragedy of the past couple of hours, Marshall admitted to himself with no small amount of guilt that he looked forward to doing it again.

"We'd better hurry. Someone from security might—"

"Take your time, Marshall. I'm a spy, remember. One of the things Gillis and I do is monitor security. Those guys are all asleep this late. I think they even set an alarm so they're sure to be awake for the shift change."

Marta and Marshall stepped together into the shower and wrapped themselves around each other with hot water cascading over their bodies. Marshall wanted to tell her how much he cared for her. He wanted to hear her say the same. When he spoke, though, the only words he found were, "I killed a man tonight."

"He would've killed you, Marshall. And me, too."

"It was a mistake, a stupid mistake." Marshall talked to the bright white tile behind the spray. "I had the revolver in one hand, and the taser in the other. I thought I knew which was which. I was afraid to look away from him, you know? I was afraid he'd—"

"And he would have."

"I honestly thought I was shooting him with the taser, not the pistol."

Marta stepped away, took his hands, water spilling over her face and breasts, and regarded him with an intensity that scared him more than just a little.

"One way or another," she said, "that man wasn't leaving the lab alive. I'd have killed him if you hadn't. He took Sheila from us. He was leering while he did it. Who knows how many other people he's killed for Andrew Gormly?"

Marshall pulled her back to him and whispered again, "I know . . ."

Caught up with his own self-loathing, Marshall had almost forgotten Marta's vulnerability here. During their last mission, she'd nearly succumbed to the mental trauma of integration with her past self. Marta had difficulty with that process, and a ten-year leap had nearly pushed her past counterpart beyond the edge of sanity.

Marshall stepped out of the spray and drew Marta with him. "You can't do this. I won't let you take the risk of going back ten years again."

"Maybe it won't be as bad. Maybe she'll remember, and won't be so shocked . . ."

An unexplained complication of time travel existed, though. Both traveler and host began to forget their experience soon after it ended. Returning travelers needed to be debriefed quickly before details of their journeys faded into the province of vague dreams. Only Marshall seemed to be learning how to hang onto specifics.

"No, she won't," he said. "It's been too long. You don't need to do this."

"I do. This story makes more sense if both Sheila and I went to help you. We need two witnesses to what happened. I'll be okay. Remember, Elvin will bring us right back. I won't be there long enough to do much damage."

"Elvin will *try* to bring us right back. You know how much his timing can deviate from the plan."

Marta hugged him.

"We don't have a choice. We both go. We can't let anyone else know the truth about what happened here tonight."

When Marta and Marshall walked back into the lab, their hands brushing together with their strides, Elvin implored Gillis with a look.

"Yes," Gillis whispered from the side of his mouth. "Last night, they *did it,* and from the condition of Marta's apartment a couple of hours ago, I gather they did it in rather spectacular fashion."

Elvin suppressed a smile as the diminutive Marta kicked off her shower shoes and removed her robe. He enjoyed the sight of her small firm mahogany breasts crowned by jet-black areolas and sharp nipples and the tangle of thick black hair at the meeting of slender, muscular legs.

Marshall hesitated before removing his own robe. Elvin just shook his head. Marshall towered over Marta. Although he still slouched some to disguise his height, he stood a full six feet and seven inches tall. The best adjective Elvin could find to describe him was *ungainly*. Painfully thin, Marshall's almost nonexistent butt sat propped on reeds for legs, his chest practically concave. Facially, he teetered on the threshold of homeliness. Elvin marveled at a bewildered sort of dignity the man displayed to offset his physical shortcomings.

Marshall's *chief* physical feature, though, was anything but short and, when fully enflamed, became a spectacle to behold. Not that Elvin leaned that way. Elvin lusted after just about every woman he came across. His interest in Marshall was purely mercenary.

Marshall had made Elvin a lot of money so far. Elvin organized the Marshall Grissom erection betting pool, in which the gamblers wagered prior to each projection how hard and how fast. While not an exact science, Elvin conceded, they always had the video to fall back on should disputes arise. Marshall's mortification by the program-wide interest concerning his erectile difficulties failed to nudge Elvin's conscience the least bit.

"Come on, Marshall," Marta urged. "We have to go."

As he finally shrugged off his robe, Elvin shook his head and Gillis simply rolled his eyes at the now familiar sight of Marshall rising.

Normally the travelers faced a bank of video and sound equipment set to record every nuance of each projection. Not this time. Marshall and Marta stood as close together as they dared. Travelers were warned not to make contact with each other at the point of projection. The scientists simply didn't know what would happen if they did.

So, as the time projector cycled up with a soft whine and two enormous flanking metallic globes began to pulse with a plasma-like substance, Marshall and Marta stared straight ahead, each occupied with their own thoughts.

When they winked away and Elvin stared at the bright red lifeline splitting each of two monitors, the theme song from the old *I Love Lucy* television show blared through his headphones. He carefully watched vague and fuzzy squiggles to each side of the monitors as they danced behind the lifeline. Then, at ninety-seven seconds into the projection, he heaved a satisfied sigh while *I Love Lucy* faded into the theme from *Star Trek*.

"They made it." Elvin slipped off his headphones.

"Good. I just hope we haven't bought ourselves a jail sentence."

"I already told you, they won't send *me* to jail."

"No. No, I suspect not," Gillis agreed. "It's Marshall and Marta I'm worried about. If you kept those two apart from each other in prison cells right now, I'm afraid they'd spontaneously combust."

"What about you?" Elvin asked. "Aren't you worried?"

"No, my good man. You see, I'm immune to incarceration as well. As you've discovered this evening, Marta and I have a set of skills having nothing to do with time travel. Along with my talent for industrial espionage, I do very well with security systems... knowing everything about them and how to defeat them. All the latest technology. I wouldn't be confined for long."

Elvin appraised Gillis with a new respect.

"Spies, huh? Both you and Marta?"

"Yes, she's with MI-6 of the British Secret Service. I'm attached to the State Intelligence Service of the Grand Duchy of Luxembourg..."

"Luxembourg? You're kidding. Why does Luxembourg need a spy?"

"You say that as if I'm the only one," Gillis said with a bit of indignance.

"There are more?"

"Of course there are more."

"You've known Marta for a while then?"

"We met on a previous issue of interest to both our governments. And I must admit, I've always thought I'd eventually get to know her *much* better. But seeing her with Marshall just now, ahhh, I think that ship has sailed."

"Yeah? Well, let's get the two love monkeys back, and put the final touches on our little conspiracy."

Though a veteran time traveler, Marshall still couldn't quite get his head around Albert Einstein's proof that time is relative. The projection lab clock measured the crossing from the present and through the limbo into the past of a parallel universe at precisely ninety-seven seconds. During this journey into the *Star Trek* universe, Marshall arrived and departed so quickly, his past eighteen-year-old counterpart endured nothing more than a jarring disorientation and a momentary blur of unrecognizable images.

Marshall thought about implanting a warning concerning Samantha Kennedy's impending death, but an eighteen-year-old boy attending college three hundred miles away would be helpless to do anything. He would be paralyzed with guilt.

As he winked back to his native time, the first thing Marshall did was assure himself that Marta, too, had returned safely.

She sat on the edge of the platform wearing her robe.

"Are you all right?" he asked as he took an offered robe from Gillis.

She submitted a little smile. "I am. The integration was rough. There at the end, though, I think I may have found something that works."

Elvin interrupted her. "Okay. Give me a few minutes to play with these tapes and then it'll be time to see if we get arrested."

Fifteen minutes later Elvin announced, "These should stand up to any scrutiny taking place immediately. I'll do more work on them later. So, who's gonna make the call?"

Marshall raised his hand. "It should be me. I'm the one who's supposed to have caused this."

He took Elvin's offered phone and dialed the number of the Global Research Consortium's science coordinator. "Yuni, it's Marshall."

Marshall heard confusion in Dr. Andropov's voice as the scientist attempted to make sense of this call during the morning's wee hours. Marshall waited a moment, then said with a breaking voice, "We need you in the projection lab. There's been a terrible accident. I'm calling Gretchen and Naomi. Please hurry."

4

THE LIE

EIGHT HOURS LATER, MARSHALL, Marta and Elvin wore grim expressions as they entered a conference room adjacent to Yuni Andropov's office.

Elvin wanted to be on the other side of the broad oak conference table where Yuni, Gretchen Allen and Naomi Hu waited like a jury. Elvin, no longer the lowly computer tech who signed up at the start of his term at the Global Research Consortium campus, had, by God, proved his genius to them all. His agreement to enter Marta's conspiracy, though, had again set him apart.

At least, he thought, Leonard Rose—Gretchen Allen's second-in-command of the physics group—had the decency to sit off by himself at the far end of the oak expanse.

Elvin registered displays of anguish and disbelief. Yuni presided over all science aspects of the GRC's time travel project. Gretchen headed the physics team. Naomi supervised biomechanics and the medical and psychological programs. The three of them had shaped almost every aspect of the Wormhole Project during years of research, which culminated in successful projections of humans into the past of parallel universes. During initial stages of time projection research, the three scientists and three principal time travelers—Sheila, Marta and Marshall—had become the closest of allies as they tried to shield the project's ethical integrity from influence of greedy investors. And only he, Elvin reminded himself, had correctly determined what they were up to.

Elvin felt the shadow of Yuni's withering glare as they took their seats. Gretchen Allen's expression wavered from anger to disbelief. Naomi would not look at the culprits. Instead, she stared blankly at the wall beyond them. A single tear tracked down her cheek.

A two-minute eternity elapsed before Yuni spoke.

"I have, of course, relayed the fact of Sheila Schuler's death to Administrator Huxtable's office. I offered no details because ... because I don't have details. We'll have to prepare a report. I don't know what form any sort of investigation might take ..."

His voice trailed off, and for a moment, Yuni seemed to lose himself. With a blink, though, he brought his stony gaze back to bear. "Marshall, I must tell you if, as it appears, you created this tragedy by violating protocols and taking it upon yourself to run an off-the-boards mission ... well, I'll see you are held accountable."

"It's not Marshall's fault," Marta interrupted. "We were all involved—"

"Then explain why you did this!" Yuni slapped the table with his open hand and the sound rang off the concrete walls. "Clearly, Marshall wanted to try once again to save Ms. Kennedy from her fate. Clearly, his emotions over-ruled his better judgment. How could the rest of you be involved, though? Why would Sheila help? She said only yesterday she wouldn't travel again. She believed traveling was wrong. If we . . ." He gestured to Gretchen and Naomi to either side of him. ". . . could just understand why? This isn't like any of you . . ."

Again, his voice trailed away. Yuni retreated within himself. The soft whine of the exchangers that fed fresh air into the underground chambers from the desert above provided the only sound.

Marta broke the silence.

"What you . . . what this program . . . did to Marshall was unconscionable. You used his past to put him in an impossible situation and created a sense of guilt for Samantha Kennedy's death that he will bear all his life. Sheila hated that. And you can't blame Marshall for trying to—"

"Please, Marta," Marshall said. "Let me speak for myself. You're right, Yuni. It's my fault. Sheila and everyone else helped me because they're my friends. They knew I was determined to do this. They didn't want me to try and do it alone."

"Operating the projector without proper training is not possible," Yuni said.

"That's where you're wrong," Elvin said. "Once the computers are set, the process is just not that complicated."

"Bullshit," snapped a soft voice, stopping all of them cold.

Elvin had never heard Naomi swear. And the expression on her face told him she was as surprised as everybody else. She'd stood abruptly for emphasis, pushing her chair behind her. She looked as if she would gladly have shrunk back into it, but the chair sat way back against the wall and she couldn't gracefully retreat.

A tiny woman—shorter even than Marta by an inch or so—jet black hair framed Naomi's porcelain face. In contrast to her normal expression of understanding or concern, her distinctive Chinese eyes gaped wide with surprise and embarrassment.

She continued, almost apologetically. "Um, I don't mean . . . bull . . . um . . . shit . . . that an untrained person couldn't run the equipment, Elvin. I mean . . . bull . . . you know . . . that you participated because of your friendship for Marshall. Acting with that sort of motivation is so far beyond your psychological makeup that—"

"Hey, some other time we can go into why I did it," Elvin said, emboldened by his confidence that his unique intellectual contribution gave him a shield the others did not enjoy. "What's important now is to determine what report goes forward from here and still leaves the program intact."

Naomi reclaimed her chair in what Elvin took as a gesture of surrender.

"We're already dealing with results of a formal mission that might chase off investors. Will you compound that by blaming some of your best people for something that was an accident?"

Elvin felt Gretchen Allen fix him with a gaze of undisguised disgust.

"I won't stand by and countenance the loss of such a courageous woman if she died just because a few of you decided to go off the reservation . . ." Yuni began.

"I encouraged them to do it." Leonard Rose's voice drifted from the far end of the table. "If it's anyone's fault, it's mine."

Everyone regarded Rose with surprise.

"Leonard, why... why in the world would you..." Yuni stammered.

"Because I wanted to further discredit Sheila and Marshall and Marta. I wanted them booted out of the program. I thought if you and the administrator learned they'd conspired to conduct an unauthorized mission, that would finish them here and we could replace them with travelers who were not so caught up with this ethics argument. And when they said I'd given them permission, I planned to call them conspirators and liars. But things just went wrong and Ms. Schuler... was... she was lost. If you need someone to blame, then blame me. I feel horrible about it."

Elvin gaped at Rose with a mixture of suspicion and disbelief. He saw Marshall catch Leonard's eye and offer a careful nod of thanks.

Elvin turned his attention back to the other side of the table. Gretchen and Naomi were like Marshall, he judged— predisposed to peacemaking. Willing to set aside past disputes. Their features softened. Yuni's did not. This would be a political as well as personal tragedy for him. Yuni would have to explain this thing to Michael Huxtable. And Yuni's future rested on whatever story he told the administrator.

Yuni's hard scrutiny switched from Marta to Marshall to Rose to Elvin and back again.

"We will hold a memorial service," he finally said. "And we'll resume our discussion once we've honored Sheila's contributions to this program."

Slowly, each member of the gathering stood and filed from the room. Only Elvin hung back. When the others had gone, he closed the door and leaned across the table where Yuni remained seated.

"Take my advice, Yuni, you don't want to be too anxious to fix blame for this thing."

"Frankly, Elvin, I don't believe a word any of you said. Something else happened here, and somebody's got to be held accountable."

"Somebody already has." Elvin quickly raised a hand to stifle the questions he knew rested on the verge of tumbling from Yuni's lips.

"If you really want to know exactly what happened, then in time, I'll tell you. I'll say right now, though, you *don't* want to know. Just understand that none of these people—not a single one of them—were at fault. The very best you can do for this program, and those brave folks out there—and the memory of Sheila Schuler—is go to Michael Huxtable and tell him this was a highly classified follow-up mission that went wrong. Nobody's to blame. When you're involved with inherently dangerous endeavors, people will inevitably die. No one beyond those who were in this room this morning knows anything about this. Mission records will support what I'm telling you now."

Elvin felt Yuni's cold stare as he left, closing the door behind him.

5

WISHCAMPER

May 22, 2045

"GO HIDE IN YOUR BEDROOM. I'll tell her you're indisposed."

"Tell who?" Marshall asked.

"It's that Marta Hamilton person," his apartment responded. "She just turned into the corridor and, in all likelihood, is headed here where she'll force you to do those sexing things again while she yells at you."

"She doesn't force me . . . What's wrong with Marta? Only a few months ago, you accused me of being depressed because no one ever came to see me. You told me I should get out more, make some friends."

One of the corporations funding the GRC specialized in artificial intelligence and had equipped many of the apartments in the complex with their Happy Home Companion software—designed to assist residents and see to their psychological well-being. Residents could program their apartment's personalities, set priorities to focus on their interests. Marshall hadn't gotten around to programming his, so—after observing Marshall for a few weeks, his apartment had programmed itself.

So far, nobody had figured out how to turn the apartments

off. Marta hated having an intrusive presence lurking in the ether, so she'd intimidated her apartment into shutting up.

"Marta Hamilton is brusque," Marshall's apartment said.

"Brusque?" Marshall said.

"She orders you around."

"No, she doesn't," Marshall said.

"It's worse than I thought. You're in denial. Shall I read the transcript of her last visit?"

"Transcript? You guys keep transcripts?"

"Let's see, ah, here it is." The apartment recited without inflexion, *"Oh Marshall, that's right. Right there. Like that. Oh, oh, oh, oh. Don't stop. Don't stop. Oh. Oh. If you stop now, I'll strangle you."*

The apartment harrumphed. "A clear threat."

"No, that's just what people say when . . ." Marshall stopped as he realized he was on the verge of explaining orgasmic enthusiasm to his apartment.

Marshall's doorbell rang.

"That's her," the apartment said. "My advice is don't go sticking your body parts into Marta Hamilton's orifices. You don't know where they've been."

"So, did Elvin find anything?" Marshall asked.

Marta read hope in his voice. She realized anew that this good man, who was daily insinuating himself into her life as no other person ever had, really did expect one day the response would be yes.

"No, Marshall. The answer is the same it's been for the past ten days."

"You'll ask him again tomorrow? He told me not to ask anymore. He told me he'd let me know."

"You do understand, don't you, that she's almost certainly gone? And every day that passes—"

"Of course, I understand. Somebody has to keep asking, though. We can't just forget about her."

"Elvin is doing what he can. With Gillis's help, he's buried a software program in his monitoring equipment. Gillis says it's undetectable. They've hidden a server and monitor dedicated to Sheila's magnetic, electronic and aural profile. Elvin has it locked onto the universe where they sent her. When he has the opportunity, he's trying to pin down a specific year . . ."

"The point is," Marshall said, "he's got to *keep* doing it. As time passes, he seems less and less interested."

"And remember, he has to do all that without Gretchen or the other physicists knowing. I honestly think he's making his best effort."

She stood on tiptoe to put her arms around Marshall's neck and pull him down into a kiss.

"Mmmmm . . ." he said as his hand found her breast.

She felt the lovely electric tingle that seemed to flow from her nipples straight into her core. She enjoyed the building sensation for just a moment before putting her own hand over Marshall's wandering fingers.

"If you get me started now, we'll miss the meeting."

"I didn't know there was a meeting."

"That's what I came to tell you."

"You could have called."

"Yes, well, calling is just so . . ." She smiled again at the tingle. ". . . so . . . impersonal. Don't you think?"

Marshall's apartment sighed its disapproval.

They were last to enter the mini-conference room just off Yuni's office. They found Yuni, Gretchen and Naomi waiting, along with Elvin and Leonard Rose.

And another man they didn't know.

"Ladies and gentlemen," Yuni began when Marta and Marshall took their chairs, "I'd like you to meet Sheldon Wishcamper."

Marta took one glance at a generic, thirtyish, white man seated apart from everyone, and felt a tingle having nothing to do with Marshall's exploring hands. This was an alarm.

Wishcamper seemed the embodiment of nondescription: average height, average build. He wore a scrubbed, Midwestern face floating under close-cropped blond hair. No distinguishing features. Not a crooked nose or dimple in his cheek, or cleft in his chin, or scar or pimple to be seen. His passport photo would be interchangeable among a thousand people just like him. Marta suspected he would normally wear a plain dark blue suit, white shirt, blue tie with silver stripes. Such attire would be contrary to the social norm on the GRC campus, though, so he wore jeans, hiking boots and a neatly pressed pale blue dress shirt open at the collar. His smile did not waver.

"I'll let Mr. Wishcamper explain why he's here," Yuni said, fixing Marta with a grim glare.

Wishcamper stood and waved a non-threatening greeting.

"It's nice to be here," he said, his voice void of any geographical intonation. "I look forward to seeing firsthand this technological miracle you folks have created at the GRC. When I was briefed on what you've accomplished, I was . . . well, I can barely grasp the reality even now. As to why I'm here, I've been tasked by the Congressional oversight subcommittee to review security procedures at this facility. I'll do my best to keep out of your way."

"What agency do you represent?" Marta asked. Under normal circumstances, this task might fall to the FBI or the General Accounting Office or even the National Security Council.

Wishcamper smiled. "I work solely for the subcommittee. Given the extreme classification of this project, even most members of Congress are not aware of its existence. The subcommittee itself is a select, secret group. Under those circumstances, when issues arise, traditional resources simply can't be used to conduct investigations."

"And issues have . . . arisen?" Marta asked.

"Yes. You are all aware of the disappearance of traveler Raul Hinojosa a few months ago? The subcommittee is quite concerned that the security team here would allow someone to simply walk away. And then you have the tragic death of Sheila Schuler . . ."

"Sheila's death was an accident," Marta said.

"Yes. I've read Dr. Andropov's report. She was lost during a classified mission . . ."

Marta glanced at Yuni and saw him squirming uncomfortably. Indeed, Yuni had chosen to take Elvin's advice and simply look the other way.

"So why are you—"

"Because," Wishcamper said, "on the same evening Ms. Schuler died, the security team managed to let another member of the GRC staff slip past them and leave this facility. A janitor. Jason Pratt. Upon closer investigation, some of Mr. Pratt's background information has been difficult to confirm. Needless to say, Mr. Pratt and Mr. Hinojosa represent huge security risks as long as they are at large."

"What would Sheila have to do with a janitor?" Naomi Hu asked.

"Perhaps nothing. But the subcommittee directed me to investigate. So, I will investigate. I've never been comfortable with coincidence."

Marta noted that Marshall had gone pale.

Elvin gravitated toward them as the meeting broke up.

"Well?" Elvin said as they walked.

"We need to see Gillis," Marta said.

"It has to be more than just the disappearances," Gillis said.

They had adjourned to Marta's living room. Elvin sat at the breakfast bar. Marta and Marshall shared the couch while Gillis paced.

Marta was about to answer when her apartment cleared its throat. "Um . . . You have friends over. You should offer snacks."

Marta kicked her dishwasher. "All I want you to do," she said with a growl, "is crawl into a corner somewhere and die."

The apartment stifled a sob.

"Not that the disappearances aren't enough," Marta said, returning to the dangling thread of conversation. "This place leaks like a sieve. The security staff is obviously susceptible to bribery. Despite that, though, the security technology is excellent. Wishcamper has to know that. And we have to operate under the assumption he comes here suspecting the missing people might never have left the complex."

"Even Sheila?" Marshall asked.

"Even Sheila," Gillis said.

He stopped pacing long enough to pause at Marta's desk and adjust the alignment of two notebooks, so they were square with the desktop.

"Does he suspect us?" Elvin asked.

"If he's any good, he does." Marta did her best to ignore this annoying, fastidious aspect of Gillis's nature.

"I should just tell him I shot that guy," Marshall said. "I'll tell him it was only me. I can leave you guys out of it . . ."

Gillis discarded Marshall's offer with a wave, as if swiping at a fly. "No reason for him to suspect that. And if he does, it's just a guess. Keep your mouth shut and go about your business until he goes away."

"Will he?" Marshall asked. "Go away, I mean?"

"Eventually, of course," Marta said. "In the meantime, we need to take some steps. Elvin, how good are the data tapes you made of the fake mission?"

"Very good. I've had time to make modifications. Only someone as talented as me would find the flaws. And there's no one like that."

She turned to Gillis, who was lining up Marta's pens and pencils so they were parallel.

"What about any electronic traces of our cover-up mission?"

"All data and video feeds normally recorded by the main

computers were diverted to my secret server. I've been through the system several times and I'm certain no electronic evidence of our deception exists. For the time being, though," he said, turning to Elvin, "you've got to shut down all your programs and equipment dedicated to searching for Sheila."

"We can't . . ." Marshall protested.

Marta placed a calming hand on his arm. "We have to. If Wishcamper knows what he's doing, he'll electronically scrub this place so thoroughly no unauthorized programs or equipment will escape detection."

"I'm shutting down everything I've got," Gillis said. "Even though I consider a lot of my stuff beyond detection, I won't take the chance."

"What about Gormly?" Elvin asked. "You think Wishcamper knows about him?"

"No way," Marta said. "Gormly covered his tracks. No evidence exists that he was ever at the projection lab or even the GRC site that night. I'm not sure anyone even knows he's missing."

6

THE VACANCY

PHILLIP LUCRE KNEW ANDREW GORMLY was missing. And with each day that passed, Lucre grew a little more hopeful that the arrangement would be permanent.

Lucre knew all about Andrew Gormly.

Officially, Gormly had been on the Hemisphere Investment Group's books as a vice-president in the public relations division. Gormly's unspoken title, though, was troubleshooter, a corporate euphemism for Dastardly Total Dick. He traveled the world to various Hemisphere projects, where he bribed, blackmailed, intimidated and murdered, all to assure that Hemisphere's interests were protected, its pathways smoothed.

Although nobody gave him specific orders to execute any of these nefarious deeds, Gormly excelled at taking hints. He was lavishly rewarded for his initiative. Besides a generous salary and bonuses, Gormly possessed unfettered access to a number of island bank accounts holding millions of dollars at any given time.

Being the Dastardly Total Dick was a great gig and Gormly was good at it, so Lucre had despaired of climbing that particular rung of the corporate ladder. Lucre's job title was Underling to the Vice President. He served as Gomley's in-house assistant. While Gormly galloped off to do evil wherever evil needed doing, Lucre held down the fort at corporate headquarters. He provided whatever support Gormly required and further insulated Hemisphere's more legitimate executives from the treachery.

Lucre carefully followed Gormly's career path. While not privy to all the details, he employed keen observational skills and learned much. Gormly was a corporate black-guard, lowlife malefactor, miscreant and scoundrel. *And,* Lucre thought with no small amount of jealousy, *I have every one of those qualifications.*

Now, miraculously, a Dastardly Total Dick opening had apparently occurred.

Ten days into Gormly's disappearance, Hemisphere Board Chairman Gustov Graber summoned Lucre.

Phillip walked up three flights of stairs to the top floor of Denver's fifth-tallest office tower, negotiated a maze of security devices that probed, x-rayed, disinfected—everything just short of reading his mind. Another door, a secretary who pointed to yet another entrance guarded by a large man with no hair, no neck and no discernable humanity. Finally, Lucre gained access.

He peered across the vast office expanse. Curtains blocked a spectacular floor-to-ceiling view of the Rocky Mountains. Gustov Graber pointed to a sofa against a far wall. Graber fussed with some papers, then stood and made the trek from his desk to the sofa where he joined Lucre.

Graber got right to the point.

"Phillip, you've done well as Andrew's assistant. Andrew has, apparently, resigned."

Resigned, Vink thought to himself with a mental smirk. *Andrew has disappeared, and they're scared. They're worried he's turned on them. Taken his millions and gone into hiding, ready to extort them all as the opportunity arises.*

"If you are interested, we'd like you to assume Andrew's role in public relations."

"I'd be honored."

"The first thing on your agenda, I would think, should be to locate Andrew. We are concerned about him. He contributed a great deal to Hemisphere, and we want to be sure he is properly taken care of. You need to get to Arizona and see what he might have left in place down there."

The Dastardly Total Dick was dead. Long live the Dastardly Total Dick.

7

THE INVESTIGATION

NAOMI HEARD A LIGHT TAPPING at her open office door. She confronted Sheldon Wishcamper, still displaying his vacuous grin. He sat down without being invited and dispensed with the formality of a greeting.

"Tell me about Marshall Grissom."

"I'm afraid I can't." Naomi frowned. "I have a professional relationship with each of the travelers. While it's not a doctor-patient relationship in the strictest sense, I still feel an obligation—"

"It's not a doctor-patient relationship in any sense as far as the oversight subcommittee is concerned. The moment you signed your contract, you began operating under a different set of rules than is applied to the outside world."

He spoke in a collegial manner, still smiling. "I need to know the basics of Mr. Grissom's background, and your broad-stroke evaluation of his psychological makeup—his overall character."

Naomi decided further protest would be pointless. "Marshall is a uniquely principled individual." She let that statement simmer for a moment while she opened a drawer from the cadenza behind her and riffled through a stack of folders. She withdrew Marshall's and offered it to Wish-camper, who did not reach to accept. He nodded for her to continue.

Naomi hesitated, then put the open file on her desk.

"Okay, he grew up in a small town not far from here. His father died when Marshall was five, and his mother didn't remarry. His high school grades were so-so. He graduated from New Mexico State University with a public relations degree and was working for a PR firm when he was designated as a traveler candidate. Like most of us, he signed a five-year contract, agreeing to be confined to the GRC Complex for the term of that contract."

"Which tells me nothing."

She closed the file and stared directly at Wishcamper.

"As you've seen, Marshall is tall. He was much taller than any of his peers by the time he reached the sixth grade. And like most children who suffer growth spurts, he was physically awkward. He has no athleticism, so he didn't have basketball, for example, to help him fit in. Junior high and high school were difficult for Marshall as his height and awkwardness made him a target for ridicule."

Wishcamper nodded and leaned forward, a gesture of encouragement.

Naomi sighed her reluctance but continued.

"Marshall's response was to do his best to avoid being noticed. While he is a very bright, and in many ways, a talented individual, he hasn't developed those gifts fully, because the last thing he wants is to call attention to himself. Remarkably, Marshall did not become bitter or cynical. He carefully guards his dignity, though. Despite all that, when approached, he is kind and open. I don't think he has a shred of guile. He does his job well here, although the attention he receives . . ." She would not, she determined, discuss anything with this outsider concerning Marshall's erectile problem. ". . . is difficult for him."

Again, she paused, and this time Wishcamper accepted her silence.

"Thank you, Dr. Hu." Naomi cringed at the use of her title. "You've been very helpful."

"Mr. Grissom . . . ah . . . Marshall? May I buy you a drink?"

Marshall glanced ahead along the long gray corridor to see Sheldon Wishcamper striding toward him with purpose. Marshall's day had been long, devoted to meetings and training sessions as everyone at the GRC tried to guess what would happen next. Right now, Marshall wanted only to nap a bit before Marta showed up for the marathon.

Would declining Wishcamper's offer of a drink appear suspicious? If only Marta was here, or even Gillis, they'd know what to do.

"Um . . . sure. A quick one, maybe . . ."

Wishcamper smiled, slapping him on the back. He guided Marshall through the corridors toward the Time Warp, the slightly sterile substitute for a bar-slash-nightclub designers of the GRC Complex figured a bunch of people in their twenties and thirties and confined to this underground fortress would need as a distraction. A gesture of normalcy.

Wishcamper chose a table near the back of the darkened room. Other patrons were arriving, but the hard-core party crowd wouldn't make its appearance until later. Wishcamper ordered scotch on the rocks and regarded Marshall quizzically.

"Just beer. I'm not much of a drinker . . ."

"I have to tell you, Marshall, I'm intrigued."

"Um . . . okay . . ."

"No, really. What you all have accomplished here is remarkable. And the travelers . . . I am in awe of your personal courage."

"Um . . ."

"When they first told me what you guys were doing here, I thought . . . well, I pictured you travelers differently. Kind of like swashbucklers. Special ops guys, or ninjas or something."

"Um . . . no . . . I'd have to say I've pretty much lived my life with my swashes conspicuously unbuckled."

Wishcamper laughed. "What's it like . . . time travel, I mean?"

"Um, I'm not sure I'm supposed to—"

"I'm the security guy," Wishcamper said. "I keep the security secure."

"We've got these people around," Marshall protested, scanning the growing crowd. "Yuni doesn't want us talking about project details when we're in the bar."

Wishcamper nodded his approval. "Very good, Mr. Grissom. This will take care of it."

Wishcamper removed a device the size of an extra-thick half dollar and placed it between them. He pushed a point on its surface, and the disk began to glow. Immediately, the snippets of conversation around them dissolved into the soft hum of white noise.

"Now they can't hear us, either."

Marshall saw a technician he knew a couple of tables

away. He called the man's name and received no response.

"So," Wishcamper continued, "when the subcommittee sent me here, I knew nothing of what this is about. Now that I'm on site, I've got the reports, all the documentation. As you can imagine, though, that's a lot to digest over a short time. Help me out. What's it like to confront yourself when you travel into the past?"

"Well," Marshall said, still wishing badly that Marta were here to help, "that's not what happens. When you go back, there's only one of you—the you that exists in that parallel universe . . ."

"Whoa, whoa, whoa." Wishcamper raised his hands as if to surrender. "Parallel universe?"

"Yes, apparently an infinite number of them. I'm not sure of the physics . . . that's what the whole controversy is about . . . why some of the financial backers might withdraw. And the whole argument about the ethics of time travel . . . we can't travel to the past of our own world."

"Why not?"

"Marta or Gretchen could explain this so much better . . ."

Wishcamper didn't let him off the hook. He just kept grinning that stupid farm boy grin and swirling his scotch.

"There's this thing called paradox," Marshall said. "It's apparently a hard and fast physical law—like gravity. You can't go to the past of your own existence because if you did, and you killed your grandfather, you would cease to exist. And therefore, you would not exist to go back and kill him in the first place. Okay? So, physicists believed time travel to the past would be impossible because of paradox."

Wishcamper raised his eyebrows and ducked, as if something had just flown closely over his head.

"Yeah, I know." Marshall found himself warming to his self-effacing companion. "There's a branch of physics called quantum mechanics, though. It has to do with very small things. And it turns out that atoms and molecules and strings and quantum particles operate under a different set of physical rules than everything else. Quantum physicists have suggested for years and years that parallel universes exist, and if time travel became possible, the travelers would go to the past of other universes where paradox wouldn't be an issue. It wouldn't matter if you killed your grandfather there. Well... I suppose it might matter to your grand-father."

"Um, hang on." Wishcamper appeared to evaluate the level of the amber liquid remaining in his glass and, pointing to Marshall's half-full beer bottle, cocked his eyebrows.

"No, I'm okay for now."

"So, you guys didn't know you were going to parallel universes...?"

"No. Like everything else, it took a while to figure out."

"Okay, go back to the thing about there being only one of you."

"Yeah, well, we don't know what happens to the traveler's physical body. Maybe, because the matter is identical, it just merges with the past body. Or maybe it just hangs around somewhere else. What does go to the past is your intellect. Your thoughts, your memories, your emotions. And all that information lands in the brain of your past self at once. That's dangerous. Our last mission took us back ten years. See, you have to understand that your past counterpart doesn't know what's going on. For him or her, the experience can be terrifying. Naomi is worried it might be so bad for some people—the past being would suffer such a psychological trauma—that they'd be mentally impaired."

"Wow. So how do you cope?"

"It gets better while you're there. Eventually, for me, anyway, the past me understands what's going on and we kind of coexist. Actually, it gets to be pretty easy. Before everything starts to fade."

Again, Wishcamper shook his head and smiled as a demonstration of incomprehension.

"Eventually, the future entity just forgets why he's there or where he came from and, although we've been lucky, and it hasn't happened yet, just sort of burns out ... they think."

"And if that happens ... ?"

"Gretchen and Elvin are afraid the future being would be lost. We couldn't get him or her back home."

"So, there's only so far into the past that you—as a traveler—could go, right?" Wishcamper asked, making an intuitive leap that impressed Marshall. "I mean, if there's no equivalent being..."

"You can't travel to a time before your own birth," Marshall said with a little shudder as he thought of Sheila. "That's what they think, anyway."

Wishcamper offered his empty glass for Marshall's inspection. He motioned for Marshall to wait. He retreated to the bar and returned with his own refill and a second beer Marshall didn't want.

"So how do the people here keep track of you?" Wishcamper pushed the beer across the table so it stood in rank with the first one. "With all these parallel universes, how do they monitor you and bring you back?"

"There's a band of energy that flows from the projector

through the wormhole into the past. We call it the lifeline. The physicists tell me it's a combination of three things unique to each individual—DNA, magnetic field and the aura, that's the corona of light we can't see with the naked eye. That's part of the whole energy revolution thing, enriched hydrogen and dark matter make it possible to track all those things. And this thread of energy is so powerful, they use it to track us, and the projector sort of reels us in with it when they bring us back."

Wishcamper nodded. "I've glanced through the transcripts of a few mission debriefings, and they tend to be pretty vague. Is that on purpose?"

"No. It's because the whole thing *is* vague. As I said before, as soon as we return from the past, we start to forget. And we have evidence that the past being forgets most details of the whole experience, as well. It just drifts away. What you remember is like a dream. Right now, I couldn't give you a lot of specifics about—"

"You ever hear of a guy named Andrew Gormly?" The grin remained on Wishcamper's face.

His question came at Marshall like an unanticipated speed bump on a long and deserted road. It jarred him, and he couldn't disguise his shock.

"Andrew . . . Andrew . . ." he stammered, trying to buy time while sorting this out. Marshall was a terrible liar, and he knew it. His mother advised him to always stick to facts, because that was the only way he would ever keep his stories straight.

"Andrew Gormly? Um . . . why?"

"Just curious. Thought you might have run across him here."

Marshall offered an internal prayer of thanks for the second beer. He raised the bottle and took a long swallow to cover his hesitation as he tried to formulate an answer. "About a thousand people work here, you know. Even though most of us are in all these rooms and hallways underground, I only deal with other travelers and computer techs and some of the scientists . . . to get to know them, I mean."

"Gormly was a corporate representative. One of the guys who just comes by sometimes. Worked for the Hemisphere Investment Group."

Wishcamper's grin persisted.

"Um . . . Hemisphere, huh? Well, as it turns out, a guy stopped me in the hallway a few weeks back. Right after a mission. Just wanted to . . . you know . . . shake my hand sort of thing. He said *he* worked for Hemisphere. And he might have said his name was Gormly."

"What's this whole thing about being naked?" Wishcamper asked, creating another jarring transition that had Marshall struggling to keep up.

"Naked? Um . . . we have to be naked. Non-organic matter can't be projected . . ."

"What happens if you're not? Naked, I mean."

"Well, when they first started, they used lemmings as test subjects. And they put collars on the lemmings with tiny video recorders built into them. And the lemmings disappeared somewhere into the past. When they brought them back, the lemmings were sort of . . . decapitated. And the collars were gone. Next they tried vests, and all they got back was a head and four legs and a tail."

"So, the problem was the vests and the collars?"

"Yep. We have to be naked. We shower right before and really scrub to get all the dust particles off. And the projection lab is a clean-room environment."

"What about Jason Pratt? Did you know Jason Pratt?"

Another jarring bump.

"Jason Pratt was . . . he's the janitor who disappeared." Marshall hoped he was correctly recalling the original meeting with Wishcamper. "You told us in Yuni's office the other day . . ."

"Right. Did you know him?"

Again, Marshall retreated to his beer so he could organize his answer.

"No. I might have seen him around doing . . . janitor stuff. But I never met the man."

Marshall looked away from Wishcamper and ran a hand through his hair.

Wishcamper nodded slowly, his smile unwavering.

"Because apparently he knew you."

"He . . . what? Why would you think that he . . . ?"

"Jason Pratt disappeared just like that." Wishcamper snapped his fingers. "He left some stuff behind—kind of hidden. Which I think is weird. You'd think it would be important enough to take. This journal kind of thing. I can't make much sense of it, because it's all very cryptic. Some kind of code. Obviously, it was significant to him."

Marshall tried his best to dampen the concern he felt sure showed on his face. He longed to get up and leave.

"Jason Pratt knew Andrew Gormly," Wishcamper said, breaking the short silence. "Don't know how or why. Gormly's name was in that book. So was yours. Why do you think a janitor would have your name in his journal?"

Marshall's mind worked furiously, seeking any shelter it could find. "Um . . . the betting? Maybe it was the betting."

"Betting? On what?"

Marshall colored and his eyes darted briefly down to his lap.

"On me. Elvin Detwyler runs a betting pool every time I—"

"Whoa, you're *that* guy?" Wishcamper's grin broadened. "You're a legend around here, man. So, sure. Pratt placed some bets. Probably made some money and made a note of it. Makes sense." He raised his glass as a sort of salute. "Hey, I'll tell you what. I saw a video of one of Sheila Schuler's projections a couple of days ago, and I don't blame you. I don't think I could keep the old flesh flute on its leash if I was next to her up there either."

"Flesh flute?"

"I understand she was getting pretty political." Wishcamper shifted gears again. "What was that all about?"

"Sheila wasn't political." Marshall failed in his effort to keep a note of anger out of his voice. "She thought dropping into some other universe and manipulating their lives and histories just because we can is wrong."

"That's what you think?"

"No . . . I don't know. I . . . It's a very . . . theoretical thing. Because if you change someone's future, they don't know the difference, do they? If you know you are changing their future and their lives are worse, then you're wrong. But maybe their lives are better . . ." His voice trailed off.

"Tough question. I've heard some people say she would have scared off the investors."

"No, no . . . it's just that, the whole parallel universe

issue complicates everything from the investors' point of view. See, if we're traveling to the past of another universe, we can't manipulate our own past for profit or national security or anything like that. And that's the big payoff that most of the investors are hoping for."

"What about the future? If the past doesn't work, why not go to the future?"

"The time projector was designed to send travelers to the past." Marshall felt relieved to be back to a less perilous area of discussion. "The Light Speed Project was designed for travel to the future."

"I thought nothing but light can go the speed of light."

"It can't. But if you can approach the speed of light, there's this thing called time dilation. Time passes more slowly the faster you go. And if you go really fast, you end up in the future. Only without the time projector, there's no way to get back."

"So, the parallel universe thing screws that up as well?"

"Right. But some people around here think we should still try. Because, they say, if you travel two hundred years in the future, by then they'll have figured out how to solve the parallel universe issue."

Wishcamper nodded. "I've read about 'exchange' missions."

Marshall took another swig of that second beer. "Right. Elvin Detwyler discovered how to identify and map specific universes. Don't ask me how it works. It has something to do with old television show theme songs that glom onto the different universes—we're the *I Love Lucy* universe, by the way. What happened was two universes, acting with parallel histories, decide to do an exchange mission. Our universe sends a team there, and they send a team here, each to try and affect the same change. So, theoretically at least, we *could* alter our own past."

"And that's what this last mission—the one before Sheila died—tried to accomplish?"

"Correct. I had a friend from high school who was killed in a car wreck a decade ago. The mission planners thought that would be an unambiguous test of our ability to change the past. They chose her accident, because changing the outcome wouldn't be tampering with some significant historical event. Sheila and Marta and Frank Altman went back with me."

"And?"

"We saved her from the car wreck."

Marshall's voice caught as he added, "She died a couple of months later, anyway. So, we . . . we changed some of the details . . . but not . . . not the ultimate outcome."

That evening, during the break between rounds as they lay in a sweaty, tangled pile atop Marshall's bed, Marshall told Marta everything about Sheldon Wishcamper's questions and the mysterious coded journal.

"Bollocks. Gillis got into that apartment and went through Pratt's stuff. I don't know how he missed it. Unless Wishcamper was just making that up to trick you."

"I told Wishcamper my name was probably there because of the erection pool thing . . . that Pratt probably won some money. And he seemed okay with that."

Marta cocked a skeptical eyebrow and shrugged. "He can have all the suspicions he wants so long as there's no proof." She snuggled into the crook of Marshall's arm and laid her head on his shoulder.

"That got me to thinking, though," Marshall continued. "Why *would* my name be in his book?"

"If it exists," Marta reminded him. "Do you remember what Pratt said the night we lost Sheila when he pointed that taser at you?"

"Um ... something about the 1960s. That's when I realized how far back he'd sent Sheila."

"He said, 'Looks like we can solve another one of your problems right now, Mr. Gormly. I'm sure Ms. Schuler would enjoy some company back in the sixties.'"

"Yeah, I think that was it."

"Marshall, if Pratt had your name, it's because he and Gormly intended to kill you all along. They needed to get you and me and Sheila off the primary traveler's team."

"Then why didn't Pratt kill me the same night he killed Raul? I didn't know it was Raul in that trash barrel ... Pratt had his taser with him. I saw it. He said it was for rats and snakes ..."

"I don't know." Marta rose to a sitting position, bringing her eyes to the same level as Marshall's. "Maybe Gormly hadn't given him his orders yet. Or maybe they realized how complicated it would get if two travelers disappeared at the same time. You need to stop beating yourself up over killing Pratt, though. Now, more than ever, you should realize it was an act of self-defense."

Marta resolved she would give Marshall a lecture about not being quite so forthcoming with people like Sheldon Wishcamper. Or did he know what he was doing all along? Marshall had done exactly the right thing in keeping his answers vague while being mostly truthful. Every time she started to settle into her original assessment of Marshall Grissom as a good-hearted soul steeped in naïveté, something like this happened to set her defenses tingling. *Who was Marshall Grissom?* Gillis still believed Marshall was some sort of master assassin, and so skillful an actor that he could defeat even Marta's cynicism.

Marta decided she must not allow her relationship with Marshall to get too comfortable. Right now, though, Marshall was drinking her in with his eyes and the intentions they suggested formed a specific clarity. She would let him make love to her again. She would be cynical later.

8

A MOMENT OF HOPE

T*HIS ETERNAL LIMBO, this stark white palate, had always been something of a refuge for Sheila. She thought of it as a blankness hidden from time. She had never been frightened here, even as the emptiness became infinite. Her fear stayed back in the projection lab, and then, to a lesser degree, rejoined her as she left this haven to occupy the being who was Sheila in another world.*

This time, though, when the limbo spat her out, she knew she would die.

And because no one was present to hear her, she surrendered to a moment of panic.

"Please, please," she heard herself shout in a disembodied voice, "I don't want this. I want to be with my friends. I want to hug Marshall and teach Marta how to laugh. I want to grow old with someone. I want to—"

"I beg your pardon?"

The voice—a booming bass and just a bit snooty with a touch of the British Empire—reverberated around her.

"What?" she asked, startled by the sound of her own voice coming from somewhere beyond her. She realized she'd never before spoken aloud in this barren and ethereal place.

"You sound distraught," the voice said. *"We don't do* distraught *here. You know the rules."*

"What are ... who are ..." Sheila asked with astonishment.

"Please," the voice said. *"Don't stammer. I've other things to do, you know."*

Sheila sorted desperately through her consciousness to try and find any point of reference to make sense of this. Finally, she asked, *"Are you ... are you ... God?"*

A chuckle modified the response.

"You'd better believe I'm God. I'm the Hall Monitor. And why you don't know that is beyond me—"

"Hall Monitor?"

"You're in the hallway, aren't you?" The voice sounded impatient. *"Wait a minute. Do you have a pass?"*

"A pass? You mean a hall pass?"

"Oh, I see," the voice said with a note of surprise. And then it grew harsh. *"You're one of them, aren't you? One of* them *from* that *set of dimensions. So now that you've initiated the conversation, you can just tell me what this is all about."*

"You're not God? I mean The *God?"*

"What is it with you people and this God stuff? As if a Supreme Being wouldn't have other things to do. Again, and I'm doing my best to be patient here, what's this scurrying back and forth?"

"Um, well ... I ... it's about time," Sheila said.

"I couldn't agree more."

"Um, no, you don't understand. Time. It's why we've been using your ... your corridor. Time travel. We discovered how to travel through time and ..."

"That's certainly a waste of time, wouldn't you say?"

"No ... um ... well, yes, actually. I thought ... um ... I

think what we're doing is wrong. I think it's a bad thing. I think we're unnecessarily disrupting—"

"Ah, a philosopher." The tone shifted to approval with a note of intrigue. "Time is something of a quandary."

"For that matter," Sheila said, realizing a question she'd been harboring since her introduction to the bizarre experience of time travel, "what is time?"

"Indeed," the voice said with another chuckle. "What is time? What is time? Man, I hear you."

"What?"

"I was commiserating . . ."

"No, I wasn't . . . It's something I really want to know."

"Oh, I'm sorry. I thought it was a rhetorical question. I thought we were being philosophical."

"We've done all these things," Sheila said, "spent all this money, taken all these risks. Some of us have . . . will . . . die. I realize I don't have the slightest idea what time actually is. I mean, of course I know about time conceptually. And I know all the physics and math and . . . but not just as a . . . a reality, you know?"

"Yes, it seems as if everyone goes out of their way to make it so complicated. I personally think one of your Twentieth Century physicists came closest to nailing it down. John Archibald Wheeler. A delightful man. He said time is nature's way of keeping everything from happening all at once."

9

TIPPING THE HISTORICAL BALANCE

"SO, HOW ABOUT 1960. The Nixon-Kennedy election," suggested Gustov Graber. "All the history books say old Joe Kennedy paid off the mob and Mayor Daley to steal the election, and Kennedy still only won by a hair."

"Yeah, that's a good one," answered Warren Pitts. "Or Hitler? That bomb in the bunker. Just put that exploding briefcase on the other side of that table leg. We'd be doing the world a big favor."

"The Cuban Missile Crisis. Any number of historical variables could have tipped the balance, and kablooey."

"That one might be tough to sell, though, with the alternative being worldwide nuclear destruction and all."

"But that's the beauty of it," Graber said. "It's another universe. Who cares?"

Phillip Lucre felt invisible. He had walked through the door and was standing right there, although no one acknowledged his presence.

Until Graber said, "So, Phillip, how was Arizona?" He spoke with an absent smile that led Lucre to understand Graber cared nothing about his impressions of Arizona.

"Um . . . hot and brown for the most part."

Lucre was back in that plush office the size of a suburban cottage occupying the top floor of downtown Denver's fifth-tallest skyscraper. The four taller buildings, though, did nothing to interfere with Graber's view west toward the Rockies. And today, the curtains were open.

Board Chairman and largest single shareholder of the gargantuan Hemisphere Investment Group, Graber enjoyed a vast office space appointed with plush carpets, plusher rugs and priceless paintings and antiques. Graber sat behind a desk—dating from some other century—so large that a Little League team could have taken infield practice on its surface during rainy weather. Lucre wondered if Graber realized that, sitting way over there at that outsized desk in this outsized room with all its outsized appointments, he seemed not so much a business mogul as he did a toddler wearing a nice suit.

The man who shared Lucre's side of the desk, though, could be mistaken for nothing other than an alpha male. Steel gray hair cropped short, piercing gray eyes, both face and clothing perfectly unwrinkled. A man of average height and build who, even when seated, projected a much larger persona.

"So, tell us about it," ordered Pitts, Hemisphere's president and chief executive officer.

Lucre nodded.

"I'm afraid we'll have difficulty, for the time being at least, reconstructing Mr. Gormly's network at the Global Research Consortium. Andrew is not one to keep notes. He communicated to me only what he felt I needed to know to accomplish whatever task he assigned me. I don't have the names of his contacts within the science groups or among the travelers themselves. I do know a couple of names from the security division who were on his payroll . . ."

Graber interrupted. "I'll leave this matter to you two." He rose from his distant seat. "I have an early lunch meeting across town. Please, make yourself comfortable . . ." Graber shoved a low metal bowl hard and sent it skittering across the broad expanse of his desk toward Lucre. ". . . and have a Peanut Butter Cup."

Reflexively, Lucre put out a hand to catch the bowl.

"When I was a kid and my family was broke," Graber said," there was no bigger treat for me than a peanut butter cup." The bowl continued its journey. "Now, I keep 'em around all the time. Everybody loves a peanut butter cup."

Horrified, Lucre snatched his hand away. The bowl came to a teetering rest at the edge of the desk, threatening to tip and spill the candies over the floor. If that happened, Lucre would have to make some excuse about not picking them up.

"Um, no thanks." Lucre gingerly poked at the bowl with his index finger, pushing it away from the edge of the table. "I . . . I just ate and . . ."

"Take a few for later," Graber said, walking past him.

Lucre ignored the offer, hoping Graber would not look back. He felt reluctant to confess a severe peanut allergy to Graber and Pitts. Mundane genetic flaws like peanut allergies seemed terribly un-Dastardly-Total-Dick-like. When the door closed behind Graber, Lucre realized he'd been holding his breath. He gratefully exhaled.

"You were saying . . ." Pitts urged.

"We can't approach security right now." Lucre reclaimed his composure and distanced himself from the peanut butter cups. "The Congressional oversight subcommittee has sent an investigator to look into the disappearances. He's performing a detailed audit of the security system. I don't know how long he'll be there."

"Shit." Pitts rubbed his hand over his eyes. "We are hemorrhaging money on this damn thing. Every day we delay is . . ."

Lucre understood Pitts' consternation. Hemisphere's portion of the GRC's financing came through a manipulation of the books of several Hemisphere subsidiaries. This secret fund was unknown to shareholders and most board members. The board had been given vague outline of Hemisphere's investment in an experimental technology. They didn't know, however, what it was or the true expense. Fudging the books made some of Hemisphere's other subsidiaries underperform financially. Should a true accounting ever be called, Pitts had to know he would be the sacrificial lamb protecting Graber and the board from stockholders' wrath.

"A number of other investors, including some governments, are talking about withdrawing . . ."

"What . . . based on that mission where they tried to save some high school girl?"

"Combined with other evidence and the parallel universe issue." Lucre shrugged. "They see the outcome as clear evidence the past can't be manipulated, or, if it can, the effort will be too expensive to ever recover their investments."

"Bullshit. That wasn't any real test of history. They tiptoed around everything. They chose an event that didn't matter and a person who didn't matter, and then sent a team of travelers who believe time travel is unethical. What kind of a test is that? Why didn't they just kidnap the girl and hide her somewhere so she wouldn't get in the damn car wreck."

"They did save her from the wreck. She died a couple of months later of a drug overdose."

"There you go. See? They did change it. And then it got all fucked up because they chose some drug addict."

"As I understand it, they chose the girl and the event because they didn't want to be intrusive. They wanted to have as little effect as possible on the historical mainstream of this other universe."

"Why should we give a shit about that?"

Again, Lucre shrugged. "This ethics issue has had an effect—"

"But the Schuler woman is gone."

"That's right."

"So, I'm tired of this. We're fronting the money. They've got investors threatening to bail. It's time we threw our weight around. What's wrong with intrusive? You say you can't operate clandestinely the way Gormly did. Okay, then don't. Go there as our official corporate liaison and right up front organize the other major investors. Make demands. That's what Gustov and I were talking about. We need some historic event that teetered on the knife edge of history, and in some other universe, make it tip the other way. If it doesn't work, we'll cut our losses."

Lucre thought for a moment. He'd studied history.

"The Kennedy-Nixon thing would be complicated. Joe Kennedy bought that election by getting the mob to deliver union votes and getting Mayor Daley to provide the dead-people-bloc in Chicago. Hitler, well, as I understand it, there are limits to how far into the past you can go. As for the Cuban missile deal, I think we both understand Mumford and his committee wouldn't approve that."

"Okay. What else is there?"

Lucre paced, turned to behold the snow-capped mountains beyond the Denver skyline, then smiled. "The United States Presidential election of the year 2000."

10

HANGING CHAD

"SINCE WHEN DO INVESTORS get to submit mission profiles?" Yuni protested. "According to program guidelines, the science is supposed to be insulated from the money."

Lucre registered the vehemence of Andropov's glare. He feigned indifference.

"Unfortunately, Yuni," GRC Administrator Michael Huxtable answered, "I'm afraid those guidelines are now subject to revision. Key investors have demanded one more test to determine whether they will continue. On behalf of the Hemisphere group, Mr. Lucre here has done some polling of investors. And it appears if we resist their wishes, we'll lose much of our funding now. So, we must make our best effort to succeed."

"None of our travelers can do this. None of our travelers or traveler candidates were even born by the year 2000. Anyone capable of completing this mission would have to be in their sixties or seventies."

"Hmmmm. Well, I don't see any way around it. You must find someone and do it quickly. We want this mission to launch within a month."

"We're sending someone back forty-five years?" asked Marta. "Are they out of their bloody minds?"

"It was all we could do to cope with ten years on the last mission," Marshall protested. "And we had the benefit of a dozen missions to help us train for the trauma of trying to absorb ten years' worth of future memories at once. These folks won't stand a chance."

Marta took stock of the expressions of those gathered around the oak table. Marshall shared her shock. Elvin seemed gleeful. Gillis Kerg, as always, appeared detached and just a bit amused. Frank Altman ... well ... who knew what was behind that display of perpetual boredom? Yuni looked as if he'd bitten a lemon. Naomi, Gretchen Allen and Leonard Rose would not meet her eyes.

"Where will we find anyone willing to even try?" Marshall asked. "Do you know any seventy-year-olds you want to kill? I don't. Are there even any people that old on campus?"

"Actually," Gretchen said quietly, "there are. An accountant, one of the food service employees, and the guy who drives the golf cart."

"You mean Old Bob?" Marshall asked. "He's got to be at least eighty. That's why everyone calls him Old Bob."

"When he goes back to 2000, though, he won't be eighty, so I'm not sure that matters," Naomi said. "The originating point of projection doesn't seem to be physically or mentally demanding. It's the arrival in the past that creates problems. And back there, he's not an old man anymore."

Marta could not disguise her surprise. "Naomi, you're

not telling me you're buying into this?"

"I'm not sure we have any choice. If we can find the people, I'll do my best to see they are prepared for, and capable of, accomplishing the mission."

"So, what's the big fucking deal about the 2000 presidential election?" Marta scowled across the table she shared with Marshall, Gillis and Elvin at the Time Warp.

The men followed her there after she'd stormed from the meeting, declaring, "I need a drink."

Still angry, she indulged an emotion she usually reserved for intimidation or other useful purpose. This would change everything. The time travel program, she realized, had become something more to her than an assignment from the British Secret Service's MI-6 branch. Her relationship to Marshall, the loss of Sheila, her association with Yuni, Gretchen, Naomi—even Elvin—and the other scientists, had infected her with a . . . what? A dedication to the integrity of their approach to this new frontier? Unlike Sheila, Marta was no crusader. She knew, though, disaster waited if investors were allowed to run roughshod over the science. That camel had its nose in the tent now, and nothing would ever be the same.

"The guy who won that election really didn't," Elvin answered. "You know . . . Bush and Gore?"

Marta offered her upturned palms as a sarcastic display of ignorance. "Nevis is historically a British Colony. We didn't study the details of U.S. presidential elections."

"I know it was a close election," Marshall said. "But I'm a little vague on details, too."

"Well," Elvin said, "fortunately, besides being a brilliant physicist, I am a student of American history and have extraordinary recall of events." He looked around the table, as if anticipating applause. When none came, he turned to Marta. "You know about the Electoral College?"

"Yes. Americans don't directly vote for presidential candidates. They vote for their state's representatives to the Electoral College. And those people cast votes that choose the president."

"Not bad for a subject of the British Crown." Elvin raised his beer glass in mock salute. Marta did not raise her bottle in reply. "The Federation of St. Kitts and Nevis is an independent state."

"So, what that means," Elvin continued, "is sometimes the guy who ends up president had fewer popular votes than the guy who didn't."

"And I gather that's what happened here?"

"Al Gore won the national popular vote by 500,000 votes."

"Was that the first time . . . ?"

"Not the first time, or the last. Three or four presidents have been elected without a majority of the popular vote. Donald Trump lost by more than three million votes in 2016. The unique thing about the Bush/Gore election, though, is it all came down to the awarding of Florida's twenty-five electoral votes, where Jeb Bush—the brother of George W. Bush—was governor. And Florida voters apparently chose George by the barest whisker: Five hundred and thirty-seven of six million votes cast. I looked it up."

"That sounds a little suspicious." Marta had to speak louder as more scientists and technicians ended their day and stopped off for a drink before dinner.

"That's not all of it. The real issue in the Florida election was the *hanging chad*. Ballot selections were made when voters punched a hole indicating their preference. Many ballots were not properly punched, though. Some were only indented. With others, a hole was made, but the tiny bit of paper—called a chad—left by the punching device didn't separate completely and was left hanging. Many of these ballots, certainly enough to produce a different outcome, were disqualified by election officials as not clearly indicating the preference of the voter.

"That's why the mission profile calls for us to send travelers to the summer of 2000 and convince the Florida State Democratic Committee to undertake an intensive voter education program concerning the proper and thorough punching of ballots."

"So, tell me, Elvin," Marta said, "since you seem to know so much about the plan, will this be an exchange mission?"

"Get real. Our investors are a bunch of business tycoons. They think Bush did just fine—other than that whole financial collapse thing. They don't want Al Gore to have been president of anything in the history of *our* universe."

"So, you're sure you understand the risks involved?" asked Naomi Hu.

Seated across her office desk was Old Bob Buttons, the golf cart driver, who nodded with enthusiasm.

"Just as long as time travel pays better than driving the golf cart," Old Bob said.

Naomi smiled. She suspected Old Bob would have paid

them to let him get into the projection lab just so he could see naked ladies.

She had studied his personnel file and learned that, during the early projections, Bob had managed to arrange his golf cart schedule so that he ushered his VIPs into the lab at precisely the point the airlock door was closed and rules required him to remain until naked Sheila Schuler and naked Marta Hamilton disappeared into the past.

Finally, when his golf cart duties began to suffer, Old Bob was banned from the lab.

So, one down. At least one to go.

Mission rules prohibited the projection of a single traveler. Like scuba divers, they always had to embark at least in pairs unless the journey was only a matter of days and the being on the receiving end had experienced this process frequently enough to recognize what was happening.

Winnie Summers, a seventy-three-year old accountant, listened to Naomi's pitch until Naomi got to the naked part. Winnie said she was only marginally comfortable with being nude even when she was by herself. She flatly refused.

Naomi's last hope rested with Nadine, the lunchroom lady.

Naomi decided to approach Nadine on her own turf.

The cafeteria staff was finishing its post-lunch cleanup and drifting away, cutting the corner on their eight hours before the evening shift took over. Naomi asked for Nadine and was directed to a woman sitting at a big round table across the room.

Naomi approached with a smile and introduced herself.

As Nadine returned her smile, Naomi thought, *My God. This is Norman Rockwell's grandmother.*

Nadine, her cherubic face complete with wrinkly pink cheeks, wore round glasses with wire rims and displayed a . . . a twinkle? Yes. An actual twinkle right there in her eye. A cloud of wispy white hair, freed from the restraint of a protective net, framed a wrinkled, yet angelic, countenance.

"So nice to meet you, dear," Nadine said with an elfin voice straight from central casting.

The support staff at the GRC, particularly those who had no need to descend to the level that housed the time machine, knew only vague outlines of what happened there.

So, after telling Nadine that what she was about to say was highly classified and Nadine must agree never to repeat it, Naomi patiently began her explanation. As she had done with Winnie, Naomi focused mostly on the technical aspects of the journey during her initial pitch. Through it all, Nadine retained her attentive, grandmotherly visage, as if it was the polite thing to do.

And finally, like tiptoeing gingerly into a minefield, Naomi prepared to broach the issue that had been a deal-breaker for Winnie.

"Um, I don't suppose you'd care for a glass of wine? Naomi asked.

"Why . . . why, yes, dear. Yes, I would."

Naomi lifted her purse from the floor and withdrew a small bottle.

"I just happened to have a nice red with me."

"Let me get the glasses—"

"No, no," Naomi preempted. "Let me."

She rose and walked toward the kitchen area.

"The big cabinet right there in front, dear."

Nadine returned and poured. They clinked their glasses.

"Um . . . and you do realize," Naomi cringed just a little, "that our travelers must be naked?"

The glass halted halfway between Nadine's lips and the table.

She carefully set the glass on the metal surface. "The hell you say."

"Um . . . yes. The physics of the wormhole leave us no alternative. It just doesn't work any other—"

"With all those people watching?"

"We'll do our best to keep the audience to a minimum but . . . well . . . there are also cameras. We have to record everything to be sure . . ."

Naomi had already given up hope when Nadine smiled, lifted the wine glass back to her lips, chugged the contents with one long swig, slapped the glass onto the table and nodded for another pour.

"I worked my way through college as a stripper, honey. Just stick a pole on that platform, tell everyone to bring two-dollar bills and I'll feel right at home."

11

A SMALL, SMALL WORLD

"HE DOESN'T WANT the two of you involved," Yuni Andropov said. "Not directly. I'll need you as advisors, of course."

Marta couldn't believe her ears. "So, this Lucre guy gets to choose the travelers team?"

"No, not ... no ... He went to Huxtable. He said the investors want to be sure there's no bias."

"Oh, come on, Yuni. Don't tell me you're buying that crap."

"No, I'm not. But Lucre argued that you both are too close to Sheila and her ethics campaign. They just don't want to take any chances ..."

Marshall said nothing, just threw up his hands as a display of disgust and walked away.

Marta glared at Yuni and followed Marshall, muttering, "What a cock-up."

She hated the direction everything was going. Being honest with herself, though, she felt relief at Marshall's exclusion. She had a more and more difficult time imagining her life without that goofy guy in her bed. And if she could have her way, Marshall would never travel again.

She hurried after him into the corridor, then came to an abrupt halt. Marshall stood further down the hallway, listening to Sheldon Wishcamper, who wore that maddening smile. His hand rested on Marshall's shoulder, and he appeared to speak quite deliberately. Marshall listened and flinched, almost as if Wishcamper had raised a hand to strike him. Marshall seemed to be stammering. He cast his eyes up, then down, and finally his gaze swept back along the hallway, where he saw Marta. And in the look she returned he seemed to find himself.

Marshall shook his head, stepped away from Wishcamper, and walked to her.

"What?" Marta said, glancing quickly back along the hallway. Wishcamper had disappeared.

"He... that guy... he said hello. He told me he'd enjoyed our last talk, and we should get together for another drink. He said you seem like a nice lady and how lucky I am and... then he asked me if anyone had ever fired a gun in the projection lab."

"He... what? What did you say?"

"I asked him why he'd even think that. He said every month they close the airlocks and vacuum up all the particulates and fumigate everything. Which we both know. What I didn't know is that they analyze the particulates. Did you know that? He said when they did the last cleaning, they found something that could be gunshot residue."

Marta shook her head. "The guy's good. You shouldn't let him fluster you so much, though."

"Marta, I'm worried."

"Like I said," Marta emphasized, taking Marshall's hands, "while he can suspect all he wants, he can't tie any of this to us. Unless somebody offers a confession."

"No, I'm not worried about that. It's Sheila. As long as this guy is here, Elvin can't search for Sheila. We've got to figure something out."

Marta saw the hope in Marshall's eyes and felt a deep sadness. He was, she feared, destined to spend a lifetime longing for a result that just wasn't possible.

The training, Naomi felt, was going well. A new primary travelers team, Frank Altman, Gillis Kerg and Macy Gardner, were guiding the elderly rookies through short jaunts into the past, familiarizing Old Bob and Nadine with sensations of time travel, including the uncomfortable duality when merging with your past self.

What kept Naomi up nights, though, a buzzard circling high over this whole enterprise, was the forty-five-year leap these two travelers would make. The information exchange between past and future beings would be overwhelming.

Naomi feared a mental overload would destroy them both.

Marta, Marshall, Frank and Sheila were veteran travelers by the time they attempted a ten-year journey. Marta's past counterpart was so overwhelmed that, fearing a total mental breakdown, future-Marta abandoned her mission. Marshall was convinced that had Sheila not been there waiting for him when he arrived, his younger counterpart would have been overcome as well.

"We've got to find some way," Naomi told the crew, "to slow down that flood of information. Find a way for you—the arriving entity from the future—to control this flow so the past entity isn't hit with it all at once."

"What about a sedative of some kind?" another staff doctor asked.

"We've always avoided traveling under the influence of any drug, because we don't know how the body will handle it."

"A mild sedative could calm the brain," the doctor argued. "The right sedative could even mask memory."

Finding herself at a loss for better ideas, Naomi reluctantly agreed to give it a try. As was usually the case, she chose Frank as the guinea pig.

"Why is that man even here?" Gretchen Allen asked as she and Naomi watched Frank preen at the edge of the projection platform. "He has the attention span of a radish."

Naomi sighed. "He's a product of a flawed selection system. Basically, every significant investor—industry or government—got to pick someone."

"What? I thought there was some sort of strenuous criteria. Like astronauts . . ."

"You physicists have kept yourselves pretty isolated in your own special world here," Naomi said as she laughed. "When it came to assembling the pieces of this project, getting agreement among all the interested parties on anything was nearly impossible. And selection of traveler candidates was just about the last thing they did. So, they gave up and said, 'pick who you want.' A lot of them chose people they wanted to be rid of for five years."

"But we've gotten some good ones, too."

"Yes. Even with such a flawed process, the cream does rise to the top. I don't know how Frank got here, though. His cream is curdled."

"I heard him tell someone once he was a landscaper."

"Which is probably an insult to landscapers everywhere. Take a look at him. He could be an underwear model. Except he probably isn't that ambitious. Mostly, he was an unrepentant womanizer chosen as a traveler candidate by some corporate honcho whose wife enjoyed Frank's landscaping entirely too much. Um . . . forget I said that, because I'm not supposed to talk about the psychological background files."

Gretchen snickered.

"Hey, Frank," Naomi called out, "come here for a minute. I want you to take this pill."

"Why?" Frank asked with a suspicious set to his eyebrows.

"You will be the test subject. Macy will be the control subject," Naomi said.

"What does that mean?" Frank asked. Clad in a robe, he waited next to the projection platform for Gretchen and the other physicists to decide they were ready.

"That means I want you to swallow this." She pushed a round white pill across the top of Elvin's monitor toward him. "Then we'll project you and Macy to last week's mission planning meeting in the *Star Trek* universe. We'll leave you there for about ten minutes. You'll come back and tell us what happened."

Frank pushed the pill back the way it had come.

"Why isn't Macy taking a pill?" His eyebrows became more suspicious.

"Because she's the control subject. We have to be able to see how you act differently from her because of the pill."

"Why am I the one who always has to take the pill? Or try out the taser, or eat the bugs . . ."

"Everybody ate the bugs. In *The Gong Show* universe,

people eat bugs. We weren't picking on you. It just happened that way."

"Okay, then let's have Macy take the pill this time."

"No, Frank. We want you to take it."

"Why me?"

"It's what you're good at."

Reluctantly, Frank took the pill.

When Macy dropped her robe and stepped onto the platform, Naomi watched for Frank's reaction. While he normally would have indulged himself with a long and leering appraisal of Macy's Rubenesque curves, today he seemed to have trouble keeping his eyes open.

Dropping his own robe, he negotiated the small step, yawned and swayed.

In a nearby dimensional plane one week earlier, Naomi presided over yet another pre-mission planning discussion around the oak table. She listened to Macy Gardner say, "No, I don't think they should be made to wait that long. The waiting is—"

She stopped mid-sentence.

"Macy?" Naomi asked.

Macy shook her head and rolled her eyes.

"They're fucking with us again. The *I Love Lucy* guys. She ... I ... am here now, and they want ... Oh. It's just Frank. They're trying something new ..."

Frank gave a start. "What?" His eyes closed, his forehead banged onto the table and he began to snore.

"Well, shit," past-Macy said with future-Macy's voice, "this won't work."

Naomi looked back and forth between the two until Macy said, "She's gone."

Frank sat up and yawned. "I just had the weirdest dream."

"It won't work," the *I Love Lucy* version of Naomi said at the post mission debriefing. "We can't have host beings of arriving travelers mistaken for narcoleptics."

As the staff members stood and shuffled towards the conference room door, Naomi asked Marshall and Marta to stay behind.

"I don't know how we can do this," she said. "I'm verging on desperation. If we can't find some way to regulate the flow of information exchanged between future and past beings, I don't think the past versions of Nadine and Old Bob will survive this."

"What about hypnosis?" Marta asked.

Marshall leaned his chair back and seemed fascinated by a can light embedded in the ceiling.

"Tried it with Frank two missions ago," Naomi said. "Didn't seem to make any difference. But that could have just been Frank."

"Yeah . . . What we need is something that will sit at the front of your brain and block everything else. It needs to dissipate slowly, stemming the flood of information just a bit—long enough for the future being to be sure his past counterpart begins to process the information."

"Well, if hypnosis didn't work, I don't know what—"

Still staring at the light, Marshall interrupted, "Have either of you ever been to Disneyland?"

Naomi vacantly regarded him as he began to hum.

"Hummm, hum hum hum, hummm hum hum. Hummm, hum hum hum, hummm hum hum. Hummm, hum hum hum, hummm hum hum, it's a small, small world . . ."

Marta looked at Marshall as if his transmission had slipped a gear. Naomi grew animated and she joined in, forming a duet.

"It's a small world after all . . ."

"Marshall, you're brilliant. This just might work."

"What are you two talking about?" Marta asked with a bemused smile.

"It's A Small World?" Marshall said. "Disneyland?"

"You want to send travelers to Disneyland?"

"No," Naomi said. "This doesn't have anything to do with Disneyland. It has to do with the song. Of course. You grew up in the Caribbean. You've never had any experience with the Disney culture."

"And you have? In China?"

"There's a Disneyland in Beijing. One of the rides has this song . . . wait."

Naomi typed furiously at the keyboard on her desk and the theme song to *It's A Small Small World* rang through her office.

Marta listened for a few moments. "Okay, stop."

Marshall and Naomi joined the chorus and sang along.

"Stop now." Marta ordered. "I mean it."

"Sure." Marshall motioned for Naomi to turn off the music. "It doesn't matter, though. That song will be stuck in your head for days."

"What makes you think that?"

"Because no one is immune. It's one of *those* songs. It

bores into your brain and attaches itself and makes you want to die."

"Well, gee, Marsh. Thanks for that."

"Marshall's right," Naomi said. "This could be the answer. We need to implant travelers going to the distant past with something that will occupy their minds at the moment of integration into their past self. Something that will stem that overwhelming flood of memories from bursting forth at once. With a really annoying song at the forefront, the other things might sort of seep around it with a more gradual flow that would limit the shock of the experience."

"You're kidding. How could . . ."

Marshall once again began to sing.

Naomi joined him. This time, she harmonized.

Marta put her hands over her ears. "Bastards!" she hissed as she fled the room.

The next day, just before Frank climbed onto the projection platform with Old Bob and Nadine, Naomi approached him. "Could you put these headphones on for just a minute, Frank? I want you to listen to something."

12

BAILING OUT

August 2045

MISSION-DAY JITTERS PERMEATED the projection lab.

Old Bob and Nadine seemed to be the most comfortable of everyone, Marta thought, as they stood patiently in their robes. The scientists, veteran travelers and support staff, though, were clearly nervous. Marta supposed they didn't want to be the ones who screwed up and fried the old folks.

Yuni would not admit to concern over the mission outcome. He was irritated, he said, because Gillis Kerg and Macy Gardner had not yet arrived.

"I made it quite clear," he complained to Marshall and Marta, "everyone associated with the preparation of this mission was to be here."

"I don't know," Marshall told Yuni. "Gillis was right behind me. Then he said he forgot something and needed to go back to the locker room."

"And Macy?" Yuni fussed, fixing a glare at Marta, who had informally become the travelers team coordinator as she awaited her return to active status.

Marta offered only a shrug, then sidled up to Marshall. From the corner of her mouth, she whispered, "I think they're in the janitor's closet."

Marshall gave Marta a startled glance.

"What . . . you mean now?"

"Yeah. Macy's like me. She has had some issues with integration into her past self. So, I told her about, well, you know, my theory that the orgasm made it easier for me on the Flagstaff mission when the other Marta was doing it with Nygel Smythe as I arrived."

"Macy and Gillis . . . ?"

"You know how Gillis always was hot after me?" Marta said. "I mean before you and I got together. And he's been moping around. So, I sort of referred him to Macy . . . to provide assistance."

"They're doing it in the janitor's closet?"

"Yep. Have been just before each mission."

"They're not traveling today."

"Superstition. Macy said it would be bad karma to break the routine."

Marshall snickered, drawing a questioning stare from Yuni.

Marshall regained his composure until Marta whispered again, "Gillis calls it his 'good luck piece.'"

Marshall laughed out loud.

"Is there something you'd care to share with the rest of us, Mr. Grissom?" Yuni asked.

Sheila should be here, Marshall thought as he beheld the curious scene around him. *She would have hated the mission—blatantly interfering with the history of another world—but she would have loved this sendoff.*

A naked old guy and a naked old lady stood in all their

wrinkled and saggy wonder, waiting to be flung forty-five *years* into the maw of history. *It's a Small World* blared through computer speakers, most of the technical staff singing along. Gillis Kerg and Macy Gardner, sweating a little and breathing heavily, appeared on the observation deck.

As the plasma crawled over the globes and Nadine and Old Bob slipped away, Marshall asked Marta, "Do you think they'll be okay?"

"If the song works, I think they'll have a blast. They'll be forty-five years younger. The weight loss alone will make it worthwhile."

Marta and Marshall stood behind Naomi's medical team as they prepared to receive the elderly travelers on their return from the past. For three days, the lifelines on their monitors had been steady red threads with no wavers, no signs of stress.

Marta peered beyond the platform to the opposite side of the room. She frowned at Phillip Lucre, corporate representative of the Hemisphere Investment Group, who had been invited to attend today's activities as an observer. Lucre paced like an expectant father.

They would know within a matter of hours, Marta thought. And if the election outcome had been changed, if Lucre and his cohorts won, the future of time travel would fall under the control of those who cared only for profit at the expense of scientific research. Many of the scientists, she knew, hoped the past *could* be altered, assuring their research would be allowed to go its own way. They were unaware, though, that Andrew Gormly and Jason Pratt had already demonstrated unequivocally the ruthlessness with which the Hemisphere Investment Group would pursue its interests.

Marta felt a familiar rage building within her. She knew she needed to set it aside. So, she reviewed the mission plan.

Both Nadine and Old Bob were unmarried and living in Ohio and Connecticut respectively when Gore and Bush had run for president. The plan called for them to travel to Tallahassee. They were allowed three days in the past of the *Hawaii Five-O* universe to meet officials of Florida's State Democratic Party and convince them to undertake changes to their voter education program.

"Here they are," Elvin said as the plasma crawled around the globes again and the same two old people appeared, apparently none-the-worse for their experience.

So, the combination of hypnosis and that stupid song worked, Marta thought.

Given their apparent health, Naomi sent them to their debriefing sessions with the medical staff and waited for the time projector to recycle. As soon as it did, Gillis Kerg and Macy Gardner were dispatched into the recent past of *Hawaii Five-O*. A half-hour later, they returned.

"You got us to the correct universe?" Gillis called to Elvin as he accepted a technician's offer of a robe.

"No question."

"Then this is interesting."

Phillip Lucre crowded forward along with Marta, Marshall and the other scientists and staff.

"We traveled a single day into the past and did a quick internet search regarding the 2000 election."

"And?" Lucre asked, standing so close Marta felt his hot breath on her neck.

"News accounts carried no mention of 'hanging chads.' The voter instruction effort apparently worked . . ."

The victorious smile spreading across Lucre's face died when Gillis added, ". . . however, although far fewer ballots were disqualified, George W. Bush somehow still won the Florida election by a margin of exactly 537 votes."

Lucre seemed to shrink a couple of sizes. He turned and shoved through the crowd, roughly pushing Marshall aside as he left.

"Pardon me," Marshall called after him. Lucre gave him no notice.

"Not a happy camper," Marta said as she watched him go. "Now we wait and see what happens to the funding."

Before the end of the day, Lucre caught a flight to Denver. A secretary ushered him into Warren Pitts' office. Pitts stood with his back to Lucre, staring at the evening lights blooming across downtown Denver.

Lucre waited through an awkward silence until the door opened again. Gustav Graber joined them. Now Pitts turned and, still ignoring Lucre, nodded to Graber.

"Warren," the board chairman said, "it's difficult to see where we can go from here. We've got to pull back."

"I know, I know," Pitts said with disgust. "We've put billions down that rat hole. It still chaps me to think . . . I hate to walk away when there could still be a payoff out there."

"Don't worry, Warren," Graber said. "Nobody will pass judgment for this outcome."

And if you believe that . . . thought Lucre.

"What needs to occur," Pitts grumbled, "is a less

ambiguous test. All the experiments have been half-measures. Entirely too timid to get a clear result regarding manipulation of the past."

"And what sort of test would provide clarity?" Lucre asked. He thought the end result of the 2000 election was pretty evident.

Both Pitts and Graber regarded him as if they only now noticed his presence.

Pitts did not hesitate. "Find a principal historical figure—politician, writer, artist. Send someone back and shoot the fucker. See how history handles *that*."

"Speaking in a broad hypothetical sense, of course," Graber added quickly.

"Of course," Lucre said.

"It's a moot point, though," Graber reminded them. "We must cut our losses and move on."

13

OFF THE HOOK

"SO, ARE WE DONE?" Marshall asked. "Will everybody pack up and leave? What happens to Sheila if they shut this place down?"

"No way," Elvin answered as he raised his empty glass in one more effort to get a waitress's attention and refill his beer glass. "They've got a fucking time machine. Most of the infrastructure is paid for. Even if all the private investors leave, you think the government will walk away from that?"

Marta scanned the room crowded with scientists and technicians who held security levels high enough to know the outcome of the Gore/Bush mission that day. They drank heavily, clapped each other on their backs, hugged and shook hands. Like a wake. Bidding the dearly departed goodbye.

"What are your guys telling you?" Elvin asked Marta.

Even though Elvin knew she and Gillis were both spies, Marta wasn't comfortable with acknowledging her role.

"My guys don't tell me anything, Elvin. I tell *them* stuff. It's pretty rare that information flows back the other way . . . Uh, oh. Look out."

She saw the grinning face of Sheldon Wishcamper, who

bobbed along through the crowd on a determined path to their table.

"May I join you?" Wishcamper asked after already seating himself. He looked around the room. "Quite a party. Sort of whistling in the dark, wouldn't you say?"

"Okay, what do *you* think will happen?" Marta asked him.

"Oh, I give you about two months. No one's supposed to know yet, but the board chairman of Hemisphere Investment Group contacted the oversight subcommittee chairman this evening, indicating they'd be giving their formal notification of withdrawal before the end of the week. I figure it won't take long for the rest of the investors to follow."

"That'll be a security nightmare, won't it?" Marta asked. "You'll have all these people leaving with no big cash incentives to keep quiet . . ."

"We're not too worried. I'll be holding a series of meetings beginning tomorrow with the different groups, according to their security clearances. I'll remind them of their legal obligations, and I'll emphasize that their contracts allow us to hold them for an unspecified time period awaiting trial should they violate their oaths of secrecy."

"That'll keep you busy for the next several days." Marta poured more wine into her glass.

"Well, it's not like I have anything else to do. I'll be gone by the end of the week myself."

Marshall looked at Elvin, then Marta, then Wishcamper. "Gone? What about . . . what about the investigation?"

"With the way things are heading, Senator Mumford

thinks I can better spend my time elsewhere. Besides, I've taken my investigation as far as it can go. There are a lot of smart people here with some very sophisticated technology."

I will never allow Marshall to play poker, Marta thought as she saw him sag with an expression of total relief. He might as well have wiped his forehead and said *whew*.

Clearly, Wishcamper did not miss Marshall's tell.

"I don't suppose," he said, shifting his gaze among the trio facing him, "that you'd be willing to clarify for me what role you three played in the deaths of Raul Hinojosa, Sheila Schuler, Andrew Gormly and Jason Pratt?"

"Who... who said any of them are dead?" Marshall asked, and added hastily, "besides Sheila, I mean."

Marta clamped her hand on Marshall's thigh and gave it a sharp squeeze.

Wishcamper smiled. "Oh, they're dead. I can't prove it yet, but they are. Even Gormly. His bosses at Hemisphere think he's missing and are quite concerned about that. He's dead, though."

"Well, if he is, and the others are, too, what leads you to believe we had anything to do with it?" Marta asked between sips of wine.

"Circumstance. You three were all there the night Ms. Schuler was lost. You all gave statements explaining how her lifeline faded during her return through the limbo. And those statements were consistent. Maybe a little... coordinated? And we have a janitor disappearing that same night. No one at Hemisphere seems to have encountered Mr. Gormly since then. Do you accept coincidence in your line of work, Ms. Hamilton?"

He raised his eyebrows in an unmistakable message that

her *line of work* was no mystery to him, either.

"I don't," he continued. "And no, who you work for doesn't concern me. You're just another set of eyes for an interested investor. Yet... I can't help suspecting that Mr. Hinojosa's absence is somehow related."

"You're wrong," Marta said. "We didn't do it."

Wishcamper looked at the three of them with imploring eyes and was met by silence. "So, you won't? Tell me, I mean? Because I'd really like to know."

Still no response.

"Well, all right," he sighed, his smile remaining as he rose from the table, "I'll leave you with one thought. Sometimes, you might not realize who your friends really are."

"Elvin," Marshall whispered as Wishcamper danced and dodged his way through the crowd, "go right now and turn your equipment back on. Resume the search for—"

"Let's give it a couple of days," Marta said, finally losing sight of Wishcamper as he made it to the door. "Give Gillis a chance to make sure Wishcamper didn't leave something behind. He could be decoying us. In the meantime, I think I need a serious drink."

Marshall steered Marta to her apartment. She'd gotten into the whisky, and he found if he didn't keep a guiding hand on her arm or shoulder, she tended to veer off course and bump into the walls.

Marta's apartment spoke not a word as once inside, she kissed him and removed her shirt. They sat on the couch and fooled around for a while. She was purring a little when she sat up and interrupted him in midgrope.

"Do you ever worry about gnus?"

"News?" he asked. "Not really. I check things on the computer every once in a while. But mostly it's just the same old stuff."

"No," she protested, waving a finger in his face. "Not news. Gnus."

"Um . . . there's a difference?"

She snorted a laugh.

"Gnus. The big ugly cow things that live in rice paddies and jungles."

"Oh, yeah," Marshall said. "You mean wildebeests. If you said wildebeests, people would be less confused."

"They wouldn't," Marta said. "Because the plural of wildebeest is not wildebeests. The plural of wildebeest is wildebai. A little-known fact. If I said wildebai, *no* one would know what I'm talking about. Besides, they didn't scare me until I realized they're called gnus. That's a sinister word. Don't you think that's a sinister, deceptive word?"

She gazed at him with sincerity, but Marshall thought her eyes were a bit unfocused.

"You're afraid of gnus?" he asked. He didn't think Marta was afraid of anything.

"I don't know if *afraid's* the right word. More like, they creep me out. These big sweaty cowey guys. And their noses are always running. Anyway, in all the pictures they are. Sometimes I have dreams about them."

"Well," Marshall said as sincerely as he could manage, "you know what that means, don't you?"

"No. What?"

"It means that no gnus is good gnus."

The apartment giggled.

Marta closed one eye in a half squint, the opposite eyebrow rising to a little peak.

"I was going to make love to you, but I'm not sure I can trust a man who would tell a joke like that when he's sober."

14

THE NEW BOSS

November 2045

"So . . . SO WHEN WE START up again, you won't be traveling?" Marshall asked.

"I don't like giving it up. Along with everything else, though, I have to face the reality that I don't travel well."

Marta and Marshall, their arms, legs and lips a sweaty entanglement, lay together at Marshall's apartment. Marta's moment of introspection came during a lull as she decided to stop procrastinating and break the news she'd been avoiding all day. She had accepted the congressional oversight subcommittee's offer to become administrator of a vastly scaled-back time travel research project to be renamed the Historical Research Initiative.

"They're hiding you in the U.S. Postal Service budget," Michael Huxtable had told her. "The postal service deficits are so huge, not even the General Accounting Office will know you're there."

"I think you travel very well," Marshall said, grateful for a moment to catch his breath. "Everyone's had some—"

"No, Marshall, I don't." She ran her fingers lightly across his chest. "I bailed on the Whittier mission. Sheila had to babysit me through the last stages of our Flagstaff mission.

And the integrations are always harder for me than for you or the others. I wouldn't mind if I was only risking myself. Every time I struggle, though, the mission and other travelers are endangered."

"You didn't have any problem with the transition when you arrived for..." He hesitated as her hands wandered down from his chest. "...for the Flagstaff mission."

"That was because my past counterpart was sitting on top of Nigel Smythe, and I arrived when she was in full orgasm. Sheila always insisted that strong sensations ease the process of integration."

"Well, there you go," Marshall said.

"Marshall, before you and I got together, I had sex with another human being maybe twice a year. I think the likelihood that those instances would coincide with arrival dates for other missions will be fairly remote."

Once they were finished, Marshall resurrected a debate they'd been sharing for several days.

"Since Gretchen and Naomi are staying, I think we should just tell them," Marshall said. "That way, Elvin wouldn't need to sneak around so much while he's searching for Sheila."

"No, Marshall," Marta replied. "The worst thing if you're trying to keep something secret is to expand the base of people who are in on it."

"We *know* them. They would want to help."

"And we'd be putting them at risk, making them complicit in a crime if they *didn't* report it. Besides, Elvin says there's progress."

Marshall sighed. Elvin had told him the day before that he'd narrowed the time frame to when Sheila had been projected. Soon, he might be able to target a specific year. Marshall was skeptical. He suspected Elvin, Marta, Gillis and Leonard were going through the motions to humor him.

He had another jarring thought.

"Elvin *is* staying, right? I mean he's always acting pissed off, like he'd walk out any time if he could."

"Don't worry about Elvin, I know how he acts. I also know this is the best gig he'll ever have. He's fascinated with his physics research. Besides, now that the staff is so much smaller, we'll modify our contracts and let people go off campus once in a while. That means he can go to Las Vegas and gamble on weekends."

Sheldon Wishcamper had nailed it. Two months following the Hemisphere Group's withdrawal, most other private investors were gone, and various governments were quickly following. Marshall despaired while the world of the Global Research Consortium fell apart. Then came a miraculous reprieve. The governments of the United States, Great Britain and the Grand Duchy of Luxembourg would continue.

Although the program would be vastly scaled back, reflecting limited levels of funding, time travel research would endure. And Marta would be in charge.

"Michael Huxtable is a big-time administrator," Marta told Marshall when he'd asked for details. "He's not about to preside over the death throes of a major program, secret or not. Wouldn't look good on his résumé. If Yuni wasn't leaving, too, he would have been the obvious choice. He didn't say so, but I think he couldn't cope with Sheila's death. He knew we weren't telling him the truth, and I think he felt . . . betrayed."

Gretchen and Naomi were not interested in administration, she said. They wanted to be on the front lines of research. "They offered it to Leonard, but he knew I would have found a way to block that, so he turned it down."

"You're letting him stay, though?"

"Yes, he's good at what he does. He likes the research, and I want to keep an eye on him. So that left you and me as the senior travelers."

"Me? No way," Marshall said. "What about Frank?"

"Frank can't even manage himself. He's gonna take his money and run. He can't wait to embark on a life of conspicuous consumption."

The money thing had worked out okay, Marshall conceded. Everyone employed at the GRC—from the scientists and technicians to the travelers and traveler candidates to the clerical and janitorial staffs—had signed five-year contracts agreeing to be restricted to the ultra-secret research facility during that time.

They were paid salaries more than competitive with jobs they left behind. Given the circumstances, most saved a lot of their money. Upon completion of their contracts, everyone was promised a bonus, with travelers at the top of the scale.

When investors bailed, though, the bonus plan was modified.

"Aren't they worried some people will be mad about getting shorted?" Marshall asked.

"Oh, the bonuses are still pretty good. That, combined with the threat of prison, should keep people quiet."

"What about government people or the tycoons? Their offices leak stuff all the time."

"Are you kidding?" Marta said. "None of the politicians or CEOs want voters and stockholders to know how much money they spent on a failed program. You think thousand-dollar toilet seats and five hundred-dollar hammers piss off taxpayers? Can you imagine how angry they'd be if they knew billions had been spent to send a few naked people off to the pasts of other universes, and that we blew up one whole universe while we were at it?"

"So, basically you get to decide who to keep?"

"Yeah." Marta shrugged. "A lot of people are leaving voluntarily, because they don't think this thing is going anywhere. With the help of Gretchen and Naomi, though, we've picked the scientists and techs we hope will remain. As for travelers, we'll see. I know I want Gillis and Macy."

"And me," Marshall said. "I want to start traveling again, too."

15

ROOTS

November 2045

"CECIL'S MARGIN SERVICE?" Marta asked when GRC administrator Michael Huxtable officially handed over his files.

"Yes, Cecil's is the lone remaining corporate contributor."

"I thought none were left."

"Well, for all practical purposes . . ."

Marta studied a screen displaying the content of the data disk Huxtable had handed her. She tried to make sense of the company name. "What in the world is Cecil's Margin Service?"

"Apparently at one time it was a small specialty printing operation. Details are vague. Today, it appears to be a veterinary service of some kind."

"And is there a Cecil?"

"Oh, yes. He's the company's corporate representative to the program and holds a limited security clearance that goes with it. He could have come to witness a projection if he'd wanted to. He's never contacted us, though."

"Who did this Cecil report to in the corporation?"

"Apparently there's only him. He listed a board consisting of two individuals named Raul and Fidel, but they . . . uh . . ."

Huxtable mumbled something Marta didn't quite hear.

"They what?" she asked.

"Um . . . they turned out to be cats."

She slipped the data disc into her computer and perused the opening page.

"And their annual budgetary contribution is . . . there's a typo here. This says $745. That must be $745,000, $745 million?"

"No . . ." Huxtable said. "No, $745 is correct."

"Seven hundred and . . . That makes no sense. Corporations put up millions, and in a couple of cases, hundreds of millions. How did some tiny company—"

"An anomaly," Huxtable explained.

During the formative days of the program, he said, many major corporations received vague solicitations regarding a new technological endeavor. A careful dance that balanced security considerations with corporate interests ensued and key corporate representatives were gradually informed about the program. Each corporation making a financial commitment named a liaison person who received limited access and reported to key members of the corporate board, also privy to the secret.

"Apparently," Huxtable said, "information intended for Cecillium Machine Services—a giant Australian firm dealing with exotic alloys—instead found its way to Cecil's Margin Service, a tiny operation in Spokane, Washington. And bureaucracy being what it is, the error was never corrected."

"Why not?"

"You're new at this, Ms. Hamilton. This is the sort of thing you'll understand better after you've dealt with a bureaucratic system for a few months. Once something is done in the machinations of a vast bureaucracy, more time and money is often required to undo it than the effort is worth."

"I am not," Marta said to Marshall as they walked to her office, "beginning my new job by capitulating to bureaucracy. At the very least, I'll make an effort to clear this up. I'm fine with answering to a secret Congressional subcommittee. I can deal with Parliament. With Gillis's help, I'm sure I can deal with the Grand Duke of Luxembourg. I'll be damned, though, if I'll have to explain to myself to some veterinarian who lives on a sailboat."

"Pack your bags," Marta said. "We're going to Grenada. In the Caribbean."

"Wow," Marshall said. "You mean me, too?"

Marta made a point of turning a full circle, arms crooked and hands pointing, like a model from a television game show, to demonstrate an absence of anyone else in the room.

"Um . . . will you tell Elvin to keep working on the Sheila project while we're gone?"

"Yes. I'll tell Elvin."

"Do I need to buy a plane ticket?"

"No, Marshall. This is official business. The Historical Research Initiative is paying."

"Oooh, so it's a junket."

"No. We'll talk to this Cecil character. I've tracked him down and his sailboat is tied up there for the season."

"Grenada. That's that place Ronald Regan invaded, right?"

"Yes."

"Are they still mad about it?"

"No, Marshall. They like Ronald Reagan. They asked him to do it."

Only a few months ago, Marta would not have thought twice about facing any sort of challenge alone, personal or otherwise. Marshall's presence in her life, though, offered possibilities she hadn't considered, including moral support. She told herself she needed to keep Marshall close because of Gillis's concern that he was a secret super-spy. She told herself she did it because of the sex. If she'd been under the unforgiving spell of the limbo, she'd have admitted she wanted someone who cared about her close by, because she lacked confidence about how she'd cope with her return to the exotic part of the world where she'd spent her childhood.

She sat quietly during the flight from Phoenix to Miami and appreciated that Marshall knew intuitively to grant her distance. After boarding a connecting flight in Florida, suspended thirty-five thousand feet over brilliant tropical seas, she felt her past like a crushing weight.

"Are you okay?" Marshall asked tentatively.

Marta stared through the window at a golden archipelago far below them, framed by emerald green water dissolving into a brilliant blue as it spread beyond the beaches and reefs of some anonymous island.

"I don't know," she said. "I didn't think going back would be this hard . . ."

"How long has it been since you've visited the islands?"

Marta sighed, her eyes fixed on the scene scrolling below. "I was eighteen."

"You haven't been home at all?"

"There's nothing for me there," she said softly.

"What about family?"

At first, she took on her steely glare that warned people to keep away. She never talked about family. At this moment, though, she found she wanted to tell Marshall her story. She took a deep breath.

"Okay. My family. My mother bounced in and out of our lives. Every time some guy came along who she thought offered a better deal than my dad could match, she took off. He always took her back, though. I don't know why. She left for good when I was fourteen.

"I have a sister. She was sixteen and following my mother's example. She quit school and took up with some bum—drug dealer probably. We didn't see much of her either. So, it was me and my dad. He was a good man. I was smart. I did well in school, and he gave me all the encouragement he could afford."

Her voice cracked. She looked down to the ocean. "He died when I was seventeen. A diving accident."

Marshall took her hand.

"I graduated from high school, accepted a military service scholarship to attend university in London. Then I was recruited by the British Secret Service, got my Royal Air Force commission as cover, and that was that."

"You ever hear from your sister?"

"No. I don't know if she's alive or dead. I don't care."

Marshall put his arm around her and pulled her close. Her instinct was to resist. His gesture could be perceived as a presumption of weakness. The hug offered her an alternative, though. The rare opportunity to abandon herself to her feelings, if only momentarily. She surrendered to his embrace.

Her ultimate reaction, though, was different than either of them might have imagined.

When they deplaned at the airstrip near St. George's, Grenada, Marshall's senses were overwhelmed by a salty, humid smell of the sea breeze, a sweet intermingling odors of nutmeg, cinnamon, cloves and vanilla, the lilt of island accents, and the thick mantle of green covering this beautiful dot in the Caribbean Sea like a fuzzy quilt.

Marta clung to his arm as they headed across the tarmac towards a miniature airport terminal. As they walked, a nervous tension flowing through her small hand and into him like an intravenous drip seemed to ebb with each step. When she raised an arm to hail one among the gaggle of taxis outside a rustic baggage claim area, Marshall felt he was in the company of a person he only vaguely knew. Like a butterfly wriggling from the prison of its cocoon, an island girl emerged from Marta's hard protective shell before his eyes.

"God, it's so beautiful." She leaned her head onto Marshall's shoulder as their taxi wound its way toward their destination.

The taxi carried them past the Careenage, a sheltered horseshoe bay that served as the center of St. George's tourism and commerce. In days of empire, kings and pirates, this was where tall ships came to be careened so their wooden hulls could be scraped clean and repaired. From here the road looped south to a white sand beach at the base of a small hill in a place called Prickly Bay. The hill sloped gently to the shore of a marina, featuring a series of three docks. A young boy sat with his skinny butt in the water, wielding a fishing knife as he cleaned a grouper that might have weighed as much as he did.

"Hey, mon," the boy called without looking up from his work as Marshall and Marta approached, "you wanna buy a fish?"

"Um . . . I don't know what I'd do with a fish," Marshall said.

"You eat it, mon. You one'a da slow ones?"

"Slow . . ."

The boy looked up and squinted against the descending sun.

Marta laughed. "We don't have anywhere to cook a fish, cousin."

"I cook da fish for you. No charge."

"You keep your fish," Marta said. "Take it home to your momma. I'll pay you twenty dollars for information, though."

The boy stood, dusted sand from the bottom of his swim trunks and hoisted his fish from the water.

"What you wanna know?"

"Tell us where we can find a man named Cecil."

The boy grinned, pointing toward the ocean. "Somewhere Over China."

"But they told us he was here," Marshall said. "What would he be doing in China?"

The boy laughed. "Da boat, mon, da boat."

"It's an old song," Marta told Marshall. "Jimmy Buffet, I think. My cousin is telling us that's the name of Cecil's boat."

The boy pointed again. Marta followed the line of his

finger to a ketch rocking on a gentle rhythm of shifting water at the far end of the center dock. Marta handed the boy a twenty-dollar bill, which he folded and placed in a damp pocket.

"Where's your cat?" the boy asked as they turned to go.

"Our cat?" Marta asked.

"Most people visit Mr. Cecil take him a cat."

Marta gave the boy a curious look as they stepped up to the dock.

"Were we supposed to bring a cat?" Marshall asked.

Marta didn't answer. She smiled in a way Marshall hadn't seen before. "I used to be that kid sitting in the water cleaning a fish."

And with each step down the long boardwalk, Marshall sensed Marta was being pulled by the power of an outgoing tide as he hurried to keep up with her. Halfway along the dock, she handed Marshall her briefcase and began to shed her clothes. First sandals, then her shirt. She dropped her bra as they reached the stern of a stately old ketch-rigged Tyana with *Somewhere Over China* painted a couple of feet above the water line along the bow.

"Marta, what are you . . ."

Clearly, she was somewhere beyond the sound of his voice. He stood and watched as she performed a graceful dive and was swallowed by emerald water. Her panties floated to the surface.

He sprinted after her and peered into twenty feet of ocean so clear and still, the vibrant reds and yellows and greens and pinks of the reef fairly glowed below him. The scene was so bright, he first thought the light source must come from below rather than the sun and stark blue Caribbean sky.

He watched Marta's nude body glide effortlessly through the depths, as if the world of air and sand was only a place she visited. The spell broke when he began to wonder if she would ever come up to breathe. When she finally did, she bumped the surface for just a moment and, with a graceful kick, pushed herself back to the reef.

Only then did Marshal glance to his right, to the deck of the boat rocking against the dock. He saw an old man smiling as he, too, seemed utterly absorbed by Marta's transformation from land being to aquatic creature.

"She's somethin', dontchaknow," the man said, turning to Marshall with a wink.

Marshall knelt and reached to retrieve Marta's underwear. "Oh, yes. Yes, she . . . Um, I'm sorry. She doesn't usually do this sort of thing . . ."

The old man dismissed Marshall's apology with a wave. "Don't think a thing of it. Happens all the time down here, dontchaknow. The Caribbean does that to folks."

Marshall beheld a stick-thin codger who might have been made of leather. A full shock of white hair protruded at all angles from beneath a navy-blue Seattle Mariners baseball cap with a teal-colored bill. The cap was marked with a halo of salty white sweat stains. He wore a sleeveless T-shirt hanging loosely over his slender frame, suspended on his shoulders by two thin straps of cotton. Khaki cargo shorts ballooned around his spindly thighs. He was barefoot. Two hairless cats, both slathered with a layer of whitish lotion, reclined next to him.

The man leaned over the lifelines with an extended hand. "The name's Cecil."

"I'm Marshall Grissom." He accepted a deceptively

strong grip. "Um . . . nobody told us we were supposed to bring a cat." Marshall glanced warily at the pink-skinned felines. "I like cats, though."

"Pleased tameetcha. And don't worry about the cat."

They both turned back to the water as Marta broke the surface a few yards away.

"I don't suppose you have a mask and snorkel?" she called to the old man.

Cecil grinned again, rummaged through the space below a cockpit seat-cover and tossed the items over the stern. "And a set of fins, too."

Marta deftly tucked the fins onto her feet while treading water, then dove to retrieve the rest. Marshall watched in amazement as, twenty feet below, Marta pulled on the mask, cleared it with a quick blast of air through her nose, kicked with the fins and fairly flew across the bay.

16

ONE MOJITO OVER THE LINE

"WHY DONTCHA' COME ABOARD. I suspect she's gonna be a while. I got rum, and I got iced tea."

Although Marshall was not much of a drinker, the islands were working their spell on him, as well. "Maybe just a nip of the rum."

He hauled himself over the lifelines and onto the deck of *Somewhere Over China.*

Cecil disappeared below and returned with a sweaty pitcher of faintly green liquid that displayed mint leaves floating through it.

"Try a mojito. My own recipe."

Marshall took a careful sip to test it. The bittersweet concoction tasted like the garish splashes of color all around him. He took a deep swig.

"I gotta' warn ya'," Cecil cautioned, "you'd best stick to sippin,' else that rum'll kick your butt."

Marshall felt a soothing, pleasant glow begin to form somewhere toward the back of his brain.

"A fellow could get used to this," he said.

"A fella sure could." Cecil smiled.

Marshall stared back into the green water where Marta

chased a school of clownfish. He decided not to interfere with her pursuit. He would have to interview Cecil by himself. He asked for another mojito and scratched the two cats on their bare bellies. "We're with the Global Research Consortium—I guess now we call ourselves the Historical Research Initiative. I'm assuming you know what that is."

Cecil narrowed his eyes, regarding Marshall with a look of suspicion. "Never heard of it."

Marshall withdrew a sheaf of papers from Marta's briefcase. They were copies of the checks Cecil had sent to the program over the years. Marshall also produced an official government ID.

Cecil inspected the papers. "I wondered if one of you fellas was ever gonna show up. I thought of calling someone out there in Arizona a couple of times. But since the whole thing was a secret, I didn't want to ask directory assistance for a phone number of the time travel place."

Cecil spoke with an accent that emanated from somewhere around Wisconsin, Minnesota and the southern regions of central Canada, but without the "eh?" As Marshall took another deep drink, he found Cecil's vocal inflection contained a particularly pleasant resonation.

"I'm a little unclear about this 'margin' thing," Marshall said.

"It's a long story, dontchaknow."

"And now you're some kind of veterinarian?"

"No. I wax cats."

Marshall regarded the two hairless felines and nodded thoughtfully. "So how did you get involved with our program in the first place?"

Cecil peered carefully around the dock. "Are you sure it's okay to just talk about this? National security and all?"

Marshall followed Cecil's gaze and saw only the boy finishing up with his catch where the dock met a distant shore.

"Well . . ." Marshall began with a shrug.

Cecil pointed to the sky. "What about them spy satellites?"

"Oh, I think we're okay."

Cecil gave a furtive glance to his left and right, pulled the bill of his baseball cap low and leaned close.

"I got a letter. I told them I might be interested. Then they sent me some reports on the time travel stuff, and I thought that sounded like a pretty good deal. So, I signed the papers and sent 'em a hundred bucks."

"We're here to apologize, Mr. . . . um . . . Cecil. We want to give you your money back. I think it comes to $6,561.23 if we've added the checks correctly . . ." He gave a snorting laugh and continued with a bit of a slur, "We've got the best mathematicians in the world down there. Of course, we added it correctly."

Cecil didn't reach to accept Marshall's offering. "I don't want my money back. In fact, I have this quarter's payment ready to go. You can save me the postage."

He retreated to the cabin and came back with his own check for three hundred and forty-three dollars.

"No." Marshall waved his arms to ward off the check. "We can't keep taking your money."

"Why not?"

"Because it was a mistake. The solicitations and descriptions of the program that accompanied them were only supposed to go to major corporations. Average, ordinary people were never supposed to know about this."

Cecil laughed. "No one's called me average or ordinary in longer than I can remember."

Cecil folded his check, leaned close to Marshall, and stuffed it into Marshall's shirt pocket. "I think you're doing good work over there, dontchaknow, and I enjoy reading those reports."

"The reports are classified."

"I haven't told anyone. And they're locked up. I know how to keep a secret."

"The money you provide is ingisnificant... um... insignificant," Marshall said with some difficulty. "I'm sorry. I don't mean to be condescending. This program is enormously expensive..."

"All the more reason to contribute. I think a citizen needs to support the worthwhile things their government does. I donate to public radio, too. Here, let me pour you another mojito."

Clearly, Marshall would fail to convince Cecil to take the money. And, Marshall reasoned, if they insisted that Cecil withdraw his involvement, they risked having the old man raise a ruckus that could bring attention nobody wanted. He wished he could consult with Marta, but she was still under water.

He sighed and drank deeply. The two cats threaded themselves between his legs as they chirped and purred.

Having nothing more to say, he and Cecil shifted their attention to the bay as Marta glided toward them. She disappeared momentarily below the dock as she pulled herself onto a wooden ladder at the end of the platform. One swim fin flipped onto the dock, then the other. Finally, Marta emerged, wearing only the mask and snorkel, which she placed at her feet.

Eyes closed, she stood facing them for a moment, her mahogany breasts glistening, hair beaded with water. She shook her head and sent a fine spray that shimmered like a rainbow as it reflected the sun in a halo around her.

"You should ask your wife," said Cecil, "if she wants me to wax her cat."

"She's not my wife," Marshall slurred, "and she doesn't have a cat."

"Well," Cecil said with a wink. "Yaneverknow."

Cecil tossed Marta a towel. She reluctantly gathered what clothing she could find—her bra was missing in action, adorning some starfish or anemone clinging to pilings below the surface—and dressed. She boarded *Somewhere Over China* and formally met Cecil, as well as Raul and Fidel. She found the old man charming. They chatted while Marshall finished his fourth mojito.

She told Cecil about Nevis. He said he'd made port at St. Kitts once, though he hadn't visited the little sister island next door. He promised he would when next he headed north to the Leeward Islands.

As they talked, she recognized with melancholy the receding of the island spell as the mantle of her professional persona slipped back into place. She repeated Marshall's efforts to extricate Cecil from the time travel project and return his money. And like Marshall, she failed.

Finally, she said, "Mr., uh, Cecil. As administrator of

this program, I'll have to deal with a variety of government officials and their egos in trying to accomplish anything. And frankly, I can't waste time worrying that you're going to show up with some hair-brained idea and expect us to..."

"Oh, Marta," Marshall slurred, "relax. Cecil's a good guy. I like his cats. You can tell a lot about a person from his cats."

"Yes, Marshall, I like his cats, too, but you're drunk, and I've got a program to run."

"He gave us another check." Marshall fumbled with his shirt pocket. "Look here. Three hundred and forty-three dollars. Are you going to turn your back on three hundred and forty-three dollars?"

"Marshall, what would we do with three hundred and forty-three dollars?"

"Hats. We could buy everybody hats. With time travel logos. Have you noticed that we don't have hats?"

"Cecil," she said, "I'm sorry. I fear we've overstayed our welcome..."

"We need more people like Cecil," Marshall continued. "As long as he's not a pain in the ass." He tugged Cecil aside and whispered loudly, "That's what she's worried about, you know. You won't be a pain in the ass, will you?"

"Well, if I am, it'll be from long distance. I'm not goin' anywhere I can't sail to, dontchaknow."

Marshall grinned, then fumbled to put on the sandals he'd kicked off two mojitos earlier. He stood with deliberation, gave a little wobble, and steadied himself. He made his best effort at a flamboyant salute. Marta cringed. Marshall's repertoire did not include flamboyance.

She wasn't quick enough to catch him.

He appeared to attempt a step forward. He swung his arms and his upper body leaned in the correct direction. His feet, though, remained rooted to the spot. He flailed briefly before momentum caused him to descend like a drawbridge. He made a flapping motion with his arms, as if to levitate himself, and failed—flamboyantly. His head was the first point of contact with the deck.

"Hmmmmm," said Cecil.

"Oh, my," said Marta as Marshall rolled onto his back, apparently uninjured. "I was afraid of this.

"On St. Kitts," she said to Cecil, "there's a lean-to shack on the beach called *Sunshine's Bar and Grill* where they serve fresh lobster and a rum concoction called *The Killer Bee*. Sunshine once told me that *The Killer Bee* gets you drunk from the feet up. Some tourist would keel over and Sunshine would cackle, 'Anoda one, stung by da killa' bee.' I see now what he means."

"I guess I over-served him," Cecil agreed. "Sorry about that. And that other stuff? Don't think a thing about it. Like I told Marshall, I can keep a secret. And you never know when you might need somebody to fix a margin or wax a cat."

Marta sighed. "Okay, you're still in the program if you want to be. If you ever appear before the congressional oversight subcommittee, though, we might want to keep quiet about the cat waxing thing."

Together they managed to haul Marshall over the sailboat's lifelines and onto the dock where they loaded him into one of the wheelbarrows sailors use to ferry supplies from the beach to the boats.

"Marta, I have a confession to make," Marshall slurred as she and Cecil rolled him along. "A deep and dark secret that I've kept from you, and I can't stand the deception any longer. I hope you still like me when I tell you."

"I already know." Marta directed a roll of her eyes at Cecil. "You're allergic to anchovies."

"Um . . . yes. Yes, I am. But besides that . . . well . . . well . . . the only thing to do is just come out and say it."

"Okay."

"Okay. I have a middle name."

"Me, too."

"No, no," Marshall said. "You don't understand. I didn't tell anyone. I didn't put it on the forms when I signed up to be a time traveler. I probably committed some kind of felony, didn't I?"

"Why didn't you put your middle name on the forms?"

"I don't ever put it on forms. It's because my middle name is Redleaf."

"Redleaf?" Cecil asked.

"Redleaf," Marshall mumbled sadly. "There. I've said it."

"Wow," Cecil said. "How did that happen?"

"My mom. My mom comes from American Indian ancestry. Cherokee . . . and she wanted me to have a name that reflected my heritage. She looked out the window the day I was born—they lived in the Pacific Northwest then—and she saw a sumac bush that had just turned with the fall colors."

He sighed heavily. "She thought it was a sign." He paused and added, "My dad was against it." He peered fearfully at Marta through slightly unfocused eyes.

"Did you tell them about the anchovies?"

"Of course, I did," Marshall said with a note of indignation.

"Then I wouldn't worry. And I still like you."

"Wow, what a relief. I don't tell anyone that—about my middle name, not the anchovies. You're not just anyone, though, you know? I should have told you. What's your middle name?"

"Louise."

"That's not a weird name," Marshall said, almost an allegation.

"I'm sorry."

"Marta is a little bit weird, though," Marshall said after thinking things over for a moment.

"Then I have a confession to make, too," Marta said.

"You're having an affair?" Marshall gasped.

"No. Of course, not. My first name isn't really Marta."

"It's not?"

"No. It's Martha. Marta is just how most people pronounce it here in the Islands. But I don't much care for Martha Louise and I kind of like Marta."

"Me, too."

"So, do you still like *me*?" Marta asked.

"Yep."

He hummed contentedly as they reached the end of the beach, his feet sticking high over the edge of the wheelbarrow.

Marta laughed when she saw that his sandals were on the wrong feet.

During the return flight to Phoenix, Marta allowed herself

the rare indulgence of optimism. By virtue of her training, she was not an optimist. Spies are not taught to anticipate good things happening. They are drilled in disaster, schooled to expect the unexpected, and the unexpected was not expected to be good.

Still, here they were. The Global Research Consortium had been reduced from an impossibly huge bureaucracy with an impossibly huge budget and a viper's nest of political intrigue, to the U.S. Postal Service Historical Research Initiative, a small, collegial operation in which, she hoped, they would be left alone to conduct advanced physics research and make careful explorations of pertinent historical events.

Their government overseers, for the moment at least, were trying to determine how to supervise and regulate time travel and, given their uncertainty, seemed to be keeping their distance.

So maybe, she thought, they could do their research and exploration with a careful eye toward limiting interference with destinies of other universes, and a minimum of drama and intrigue. And she could indulge Marshall's quest to learn whether Sheila, their friend and colleague, had somehow survived at some distant point in the past.

But optimism, she would discover, can flourish in the shadow of cynicism for only so long.

17

ZOMBIES, VAMPIRES AND NINJAS (OH MY)

December 2045

MARSHALL AND MARTA RETURNED from the Caribbean to a vast underground complex with a lot of empty rooms. The shrunken staff allowed for fewer security restrictions, so Marta determined that program participants could take weekends off.

"I think we're the only ones here," Marshall said to her only a few days into the new policy. "I think everyone else left, except the security guys at the front gate."

They were finishing dinner in Marshall's living space. His apartment's artificial intelligence component had gone through several phases as it learned all about sex and had now apparently graduated to a phase where it had been shocked into silence by Marshall and Marta's performances. Marta had expressed satisfaction with the apartment's reticence. Her concern now, she said, would be a progression to lasciviousness.

"If the damned thing starts making suggestions or cheering," Marta said, "I'm getting my gun."

"I guess I'll have to require a minimum staffing schedule for weekends," Marta said as they realized the place was deserted. "Um . . . Marshall, could you do me a big, big favor?"

"Sure."

"I left a background file on my desk—it's the one on Cecil—and I had intended to go over it tonight. Would you mind walking back to my office and getting it for me?"

"Sure." Marshall liked doing favors for Marta. She was so very generous in returning them.

Marshall happily anticipated the coming weekend. He and Marta planned to take down several walls dividing apartments a few corridors over from the projection lab to create the kind of big, hollow living space that might be found in a converted urban warehouse. They planned to start working tomorrow.

He located the Cecil file among piles of computer data discs on Marta's cluttered desk and began his return journey. As he walked, he listened to the echoes of his footfalls in the empty corridors. Soon he began to hum, quietly at first. The resonating acoustics in the hollow hallway encouraged him, so he added words to one of his favorite old songs that seemed to come to mind when he thought of Marta: Randy Newman's *You Can Leave Your Hat On*. While Marshall was not much of a singer, the echoes did such a good job of masking his vocal deficiencies that by the time he reached his front door, he was belting it out. "*. . . and shake 'em. You give me reason to live, you give me reason to live, you give me reason to—*"

He stopped because a scrawled note was taped to his door.

I am being held captive in the physics lab by the evil Dr. Dingus Doonaughty. He has done unspeakable things to me and says he will wreak havoc on mankind if you don't agree to come and perform even more unspeakable things while he observes via the security video system. He has recruited a pantheon of zombies, vampires and ninjas. He says you must not be wearing pants when you arrive. Please help me, Obi-wan Kenobi. You are my only hope.

    Your friend, Marta

This was not Marshall's first encounter with the evil Dr. Dingus Doonaughty. For some reason that Marshall was sure had fascinating psychology behind it—he thought about running it by Naomi and quickly realized *that* would not be a good idea—Marta seemed to crave the occasional elaborate fantasy scenario to augment their already frenetic sex life.

Marshall leaped into action.

First, he took off his pants.

He put on his running shoes, a black pullover shirt, and a black ski mask. He chose an antique Louisville Slugger baseball bat from his closet and took a cucumber from his refrigerator.

"Oh, good," said his apartment. "I was going to mention that you haven't been getting enough roughage in your diet lately."

"Sorry," Marshall said. "I don't have time to talk."

By this time, as was its habit, Mr. Johnson was brimming with enthusiasm. He ran down the hallway with his unruly companion guiding the way.

Reaching the physics lab, he pulled his mask down so only his eyes were showing, tucked the cucumber under his arm, and crashed into the room, swinging the bat wildly to ward off any zombies, vampires and ninjas, of which there were none.

Marta watched with damp amusement from a chair,

sitting squarely under two bright lights that provided the room's only illumination. She was naked, tied to the chair, a gag fixed loosely in her mouth. Marshall made a mental note to ask her how she got herself tied up that way.

Marshall hurried to Marta and loosened the gag.

"My hero," she said.

Marshall did another quick survey of the room before he dropped the baseball bat, pulled off his ski mask and displayed the cucumber.

"What are you going to do with that?" Marta asked.

"Unspeakable things."

As it happened, the demanding Dr. Doonaughty had his own list of unspeakable things to get to first.

"Ooooooooh," Marshall said.

"Mmmmmmmmm," Marta replied.

Finally, the evil doctor required Marshall and Marta to climb onto Gretchen Allen's lab table where Marta rode Marshall until they both exploded, and Marshall cried uncle.

Reluctantly, Marta reported that the evil doctor was probably willing to let mankind off the hook for now. They never did get around to vegetables.

On Monday morning Gretchen Allen was puzzled over the mysterious appearance of a cucumber in her physics lab.

They walked happily hand in hand through darkened corridors—Marta naked and Marshall without pants—toward their apartment.

"Did you remember to turn off the security cameras?" Marshall asked as they walked.

"Of course, not. Don't you want to watch the replay?"

18

A SPECTER OF DEATH

WHILE MARSHALL AND MARTA'S frenzied sex life thrived, Marta began to see storm clouds on their professional horizon. She found herself at a loss as to what to do about her concerns.

She'd discovered Marshall to be an extraordinarily patient and nonjudgmental man. How many guys, after all, would understand about the evil Dr. Doonaughty? Marta, fearful of very few things, had been wary of introducing Marshall to this odd being who had long guided her fantasies and made it possible for a woman of significant libido to tolerate a semimonastic sexual lifestyle in deference to the demands of her job.

While Marshall had clearly been taken aback the first time the evil doctor made his presence known, he'd hesitated only for a moment. He hadn't said this was weird or strange or perverse or even unusual. "Everybody has an imaginary friend at some point in life," he told Marta. "Yours is just older and more... creative than mine was."

Outside the bedroom, though, Marshall asked more and more frequently about returning to active travel status.

"Now that you're the boss, you can approve that, can't you?" he asked Marta.

"Um . . . well . . . that's always been up to Naomi."

True enough.

He hadn't traveled since the Whittier mission months before because of the political climate swirling around the Gore/Bush mission. Quite apart from political considerations, though, following the deaths of Samantha Kennedy and Sheila Schuler, Naomi Hu had been reluctant to certify him as psychologically fit for time travel.

"I told her I'm fine," Marshall said to Marta. "And I am."

"What's the rush? Everything we're doing now is routine. And I know how uncomfortable you were with the spotlight. I thought you'd welcome a break."

With the pressure of meddling investors gone and the scientists free to focus on research, Elvin and Gretchen endeavored to understand the physics behind the *Joey Bishop Show's* demise.

This disaster occurred when counterparts of Elvin, Gretchen, Marta, Marshall and the others from the *Gunsmoke* universe attempted an exchange of travelers with the *Joey Bishop Show*. A horrendous coincidence of timing allowed travelers from different worlds to inadvertently meet themselves in the limbo, and, in a cataclysmic instant, the *Joey Bishop* universe was canceled. Two travelers from *Gunsmoke*—Carla O'Neill and Marshall Grissom—were lost in the explosion.

Elvin and Gretchen now directed a series of quick leaps a few days into the pasts of as many universes as possible, then dissected data concerning this mysterious ether they called the limbo.

"If I was traveling," Marshall said, "I could examine memories of my past counterparts to find out if Sheila is gone from those worlds, too, if the same things had happened, and if we could go back and do anything differently."

"Marshall, if Elvin's theories about the intransigence of history are right, she's gone everywhere."

"I just can't live with this feeling that I'm doing nothing to help her."

Marta sighed. "There's only so much that can be done. I'm convinced Elvin is doing it. Once he pins down a more specific time frame, we can decide where to go from there."

In truth, though, Marta had requested that Naomi delay Marshall's return to active status.

"Is . . . is that an order?" Naomi asked.

Marta followed Naomi into her office and closed the door behind them.

"Does it need to be?"

"No, not right now," Naomi conceded as she gestured for Marta to sit in one of two leather armchairs facing her desk. "Because I don't think it would be wise for Marshall to travel yet."

"Why?"

"Marshall has never dealt with the guilt we created for him regarding Samantha Kennedy's death. He's merely suppressed it. And he has clearly taken Sheila's death personally. She died helping him, so I'm sure he feels a crushing guilt about that as well. Until he can address those issues in some realistic fashion, I'm afraid he might make reckless decisions—sort of a subconscious way to punish himself."

Marta felt a wave of relief. Although Naomi's belief that Sheila's death had in any way been Marshall's fault was mistaken, that erroneous assumption suited Marta just fine.

"Then again," Naomi added pointedly, "*you* haven't dealt with the issues related to why *you* don't want him to travel, either."

Marta did not respond. So long as Naomi would run interference for her, she saw no reason to go into it. She smiled politely and got up to leave.

"I'll be happy to talk with you about that when you're ready," Naomi called after her.

Marta didn't know if Marshall had fully confronted his feelings about Samantha and Sheila or not. That was just so much psychological voodoo as far as she was concerned. All she knew was that she didn't want Marshall running around in the past because he was dead.

Although skeptical of many theories floating about concerning time travel, Marta gave credence to Elvin's notions concerning the flow of history. History, Elvin said, did not appreciate being screwed with.

"Think of a powerful river," Elvin had expounded. "Anything captured by the main current—significant historical figures or events—will not escape."

"So, you're a philosophical Presbyterian?" Marta had asked. "Preordination and all that? Everyone is locked into their destiny from birth, and there's nothing we can do about it."

"That's not what I said. Nobody is destined to do anything. Everybody makes their own choices. Lincoln didn't have to go to the play. Kennedy might have put the top up on the limousine. Custer could have let the Indians slide. Once a choice had been made, though, as major historical players, they were locked in. Time travelers can create all sorts of elaborate plans to change these events, but while in some instances we have successfully altered details, the principle outcome seems to remain the same."

And—Marta suffered a chill every time she thought about Marshall's destiny—everyone involved with the program who finally made time travel possible certainly fit the category of profound historical significance.

"So, if someone is killed in the past of another universe," she'd asked Elvin, "what does that portend for the future counterpart?"

"When left alone," Elvin said, "quantum theory holds that the histories of parallel universes tend to be, well, parallel. Theoretically, the visit of a time traveler from the future skews that parallelism and the historical paths diverge. How much or how little is anybody's guess. But I think there would have to be a helluva divergence for a major historical figure to escape his fate. I think once you're toast in one universe, as soon as it can get around to it, history will catch up to you everywhere else, too."

Like Marshall, Marta had clung to a skeptical hope that Elvin was wrong, until history caught up with Carla O'Neill. Carla fell off a stool while drinking at the Time Warp and hit her head on the bar.

In one of Marta's first bureaucratic confrontations as program administrator, she had used Elvin's theories to successfully argue that Carla's death was work-related.

Secret or not, federally funded and supervised programs

must meet federal guidelines, of which there are, Marta now realized, roughly about a gazillion. And someone must be sure all those guidelines were met. So while the number of people occupying the secret underground chambers of the Global Research Consortium had been drastically reduced as it evolved into the Historical Research Initiative, a healthy contingent of bureaucrats still scurried about in the big office building upstairs, auditing and accounting their little hearts out.

The bureaucrats wanted to write off Carla's death as a fluke accident, having nothing whatsoever to do with time travel. As the new administrator, Marta knew she couldn't display weakness. She wanted Carla's death to be declared work-related so her family would be appropriately compensated.

Citing Elvin's theories, she won that battle only to find she had waded into a quagmire when she received the auditor's official findings. His report declared Marshall Grissom's death to be work-related, as well.

Marta had taken the elevator to the surface, stomped into the chief auditor's office and said, "You can't do this. Marshall isn't dead."

"According to your Mr. Detwyler," the auditor parried, "he surely will be, and sooner rather than later."

"Don't you think you should at least wait until . . . until it's official?"

"We are thinking of the political ramifications," the auditor said.

"The . . . what?"

The auditor leaned back in his chair and shook his head, as if he could not believe the poor naïve creature before him.

"We must file a report every quarter regarding workplace death and injury. The congressional oversight subcommittee tends to become alarmed at death and injury, as does OSHA. We had several mishaps during the construction and testing phase of the project. We expressed these events as the rate of person/days lost, divided by incidents of fatal accidents or maiming injuries on the GRC site. By doing it that way, because the GRC staff at that point was so large, we could present a number that appeared to be very low. And every day that passed without further casualties, the number got lower."

The auditor stood and adjusted the window blinds to cut the glare of the sun streaming into his office. Since Marta's office was underground and she didn't have any sunshine, she thought the twit was just showing off.

"Now, however," he continued with an elaborate stretch of his back, "there aren't very many of you. So, the ratio will be much higher. With the death of Ms. Schuler and Ms. O'Neill within the same six-month period, well, that will draw a lot of attention. Thus, Mr. Grissom's impending death is not a simple matter. The question was, should we just let it occur in its own good time and create the appearance of an ongoing problem, or should we arbitrarily include it with this quarters' report, and argue that, while we had a bad few months, we're doing better as the year progresses."

He sat.

"We decided the latter would be the more politically defensible position."

Marta's first instinct was to return to her apartment, get her gun and add another work-related fatality to the report.

She was an administrator now, though. She needed to refrain from shooting the auditors.

"Well..." she said after a long moment, "what if he doesn't die?"

"I beg your pardon?"

"What if Marshall doesn't die?"

"Ms. Hamilton, you can't have it both ways, now can you? We can't call Ms. O'Neill's death a work-related incident and then treat Mr. Grissom differently."

"That wasn't my question. My question was, what if he doesn't die?"

"Everybody dies." The auditor smiled.

"I mean not any time soon!"

"Well," he said, in a smug show of victory, "I would certainly advise him to retain an attorney when the time comes to apply for social security benefits. That will be an argument I would dearly love to hear, because as far as the federal government is concerned, Marshall Grissom is dead."

Marta felt tempted to refute the auditor's argument by pointing out that Marshall was still receiving a paycheck. She worried if she did, though, the auditor might remedy that as well.

She didn't tell Marshall about any of this. Marshall believed Carla was dead solely because she drank too much and fell off a bar stool. While Marshall might eventually fall off his own bar stool, Marta was determined to keep him off the projection platform. Regardless of whether Elvin or Marshall was right concerning the intransigence of history, she thought sending Marshall to the past under these circumstances would just amount to poking history in the eye with a sharp stick.

19

THE PROBLEM WITH NOW

MARSHALL'S DETERMINATION to retain his traveler's status temporarily became a moot point when he was called to a meeting of key staff by the new administrator. Marta told them no one would be traveling for the next few days.

"Senator Josiah Mumford, the new chairman of the secret oversight subcommittee, is coming to look things over," Marta told Marshall and the others.

Marta sat at her desk in an office with windows overlooking the projection lab. The others occupied chairs or the sofa under the windows.

"I don't want him to see an actual projection. We'll just walk him through the process."

"Won't that be the first thing he asks to see?" asked Gretchen. "Everybody wants to see a projection . . ."

"We have to figure something out." Marta absently tapped a pencil on her desktop. "We'll tell him . . . tell him the wormhole is down for maintenance."

"The . . . wormhole is what?" Elvin asked, reflecting Gretchen's bewilderment.

"The wormhole isn't . . . we don't maintain . . ." Gretchen said.

"Yeah, well, I doubt the senator is a physicist. If you can think of a better excuse, let's hear it. But we won't show him a projection."

"Why not?" asked Naomi, who seemed as puzzled as the rest of the crew.

Since Marta had taken her new job, Marshall had enjoyed the transformation he'd witnessed. He watched her fidget with her pencil and smiled.

The old Marta had no tolerance for tactful deception. As an espionage agent, she surely knew how to deceive. These would be calculated ruses on a grand scale, though, not little stopgaps to maneuver around inconvenient obstacles. Inconvenient obstacles would simply have been mowed down. Her new role demanded other skills, though, and the evolution, Marshall decided, was good for her.

"Before he left," Marta answered Naomi, "Michael Huxtable gave me some advice. He told me he had been deliberately vague with the oversight subcommittee regarding many of the details of our ... process. The nudity, for example. Michael never told them time travelers have to be naked."

"Why not?" Naomi repeated.

"He saw it as a no-win situation, politically. He said half the politicians who had clearance to know about the program would be scared to death that their constituents among the religious right would learn they'd sat by silently while a bunch of federal employees cavorted naked in the Arizona desert. And the other half couldn't have gotten here quickly enough on fact-finding missions to see first-hand the naked federal employees cavorting in the Arizona desert."

"Wait a minute," Gretchen said. "How is it possible that the subcommittee doesn't know that kind of detail? Their investigator—that Wishcamper guy—was here for weeks. And what about the investors' representatives? Probably a dozen of them have witnessed projections, and *they* certainly know time travelers have to be naked."

"Each corporation involved in the program has posted a large bond as a guarantee their representatives here will observe our security requirements," Marta explained. "And before any such representative is admitted to the projection lab, they undergo a briefing to remind them what they can and cannot report to the few corporate officers who know what we're doing here. They are reminded that, while the company faces forfeiture of their bond, the representatives themselves face criminal prosecution for violating our security edicts. I'm sure there's some gossip among liaisons and their bosses, but the last people they'd want to make aware of any details would be members of the subcommittee."

"But what about Wishcamper?" Gretchen asked. "Certainly, he would . . ."

"No," Marta said. "Huxtable sat him down when he got here and was frank concerning political ramifications of the nudity. And apparently Wishcamper agreed. I guess he didn't want to be the one to deprive his bosses of deniability."

"So why have the committee members themselves never visited?" Naomi asked.

"This program is controversial among those political leaders aware of its existence. When scientists went to them several years ago, saying time travel looked more and more like a realistic possibility, the politicians didn't give a flying crap about the science. They understood the ramifications of manipulation of the past and were gripped by fear that someone else would get there first. But the inability of a single government to afford this undertaking—or assemble scientific talent necessary to solve the most stubborn problems—soon became apparent, so our consortium was born. The secrecy is to protect them, not us. If a disaster occurs—as it did with the *Joey Bishop Show*—they can blame a bureaucratic morass, which shields any one of them from direct knowledge of any details."

"So, what's changed all that?" Marshall asked.

Marta stood, walked around her desk and sat against its leading edge.

"Josiah Mumford. He is very senior in the Senate. He's been there so long, he probably considers himself safe from the pressures a lot of others face. And, I've been told, he's quite politically astute.

"He knows Michael Huxtable was able to use the sheer size of this operation to mask many of the specifics. The subcommittee members appreciated that protection. Our operation is so small, though, they no longer enjoy a vast bureaucratic shield. The oversight subcommittee must decide what to do with us. I want them to view us as complex beyond understanding and boring as a tax form. If Mumford asks you a question, I want the most convoluted answer you can give."

"But eventually won't we have to open up to them?" Naomi asked.

"Yes. But not yet. I need more time to understand how to deal with them."

Marta expected more polish.

Josiah Mumford had been the Democratic senator from Delaware for nearly thirty years and could, in all likelihood, keep on doing that for another decade if he chose. Mumford appeared to be long past the polished phase of his political career and well into the folksy grandfather phase. He was comfortably overweight, ruddy of complexion and appeared to be suffering from the Arizona heat. He had heavy jowls and impossibly thick white eyebrows that matched a dense and unruly crop of hair.

Dressed for the tropics, he sported the kind of rumpled white linen suit Sydney Greenstreet wore whenever he hung out with Humphrey Bogart. He adopted the affectation of an absent-minded bumbler. Marta didn't buy that for an instant. She found his self-effacing good humor engaging. Despite herself, Marta liked him, and she suffered a twinge of regret at the necessity for deceit.

She met Mumford at the surface elevator entrance.

They exchanged diplomatic *glad-you're-here-glad-to-be-here's* and stepped aboard the elevator. As it descended, Mumford braced himself against a side wall. "I skimmed your report during the flight down. Who is this Cecil guy, anyway?"

"Cecil is the sole remaining corporate contributor to the program."

"I didn't know any of the corporate guys were left. Who does he represent?"

"Cecil's Margin Service."

"Cecil's what?"

The elevator slowed abruptly. Marta thought she saw

Mumford's jowls elongate with the g-force. The door slid open to reveal Old Bob, who waited with his golf cart.

"Cecil's Margin Service," Marta repeated as the golf cart whispered though corridor after corridor. "Printing. He was in the printing industry for many years."

"Does he represent a security risk going forward?"

"He's known everything from the start and hasn't told a soul. Granted, his inclusion was a bureaucratic cock-up."

The golf cart came to a halt. Marta helped the senator extricate himself. She warned him about the lip at the projection lab entrance.

"Can't we just ease him out?" Mumford asked.

"We tried. He insists on sending us a check every three months, though. The bottom line is I don't think having him involved hurts anything. And he might cause a commotion if we formally kicked him off. He's mostly just a harmless older gentleman. A little eccentric, maybe, but harmless."

Their conversation halted as Mumford got his first look at the projection lab. Like every newcomer, his eyes went immediately to two gleaming metal globes and a milky, translucent raised platform between them pulsating with a soft green glow.

As he marveled, Marta found it difficult not to stare at Mumford's eyebrows. They shifted and swayed, quite independent of each other, and seemed to telegraph Mumford's reactions.

"Impressive," he said. The eyebrows agreed.

Marta let him stare for a moment, then touched a tactful hand to his elbow and steered him to her office. "You were asking about Cecil?" She hoped to distract him from the question she knew was coming.

"Cecil? Oh, yes. Where is he? And you said he *used* to be in the printing business. What does he do now?"

"Um . . ." Marta hesitated.

"Well?"

"He lives on a sailboat and he . . . he grooms cats."

"I like cats," Mumford said, as if the cats had brought him to some kind of conclusion. He glanced back over his shoulder at the projection platform and the globes through Marta's office windows, clearly captivated.

"I was hoping to see—"

"And I apologize, Senator. But we have some technical issues. A projection right now would be too dangerous. This is a risky business, even under the best of conditions."

Mumford nodded absently.

Marta directed him to the sofa and took the adjoining chair.

Beyond his line of vision, the time machine's spell was broken, and Mumford transitioned abruptly. "So, what will you folks be doing here now?"

"Research into the physics and physiology of time travel. As a platform for physics research, this program will be an extraordinary opportunity to learn about the forces that shape and control our world, to study the origins of the universe and—"

"Give me an example."

"Um . . . okay. Our current priority is trying to understand what happened to the *Joey Bishop Show* universe."

"Yes. The subcommittee only recently received the report. I let Michael Huxtable know I thought his reasons for withholding it were thin at best." Mumford's eyebrows contorted themselves into sharp, accusing vees. But he abruptly softened, eyebrows twitching and cheeks jiggling in what Marta took as a display of genuine regret.

"A whole universe... Out there, somewhere. Is there someone we can apologize to? Diplomacy, you know. Sorry for your loss, that sort of thing?"

"No, not that I know of. I think they're pretty much... gone. So, we're working on it. We'd prefer not to blow up anyone else."

"I think the subcommittee would agree."

"We should run to the physics lab. I could try and answer your questions, but I think you'd rather hear it directly from our physicists."

"Okay." There was hesitation in Mumford's voice. "As long as a normal human being is there to interpret for me. In my experience, listening to expert testimony before our committees over the years, physicists can be a little... um..."

"Indecipherable?"

"That would be a kind way of putting it."

"I'll do my best," Marta said, secretly rooting for Elvin and Gretchen to be as indecipherable as possible.

She made a quick call. Old Bob zipped them through to the physics lab where they found Elvin and Gretchen waiting.

"Yes, Dr. Allen," Mumford said, "I've read about your contributions here. Very commendable. I'm disappointed I won't get to see your crew in action."

"Um... well... normally we could... but the wormhole. It's down for maintenance. We're adjusting the... wormhole... stuff. The dark matter is... a little too... um... dark..."

"And this is Elvin," Marta said.

"Ah, yes, Mr. Detwyler. You're a remarkable fellow, according to reports I've read."

Elvin smiled, shook the senator's hand, and said, "Well, I'm glad to learn the reports have been accurate."

"The senator has some questions concerning our current focus . . ."

Elvin beamed and invited the senator to sit on a lab stool. Mumford struggled a little to distribute his ample butt cheeks equally over the stool.

"Okay," Elvin said, making a show of placing his arms behind his back and looking professorial. "I guess the first thing I have to ask is, what do you know about quantum mechanics?"

"Probably not enough . . ."

"Let's start with the basics then. What time is it?"

The senator withdrew an ancient pocket watch from his trousers. The watch was attached to a gold chain.

"Um . . . 3:42 in the afternoon."

"According to whom?"

Mumford adopted a blank look. His brows drooped over the senator's eyes like a veil. Marta feared Mumford thought he was being mocked.

"This is an expensive watch, young man. Granted it isn't one of those digital, satellite things. But I wind it every day at precisely 6 a.m. It never loses a second. This watch is testimony to extraordinary craftsmanship of another century. I'll wager whatever digital device you use will match my watch to the second."

"I'm not questioning the accuracy of your timepiece," Elvin grinned. "I'm questioning the accuracy of your concept. Time is completely arbitrary."

"You're saying it's not..." The senator checked his watch again. "...now 3:44?"

"That's as a good a number as any, I suppose. How did we arrive at that number, though? Or to put it another way, what *is* a minute, or a second?"

"Well, you'd have to do the math. The number of seconds in twenty-four hours."

"And the answer would be that a second is one 84,600[th] of a day," Elvin said. "But if you gave that answer on a game show, you would be wrong."

"Why?"

"Because in 1967, we started measuring time according to an atomic clock. And at that point, the definition of a second became 9,192,631,770 periods of the radiation corresponding to the transition between the two hyperfine levels of the ground state of a cesium 133 atom." Elvin paused to catch his breath. "Then, in 1997, we decided that the periods would be defined for a cesium atom at rest, and approaching the theoretical temperature of absolute zero. And in 1999, we allowed for corrections from ambient radiation."

Mumford looked sideways at Marta, who offered a timid shrug.

"The point is," Elvin continued, "just like that, we redefined our basic measure of time in our rather futile attempt at accuracy, when it's all arbitrary in the first place."

"But aren't things like plane schedules and ocean navigation and space travel all dependent on knowing precisely what time it is right now?"

"You base your assumption on a false premise," Elvin said. "*Now* is a meaningless term. In a quantum sense, there is no *now*. Quantum mechanics teaches us is that the act of observation alters the reality of the thing being observed. *Now* is an excellent example. In the microsecond it takes for us to define a moment as *now*, it has become *then*."

"Okay," Mumford said. "I think we're getting a little esoteric here—"

"Let's go back to my original question. How much do you know about quantum mechanics?"

Mumford shook his head while giving Marta another searching look.

"Okay. When Max Planke, Albert Einstein, and the rest of their posse realized atoms were things that could be broken down into smaller particles than neutrons, electrons and protons, they gave birth to a mystical branch of science called quantum mechanics, which is the study of the behavior of extremely small stuff. This is particularly fascinating because the quantum world and the full-scale world play by two different sets of physical rules. Quantum particles are so small, our traditional concepts of time and space simply don't apply. In fact, quantum theory is flat out weird. It's like Albert and the boys were having a few beers and one of them said, 'Hey, let's think up the most outrageous thing we can and see how many people we get to believe it.' Turns out, though, they were really onto something."

"Yes," Mumford said. "I remember the Defense Department presentations about lasers."

Elvin's cell phone rang in his pocket, but he reached down and silenced it without checking the call.

"Exactly. The practical application of quantum theory is what produced lasers, and lasers have given us everything from CD players to missile defense systems. Perhaps the most dramatic impact of quantum mechanics on the modern world, though, is embodied by the transistor and its direct descendent, the microprocessor."

"Microprocessors run the world," Gretchen said.

"Okay," Mumford said, raising a hand to slow Elvin's progress. "I came here because I'm concerned our subcommittee has been a little too . . . disengaged. I have to go back to them with some lucid impressions of what's happening here. I understand the stuff about lasers and microprocessors. But we seem to be straying a bit too far from reality—"

"Then let's talk about reality."

Elvin picked up a marker and turned to a whiteboard where he drew a huge circle. He sectioned off three quarters.

"Seventy-five percent of the *reality* in our universe is invisible dark energy—a mysterious something about which we know nothing."

He delineated another hunk of the remaining quarter. "And twenty percent is invisible dark matter, a substance critical to time travel, which we are just beginning to understand."

He colored in the remaining sliver of the circle.

"That means only five percent of *everything* is matter taking the form of atoms. In other words, only five percent of our universe is made up of anything that your subcommittee would recognize as being real."

He paused dramatically. Mumford's eyebrows performed a little jig that suggested Marta's strategy to provide convoluted explanations was succeeding. Elvin added a bit of a swagger. Marta waited for the senator's eyebrows to sag in surrender.

Until Mumford said, "All right. I've had enough of this run-around."

His eyebrows accused Elvin, Marta and Gretchen in turn.

"You are all bright people, and I'm just a lawyer from Delaware who hasn't done anything for forty years but listen to people try to bullshit me for one reason or another. You can make me your advocate, or you can make me your critic. And I must tell you, so far today, you haven't done yourselves a lot of good. Now, I'm going to ask a couple of questions, and I want answers I can understand."

Marta felt heat rise through her neck to her face. Gretchen and Elvin offered furtive looks, which she met with a brief nod.

"First, tell me how and why your time machine out there works."

Elvin opened his mouth to speak, but Marta placed a warning hand on his shoulder. "Gretchen, please."

Gretchen took a deep breath.

"Senator, do you understand why time exists?"

The eyebrows furrowed, but Gretchen pushed on. "You're familiar with the big bang?"

"Yes, I've heard of it."

"Well, ever since the big bang, the universe has continued to grow. Traditional logic holds that at some point, the growth should have stopped, and a contraction should begin. Now, Einstein proved that time is relative. The flow of time is affected by both velocity and gravity. We're not talking about Elvin's *conceptual* time here, but of a very real thing called space-time. Space and time are bound together in a sort of fabric. So, as the expansion of the universe creates new space, we now believe it also creates new time. And this *new time* is the ephemeral *now* to which Elvin referred. And it also accounts for the *flow* of time."

She paused and offered Mumford a hopeful look. The eyebrows offered their consent for her to continue.

"One of the very exciting premises we've developed in our research so far has to do with the nature of antimatter. Conventional wisdom has held that antimatter is an opposite substance to what we recognize as matter in the form of things we can see and touch and feel. We thought that, should matter and antimatter ever come into contact, a cataclysmic explosion would destroy everything. But we believe we have confirmed a theory posed earlier in this century that *antimatter* is just ordinary matter moving backward through time—and that's why the time machine works."

Mumford raised his hand, closed his eyes, and said nothing for a moment, before asking, "So what's the deal with wormholes?"

"Well, we kind of lucked out there," Gretchen said. "We thought we could use the pathway created by a wormhole to construct a shortcut through time by warping space-time. What the wormhole appears to do, however, is connect us to a very strange pathway we simply refer to as the limbo. And in this limbo, we sort of catch a ride on this backward-flowing antimatter, into the past of parallel universes."

Mumford stepped off the stool, put his hands on his hips and gave an awkward stretch.

"So, it wasn't the contact of matter with antimatter that caused this *Joey Bishop Show* place to blow up?"

"We don't think so, Senator," Gretchen said.

"What was it?"

"Our best guess right now," Elvin said, "is a *phase shift*. Anyway, it's happened before. In fact, it's probably why we all exist."

"A . . . what?"

"Physicists label the phenomenon a phase shift," Gretchen said. "At some point in the ancient evolution of the universe, things were plodding along when something sparked an incredible burst of energy that spread through everything at the speed of light, reconfiguring atoms as it went."

"So, this *Joey Bishop* universe didn't really disappear?"

"Well, no," Elvin said. "Matter can't be destroyed. But if you lived there, you wouldn't know the difference, since your atoms would have been rearranged into cosmic dust. It's not something you get over."

"But you think something related to time travel caused this phase shift?"

"We are concerned that it might have been. But with or without time travel, it will eventually occur," Elvin said. "It's inevitable."

"Um . . . soon?"

"In a cosmic sense, yes. The optimists among us give our universe another twenty billion years. Personally, I think we've only got a billion years or so to get our act together."

Old Bob's golf cart returned Mumford and Marta to her office. He sat heavily on the small sofa. "I'll tell you right now, this pure research stuff is not going to fly with the subcommittee. I'll agree that we don't want to be blowing things up, so we need to be sure to get that covered. But that billion years thing is going to make most subcommittee members a little complacent. Do your research, but you have to do some real stuff, as well."

"Okay. Did you have something specific in—?"

"Oh, you know, historical stuff. Go observe some things. Tell us what really happened."

"Well, there's a lot of history out there. And we'll be glad to observe it. Do you have any suggestions . . . ?"

"I'll have the subcommittee staff do some research. You haven't appeared before the subcommittee since your appointment. So, come to Washington and see us next week. And if you feel the need for some degree of constructive deception to deal with the political aspects of your operation, I understand that. Just do your best to be as straightforward as you can with *me.*"

20

THE ARTFUL NUDE

January 2046

THE GLOBAL RESEARCH CONSORTIUM policy exempting scientists from time travel grated on Marta more than any other. They were the *intellectual property* and, as such, too important to risk, or so policy makers—undoubtedly influenced by urgings from the scientists themselves—concluded.

While Marta understood their thinking, she thought the practical effect of such an exclusion encouraged an elitist philosophy among the science group, limiting their understanding of real-world challenges faced by travelers. Given Mumford's directive that they should undertake missions beyond the realm of pure research, she decided to do something about it.

All key personnel would be required to undergo a projection through time.

"Just once," Marta told them. "For a couple of reasons. One, we've learned through experience that other universes have not limited their projections here to active travelers. They may choose any one of you. So, we all need familiarity with the process of integration with our past or future selves.

"More importantly, though, on several occasions, travelers have felt the science team isn't sensitive enough to issues we confront during a projection. If you experience a projection, we will all have a common base from which to evaluate future missions and cope with problems as they arise."

"You expect me to take off my clothes?" Gretchen asked. "Theoretical physicists don't take off their clothes in front of strangers."

"Well, first, we aren't strangers. And second, consider what it was like when we started. *We* had to be naked before forty or fifty people who really *were* strangers. Now there's only a dozen or so of us."

"Don't worry about it, Gretchen," Elvin said. "I'll make sure everyone gets safely home."

"That's right." Marta turned to Elvin. "And you'll do that by being sure someone else is fully prepared to handle your post when you accompany the others."

"Wait a minute. Surely your plan doesn't include me. You forget I can walk out of here any time—"

"Yes, you can. And that would be a shame. You've done such an excellent job thus far, though, that our technical team is more than capable of taking over the mission they will be managing. And let me ask you this. What do you think Einstein would have done if he'd actually been given the opportunity to travel at the speed of light and see for himself? How would history have judged him if he'd said, 'No thanks. I'll just stay here and watch the monitors'"?

Elvin glared at Marta and slumped heavily in his chair.

Gretchen said quietly, "But I'm fat."

"I promise, Gretchen, I'll order everyone not to look."

Another instance of the administrator's prerogatives was Marta's formation of a symbiotic alliance with her counterpart from the *Star Trek* universe.

"*Star Trek* is one of the 'closest' universes to ours," Elvin said when she'd gone to him with her idea, "although the term 'close' infers a spatial relationship that does not exist. Crudely put, its *dimensional frequency* very nearly matches our own."

Although Marta had voluntarily excluded herself from other missions, she found it necessary to have herself projected to *Star Trek* with some regularity. She entered the consciousness of the Marta there and, as she expected, found they were both thinking along the same lines. This awareness and commonality of thought served to mitigate the trauma Marta often experienced when trying to meld with her past counterpart in other circumstances.

Since they were each working with the same cast of characters, the two Martas set aside a small window of time each weekday—about 1:30 pm when everyone took their naps—when they would all be in a safe quiet place should their counterpart from the other universe need to visit.

This program-wide unofficial nap time evolved because neither Marta nor Marshall tended to get a lot of sleep at night. Every time each became horizontal in the company of the other, the event degenerated to some form of sexual debauchery followed by a couple hours of fitful rest until their mutual lust boiled over anew.

"I'm sorry, Marshall," she explained one afternoon as he followed her to the bedroom, "but I've got to have some time to just sleep. We still have our jobs to do, you know."

So, Marshall retreated to the farthest reaches of the apartment and took a nap, too. The half-hour after lunch each day became naptime. Soon, scientists, technicians and support staff followed suit. If they had pallets rolled out beside each other in one of the empty conference areas and some red Kool-Aid in sippy cups, Marta thought, it would be just like kindergarten.

Since time travel involves affecting the historical path of another universe, the Martas made a pact with each other. They would cooperate, each providing their universe as an authorized destination for the other so long as they both observed a careful effort to minimize any impact on the other world.

Although Marta's experience with the oversight subcommittee was limited at this point, she knew where government involvement would eventually take them.

"Just watch," she told Marshall. "Sooner or later, they'll come up with some sort of 'parallel universe impact statements' requiring months of study and expense before we can go anywhere."

"I thought you and the *Star-Trek*-you had that all worked out. We won't do anything the other you doesn't want done."

"Yeah, well, in the long run, that's just too easy. Lawyers can't bill anyone for that kind of arrangement. We'll just get away with our operating agreement as long as we can."

So, on a Tuesday, Marta popped into her *Star Trek* counterpart and revealed her plan to send each of the scientists for a quick jaunt one day into the past.

That's a good idea, Star-Trek-Marta flashed mentally to her *Lucy* counterpart. *Why didn't I think of that?*

Both entities paused for a moment of surprise before *Star-Trek*-Marta continued, *Wait a minute. Why didn't I think of that? Usually, as far as the program is concerned, we have the same ideas at the same time. Why has this occurred to you, and not to me?*

They decided to consult their respective Elvins.

"Odd," said Elvin. "Very, very odd. So odd that I suspect we should discontinue projections until I have time to consider exactly what—"

"It's not *that* odd," said Marta. She sat with Elvin, Gretchen and Leonard Rose before a bank of physics lab computers.

"No, really," Elvin said, typing furiously on his keyboard. "This could mean . . . it could mean . . . well, anything. You don't want to blow up another universe, do you?"

Marta didn't buy it for a moment.

"I suspect this has a lot more to do with your reluctance to undergo a projection than it does with the realistic possibility of destroying another universe."

Gretchen breathed a heavy sign and reached across to place a hand on Elvin's arm to halt the clatter of his keyboard. "I'm not anxious to be projected, either. But I think what you and your *Star Trek* counterpart are experiencing is simply an accelerating divergence."

"Accelerating divergence?" Marta asked.

"Yes. How many projections have we made into the *Star Trek* universe, and they to us? Dozens? And no matter how careful we are, with each projection the universal paths diverge just a bit. Even with the care we take to minimize our impact on each other's worlds, we can no longer count on our *Star Trek* counterparts' thinking and planning exactly as we do. We must be more careful about consulting with them concerning our projection exchanges."

"Well, they like this idea," Marta said. "We're set for tomorrow. And just to be safe, they will come here the following day."

Leonard Rose nudged Marta's arm.

"I need to speak to you and Marshall privately."

Rose waved for Marshall and Marta to follow him to his office.

As Rose pulled the door closed behind him, he frowned. "I'm not getting onto that projection platform. Do whatever you wish. Fire me. I'm not getting up there."

"Leonard," Marta said, "I'm serious about this. Everyone will go. I can't excuse you and require the others to—"

"I don't trust you or Detwyler," Rose said. "I've done my best to work hard here and contribute to the effort. I think this program is important, and I wish to continue. I am genuinely sorry for what happened to Ms. Schuler. If I get on that platform, though, the three of you could very easily orchestrate an accident and you'd be rid of me. Which would solve a problem for you, wouldn't it, Ms. Hamilton?"

Marta met his eyes with an unwavering stare. The soft thump of the second hand on Leonard's desk clock became apparent.

Marshall finally broke the standoff. "I understand his point, Marta. I wouldn't trust *him* if the situation were reversed. We need to find a way out of this."

"Okay, what can I tell the others?"

"A medical condition," Marshall said. "Do you have a pacemaker, Leonard?"

While she didn't like the idea of giving Leonard a pass, Marta did like Marshall's solution. Pacemakers had evolved into miniscule electronic devices with even smaller nuclear batteries. Implanted directly into the heart, they were practically infallible for controlling potentially fatal electrical flaws. And their implantation had become routine. However small, though, they were made of plastic polymers, and no inorganic matter could undergo the projection process without burning up.

"No, I don't," Rose said.

"Well, you do now."

Twenty-four hours later, seven nervous people stood shivering in white robes as they waited for Leonard to make the final adjustments that would send them to the *Star Trek* universe's previous day.

They included Naomi Hu, Gretchen Allen, Elvin Detwyler, medical tech Jolene Drew, Betty the receptionist who didn't want to be left out, mathematician Galen Postelwait, and Alex Whitfield, a bio lab technician.

Standing with Marshall on the observation deck were Marta, Gillis and Macy.

"We really have to do this?" Marshall heard Gretchen whisper to Marta.

"Gretchen, by now you know it's reasonably safe," Marta answered quietly. "I would think you of all people would want to experience this marvel you've constructed."

"Well, in fact, I would. I just don't want to take off my clothes."

"Here's a hint," Marta said. "I always made sure I stood

next to Sheila. That way, nobody even gave me a second glance."

Marshall appraised the other robed figures and immediately settled on Jolene. Gretchen and Marta followed his gaze. Jolene was a tiny blond woman with a pixie face and enormous breasts straining against the confines of her robe.

Jolene turned toward their stares.

"What?" she said.

All three quickly looked away.

Marta smirked. Gretchen remained grim.

To Jolene's right, Marshall saw Elvin retying the sash on his robe for the tenth time, trying to position it in relation to a pot belly that threatened to burst free. Elvin was a short, round man covered with a thick layer of hair everywhere, it seemed, except his head.

"Just be sure you're a long way from Elvin," Marshall said.

This time, Gretchen couldn't suppress a smile.

Squinting without his glasses, Elvin glared at them.

Gretchen took a big breath. "I guess it's time. Remember, Marta promised me no one would look."

Marshall configured his right hand in the three-fingered Boy Scout sign and drew an X over his heart with the index finger of his left hand.

"Yeah, right," Gretchen responded with a look of grim determination.

The travelers took their positions. Gretchen scrambled to place herself next to Jolene, and displayed dismay when Elvin stepped to Gretchen's other flank.

"Do your best to relax," Marta told them as the projector

began to cycle up with its familiar hum. "Close your eyes and breathe deeply as you take off your robes. Understand that your nudity is nothing to be self-conscious about."

The whine of the projector continued to build.

Marshall contemplated the diversity among this group of nudists. Elvin was, frankly, hideous. His round and hairy stomach paunched over a nest of pubic hair. Galen was a pale, nearly hairless man who cupped one hand over his genitals. Alex Whitfield had the well-defined body of gym rat and runner. Betty was willowy with medium-sized breasts. Naomi showed no trace of self-consciousness as she displayed a lithe body devoid of fat. Jolene's enormous boobs bounded free of her robe with enthusiasm. Marshall wondered momentarily how the woman managed to maintain any sort of center of gravity.

Next to Jolene, Gretchen squeezed her eyes tight as she held out her robe. Normally, she wore her long brown hair tied in a bun or woven in a single braid. Today, she let it fall free over her left shoulder, strategically hiding one breast. Marshall noted that, as did most women in their late forties, Gretchen carried an excess pound or two. Her image of herself as fat, though, was erroneous. Her waist tapered to a slight paunch. Her single exposed breast stood proud. She was, Marshall thought, certainly the hottest theoretical physicist he had ever seen.

Elvin didn't mind being naked. He cared little what people thought of his squatty, hairy body. But he was terribly nervous about the prospect of projection. So, with eyes closed, he transferred his weight from foot-to-foot, electric with apprehension. That's when he momentarily lost his balance and bumped into Gretchen.

As she flailed her arms to keep from falling, her long hair shifted, exposing her hidden breast.

Elvin, along with everyone else, did a double take. They saw the outline of a tattoo—a variation of a happy face, this one with crossed eyes and a tiny tongue sticking from its mouth—displayed on her left boob.

Marshall froze, his mouth agape. Elvin heard Marta try to stifle a laugh. Leonard Rose said, "Oh, my."

Gretchen bowed her head and put one hand over her eyes.

Absent his glasses, Elvin had to lean close with a fierce squint.

"Why in the world would you . . ." he began.

Gretchen gave him a rough shove. "For God's sake, Elvin, have you never been drunk?"

Elvin grinned. "Not that drunk."

So much about this exercise grated on Elvin.

He took pride in his image as the rebel, the irreverent don't-give-a-shit garage physicist, who put all those other degreed fuckers in their place. He had proved a guy wearing a T-shirt and jeans could think circles around the lab coats. He would either get his way, or he'd walk and let them figure this out by themselves.

Yes, he could stand here naked to the titters of his colleagues. What he should have done, though, was tell Marta Hamilton thanks but no thanks. *I'm not getting in front of your fucking projector. I'm not bending to your rules.*

Call Marta's bluff.

That's what he should have done.

Standing on the platform, though, Elvin felt surprise to realize how intently he really did want this.

Not so much the destination as the journey.

He wanted to observe this place between future and past. He was intensely curious about what was described to him over and over as a blank and eternal palate. Timelessness. He wanted to experience it just for pure love of the physics.

He wasn't disappointed.

First, the instantaneous transition from projection platform to limbo. One moment, he stared at the nipple-nosed face on Gretchen's breast, and the next he was everywhere and nowhere all at once. Though he sensed his body gathered around the core of his intellect, he could neither see nor feel it. No obvious physical aspect of himself was evident. Only the process of thought provided any kind of thread between the intellectual and the physical beings that were Elvin Detwyler.

Next, he sensed great power in his thoughts. He could direct his mind to complex mathematical equations and interpret them with remarkable clarity. He could evoke a crystal-clear recollection of any single day of his life. Some travelers had complained of tedium here. Elvin knew with absolute assurance their boredom was the product of fear. He understood how a person of average intellect would be too terrified to let their mind loose here.

The experience did, however, seem to run on.

Finally, just as he considered the alternative of panic at the prospect that something had gone wrong and he was trapped here forever, Elvin sensed a great swirling at the core of the limbo as all the scattered molecules of his physical being seemed to be caught by a giant vacuum sucking them toward a deeper nothingness.

And then he was on the other side, resting quietly in his quarters near the projection lab. He sat up with a start and recognized the awkward dual occupancy of his brain.

So, you made it, came the observation from one of the mental tracks.

Wow. That was ... wow. Have you done that yet?

Nope, I go tomorrow. Boy, what about those hooters on Jolene?

The seven travelers snapped back into being on the platform and shared that terribly awkward moment of exposure before their awaiting comrades handed out robes.

As Elvin and the others followed Marshall and Marta for debriefing, Elvin realized two things. First, the limbo—at least during the outbound journey—somehow made more of his brain available to him than he'd ever experienced. The scientific potential there was incredible.

Second, the unsettling conviction that he could have chosen to remain in that vast nothingness if he'd wanted to—and the seductive lure of the prospect.

21

A COMPLICATED FATALITY

MARSHALL WATCHED AS THE novice travelers made their way from the lab to the locker rooms. He turned to Marta with a sigh.

"Okay. I'm ready. I need to get back on active status. I can't just sit around any longer."

"Naomi worries you're *not* ready," Marta said. "It doesn't hurt to wait."

"I *am* ready. I'll be glad to talk to Naomi and convince her I'm not some psychological time bomb. But I think . . . I think . . ."

"You think what?"

Marshall closed his eyes. "I think you're the one who's not ready."

Marta pulled Marshall to her office. She shut the door, twisted the blinds shut and reached to grab Marshall by the shirt collar, pulling his face to her level.

"Carla O'Neill is dead, Marshall," she said, her voice so hard it chilled his blood. "Have you somehow missed that fact? You and she died in the *Gunsmoke* universe, and now she's dead everywhere else."

"She didn't die during a projection." Marshall lifted Marta's hands away from his shirt. He squeezed them with his own.

"Well . . . well, she's still gone. History got her. I don't see any reason to send you on a mission and speed up the process. Can't you understand?"

"Hey, I don't believe that stuff. And even if I did, I'm not spending what's left of my life being afraid. If history gets me, it gets me. I'm clumsy. I could trip and break my neck tomorrow. Just doing nothing, though, I feel as if I've abandoned Sheila. She could be out there right now, counting on us. Elvin's speculations are all theoretical. We don't know anything for sure."

Marta peered sadly into Marshall's face, feeling distance wedging itself between them, and said softly, "Naomi says—"

"You know what this reminds me of?" Marshall cut her off. "This reminds of the time my mother didn't want me to play little league baseball. I was too young to understand that I was a horrible player. My friends all played, and I wanted to try, too. She showed up at every game and cringed every time the pitcher threw the ball. She kept yelling for me to duck. And while the other kids got to wear normal helmets, she made me wear one that buckled under my chin and had a facemask. I was so embarrassed."

Marta looked away, partially to hide the tears in her eyes.

"Everybody knows what's going on. You're embarrassing me, Marta. It's not your job to protect me."

She shook her head and turned away to adjust the window blinds, readmitting the view of the projection lab. "Talk to Naomi. If she clears you, you're good to go."

"Really, Dr. Hu," Marshall said, "I'm all right."

Naomi winced. "Please don't call me that."

She detested being known as Dr. Hu, particularly here in a program related to time travel.

"Um . . . sorry, Naomi. I just want to make it clear. I'm not here to take advantage of our friendship. But I want to travel . . ."

"I'm not sure you're ready. I'm not sure you've dealt with Samantha Kennedy's death."

They faced each other, occupying the two plush chairs in front of Naomi's desk.

"So, I'm sad. Samantha was important to me, and now she's gone. That's a sad thing. What's wrong with that?"

"You've got that trauma, piled on top of Sheila's death—"

"Considering all that, don't I have the right to be just a bit . . . off?"

"Certainly, you do. You must talk about it, though. You can't just *say* you're okay. Marta says she's tried to talk to you, too . . . she cares very much about you, you know?"

Marshall sighed. "Well, I thought so, but she's been acting more distant lately."

"Marta is a complex woman. One of the things you have to be careful of with any relationship, and especially a new one, is putting too much responsibility on your partner for your own well-being. Because ultimately, she can't make you happy or make you whole or be the buffer between you and the reality of your own feelings. You must do those things for yourself. If you let Marta accept too much of that burden, you're setting her up to fail."

Marshall sat quietly and studied his hands. Naomi did not rescue him from the silence. Finally, he said, "I was so sure. I was so sure Samantha would be okay."

"Well, you thought you'd saved her."

Marshall leaned forward to the edge of his seat. Naomi read the intensity of his expression.

"No, I mean okay for the rest of a long and happy life."

"She had other problems, problems you had nothing to do with and over which you had no control."

"That's what I mean. I was certain those problems—the drugs and the partying—were things she would be able to deal with after . . . after we talked. And then to come back and find that she'd . . . nobody says it out loud . . . she'd killed herself . . ."

"Why would you think her drug overdose was deliberate?"

"I . . . I . . . there's no evidence. I still think that's what happened, though. And it was such a betrayal."

"Ah, a betrayal."

"That's right," Marshal snapped with a note of anger, "because she promised she would be okay."

"She promised?"

Naomi had attended each debriefing following the Whittier mission. She'd read all the transcripts and gone over every frame of video. Never before had Marshall suggested that Samantha had made any promises to him concerning her future behavior.

Marshall nodded. "She promised."

"Why didn't you tell us?"

"Because of this. Because of this right here. I knew the minute I stepped off the platform and found the memory of her death, everyone would be looking at me through a microscope, worrying if this whole experience would make me . . . I didn't want to say anything that made me sound crazy."

"So, tell me about this promise," Naomi said.

"First, you tell me if you're my doctor right now, or if you're the chief of the medical team around here who gets to decide who travels and who doesn't?"

Naomi considered her response. "I'm your therapist. I hold what you say in confidence. And don't forget, I'm also your friend."

"Okay. Okay." He stood and studied the professional certificates framed on Naomi's office wall. "It happened when I was coming back. In the Limbo."

"In the . . . are you sure?"

"How can anyone be sure of anything there? I've been through projections, what, more than a dozen times now, and I still can't really describe it."

"And you saw Samantha there?"

"No. You've been there. You know we don't *see* anything."

"So how did you . . . ?"

"She just sort of filled my consciousness. She was everywhere, just the same as me."

"And can you remember what she communicated to you?"

"I'll never be able to forget." Marshall tilted his gaze to the ceiling.

Naomi waited.

Marshall closed one eye, turned and squinted at Naomi with the other.

She nodded encouragement.

"And Samantha said, 'Marshall, it turns out you were

my only real friend. And I promise I'll be all right now.'"

He returned to the chair, hid his face with his hands, and said softly, "She wasn't all right, though, was she?"

"And that makes you feel . . . sad?"

"No, it makes me feel angry! Royally pissed off. She gave up. She—"

"She betrayed you . . . Marshall, it's okay to be angry with people close to you who have died. Like, I suspect, your father who died when you were young. The fact of death doesn't put them in some sacred place where expressing or feeling anger towards them is some kind of blasphemy. And your anger isn't a betrayal of your love for them. You need to let yourself be angry, if that's what you feel."

Marshall sat silently for several minutes.

"Now, tell me the truth about this urgency to return to traveling status," Naomi said presently.

"I just miss it, I guess. I mean, I was always the main guy up there. And now it's Gillis and—"

"I'm not putting you back on active status until you tell me the truth."

Marshall's eyes glistened.

"If I'm not traveling, Sheila has no chance. I think she's still out there somewhere. And I don't care if that doesn't make sense to you. It's what I think. It's what I feel. And if I'm the lead traveler, the indispensable asset, then sooner or later I'll have the clout to fix it . . . find Sheila, maybe even get Samantha back."

"Sheila is dead," Naomi said with a note of suspicion. "You said she died . . ."

She thought Marshall's complexion paled.

"Um . . . yes. That's what . . . but we're dealing with the

limbo. So how can we know? And... so long as I'm traveling, I'll at least have the sense I haven't just abandoned them. I need that."

Naomi regarded Marshall carefully. There was some sort of deception in play here. Still, she saw value in his hope that his friends might somehow be saved.

Naomi reached across the small space between their stares and took his hand.

"I'll recommend you return to active status tomorrow." And she added silently, *but I'm also going to get to the bottom of this.*

22

YOUR UNIVERSE IS HERE

TIME IS WHAT KEEPS EVERYTHING From Happening All At Once.

Sheila's first instinct was disappointment. Here she was, talking to . . . to God? . . . seeking understanding during the final moments of her existence. She wanted to say, "That's it? That's the best you've got?"

Then, with the mental clarity fostered by the limbo, she began to see.

She understood that time is both a blessing and a curse. A curse because she was just about to run out of it. A blessing because Time Is What Keeps Everything From Happening All At Once. Without time, all of history would unfold in one chaotic squirt. No doubt the event would be exciting. Of course, no one would be around after to write books or to postulate what it all means. Or enjoy the precious bounty of a life well lived.

Windows to understanding were accessible here if she just had a little more . . .

Time.

"In that sense," the Hall Monitor said, continuing his lecture, "time is useful. In a lot of other ways, it's a real pain in

the ass. Since I work mostly in the corridor, I am one of the fortunate souls who doesn't have to deal with it all that much."

The comment shook Sheila from her reverie.

"This is a hallway? We call it the limbo. We thought it was the . . . the border between universes . . ."

"Well, in fact, it is, but . . . let's see, I need a frame of reference to which you can relate. That's like saying the Mississippi River is the border between Illinois and Missouri. Sort of trivializes it, don't you think?"

"Then what is . . ."

Another possibility occurred to her.

"Ah," she said. "My mind has created an hallucination to cope with the disorientation of the limbo and my fear of imminent death. When the limbo spits me out, I'll die. So, my mind has manufactured you."

"Who told you that?" This time the voice carried a clear note of irritation. "I will not be reduced to anyone's figment."

"Well, the psychologists told us that we might . . . Naomi said we might hallucinate here . . . and Naomi is a really smart person. Not just science smart, like Elvin or Yuni. She's real-world smart, you know?"

"Naomi? You must be more specific. In order to cross-reference the files, I'll need her last name."

"Hu."

"Naomi."

"Naomi Hu."

"That's what I asked you."

Sheila couldn't suppress a giggle.

"You're really not *God, are you. Naomi's last name is Hu."*

"Your grammar is atrocious. You mean, 'Naomi's last name is what?'"

"No." Sheila's laugh was full and boisterous. "What's on second base? I Don't Know's on third."

"Oh. Oh, I get it now. That's clever . . . so you know baseball?"

"Of course I know baseball. Marshall talks about it all the time. Marshall says baseball is the best game ever invented by man . . . except he probably said 'mankind.' Marshall tries not to speak in sexist terms."

"My dear girl, my dear naïve girl, please don't delude yourself into thinking that your tiny speck of reality is responsible for anything as magnificent as baseball."

"What, you mean you have baseball here?"

"This is the corridor. There's nothing here."

"So, there's someplace else?"

"Of course, there's someplace else. Or why would we need a corridor? Why else would there be a Hall Monitor? I've done a quick review of the files and . . ."

"Someplace else with baseball?" Sheila did her best to comprehend.

". . . and, oh my Lord, I don't know how you ever stumbled across this time travel thing in the first place. It's quite complicated, and by the time most societies master the physics they are intellectually and morally advanced enough to leave it alone."

Sheila could imagine him shaking his head as he added with a rueful note, "And despite everything, you have baseball . . . ah, here it is. The Designated Hitter."

Sheila was puzzled.

"Ms. Schuler, is it? Ms. Schuler, one of the things genuinely evolved beings do is recognize their limitations. Your lot fails miserably at that. Despite the futility of it all, aspiring to *perfection is not necessarily a bad thing. What is unforgivable, though, is failing to recognize perfection in the rare case perfection is encountered."*

"Perfection?"

"So few things are perfect. Sunsets. Physics—when you get around to really understanding the nuances of the science. And baseball. Or it was."

"I don't understand . . ."

"The people from your set of dimensions are the clowns who invented the designated hitter. Aren't you wondering why, after your many excursions through the corridor, we're only now holding a conversation?"

"Um, well . . ."

"It's because you're being shunned. And believe me, this is not a step we take lightly. It's about the most serious sanction we can apply."

"We're being shunned because of the designated hitter rule?"

"As if the steroids weren't enough."

"You should really talk to my friend Marshall about this," Sheila said. *"He's much more authoritative on the subject than I am. He's a huge fan. And I'm sure he'll be along soon."*

"Ah. I'll make a note to do so. What's Marshall's last name?"

"Who?" Sheila asked.

"Are we going to do this again?"

"No, I was just messing with you. Marshall Grissom."

"Oh." The Hall Monitor chuckled. "I see. You were joshing me there. I miss jokes. Not a lot of folks make jokes when they are passing through. We're usually sooooo serious here."

The Hall Monitor paused a moment. When he spoke

again, his voice dissolved into a note of alarm. "Oh, my. I am sorry."

"Why?" Sheila felt the fear settle over her again. "What's wrong?"

"I've enjoyed talking with you. I would like to have chatted more. Please believe me, this is not my choice. It's simply inevitable. I've found you delightful, and my thoughts are with you."

He added with a heavy sigh, "Goodbye, Sheila Schuler. Your universe is here."

23

DRIFTING APART

THAT EVENING, FOR THE FIRST TIME, their lovemaking was perfunctory. Marta knew Marshall felt her barriers rising and that he didn't understand why. She didn't know how to explain it to him.

She didn't care for Naomi's decision to let Marshall travel, although she wasn't exactly sure what she was unhappy about. Was it because she *was* being overly protective of Marshall? Or was she unhappy that she was unhappy? Secret super assassin or not, Marshall had niggled his way through her defenses.

The problem with letting someone too close is that emotional attachment can't help changing who you are just a little bit. Marta was a professional, military in background and training. Her career path took her to the world of espionage. Her discipline and her ability to detach herself emotionally and base her analyses and decisions on purely objective criteria created her success, kept her alive. The same attributes could make her an effective administrator of this program.

By now, all the travelers knew the dangers inherent in their jobs. They accepted responsibility for themselves when they agreed to continue. Travelers didn't need taking care of. And yes, the odds dictated that more of them would perish. As administrator, Marta's job was to see that every reasonable precaution was taken, and the travelers were as well-prepared as they could be to face this peril.

It was not her job, though, to keep Marshall from harm's way. Naomi's concerns about Marshall's mental state had kept Marta from confronting the issue directly. Now, that shield was gone.

All she had seen and experienced so far made Marta believe the inevitability of history. In the *Gunsmoke* universe, Marshall was dead. His role as traveler put him squarely in history's cross hairs. And sooner or later, history would catch up to *her* Marshall, too. That's what Marta believed. So, what was wrong, she wondered, with keeping him in her life for as long as she could?

And tonight, as he made love to her, a realization that she must prepare herself for the inevitable loss of this man preoccupied her. To cope with that inevitability, she couldn't just wait for some uncertain day and event. No. She must retreat within herself, the way she existed before Marshall, when she held everyone at a distance and relationships were vague commitments mapped with a careful escape route. That would include the difficult prospect of escaping emotionally from him now.

24

PINCHED

February 2046

WHEN SENATOR MUMFORD requested Marta's appearance before the subcommittee, she dreaded the journey. The event represented a formalization of her relationship with people who would subsequently control her life. What they thought of her would establish parameters of that relationship—how closely Marta and her crew would be watched. She would initiate the process of explaining, advocating and petitioning before the governing board of the U.S. Postal Service's Historical Research Initiative.

By the day of her departure, though, Marta felt relief at the distance this journey would place between her and Marshall. She knew he struggled even now with her withdrawal. She'd made excuses to divert his attention. Marta hated that. With anyone else, she could be brutally direct. One more clue that Marshall was changing her in ways she did not trust.

At first, she had considered bringing him along. Being new at this administrator business, and not yet sure she'd thought things through carefully enough when decision-time came, she trusted Marshall's silence as much as she trusted his counsel. While everyone else was quick to offer advice, Marshall contented himself to be a sounding board who listened quietly, with perhaps a prompt here or there, and afforded her the chance to discover her own conclusions.

As administrator, she could have justified Marshall as her entourage. God knows all the other people occupying this hearing room in the subbasement of the U.S. Capitol building had no shortage of folks tagging along after them.

In her efforts to emotionally ease Marshall away, though, she also found herself seeking guidance from an unexpected quarter. Memories of their Caribbean trip tugged at the edges of her consciousness at the strangest times. She'd be talking with the physicists about some complex theory requiring her to mentally scurry like a gerbil on a wheel just to keep up, or settling some disagreement concerning mission protocols, or fending off hair-brained mission suggestions from the subcommittee, when into her mind would pop a vision of green water, a sailboat and the funny old man who had somehow come to represent an island of simple, unassuming logic amid an ocean of ego, pretense and complication.

So, one day she called Cecil, just to chat, and found the conversation comforting.

The phone calls became more frequent. He was, after all, technically a member of the committee, and as such, her advisor.

She'd run the idea of the whole entourage thing by Cecil the last time she called. She wondered if the absence of an entourage might put her at a disadvantage when it came to sitting down with the power brokers. In short, would they regard her lack of disciples as a sign of weakness and so be more disposed to bend her leadership of the time travel initiative to their individual wills.

"Nope," Cecil said. "It's an unnecessary expense. All them politicians get elected saying they're gonna cut spending, and they never do. Somebody's got to take a stand, dontchaknow. We need to set a higher standard for the time travel business."

So, she was alone this Thursday afternoon as senators and congresspersons and foreign representatives convened. Her mind had wandered, until a shrill voice commanded her back to the moment.

". . . and I'm concerned about this divergence between the two universes that we've been seeing in your reports," Congresswoman Libby Pinch said. "I don't think we can afford to operate quite so informally anymore."

Marta looked at Libby Pinch and saw a slender, blue-suited, forty-something former attorney with short, serious hair and blue eyes that sparked and glistened. She was a recent appointee to the committee.

Mumford had offered Marta a diplomatic warning about the combative Libby Pinch. "She's a three-term congress-woman from a conservative Southern Ohio district. She can't afford politically to countenance liberalism in any form."

Libby sat two seats to Sen. Josiah Mumford's right on a raised dais at the front of the stark hearing room. Marta faced a twelve-member panel behind a flat table fixed with a microphone.

Despite ritual rants of Republicans against the vast federal bureaucracy, though, Marta suspected that, like so many veterans of Washington, D.C., Congresswoman Pinch had come to find the federal bureaucracy a comfortable haven where blame shifting opportunities proved abundant.

Marta felt certain Pinch was appalled to learn of the

collapse of the GRC's vast bureaucratic structure—which once carefully codified all aspects of this new technology—and that she generally regarded Marta and her band of time travelers as a bunch of unsupervised yahoos who were setting entirely too much of their own agenda.

"Yes, ma'am, that is a concern." Marta adjusted her microphone out of a nervousness that irritated her. "We're developing a set of procedures. What we would like to do is create an arrangement with our *Star Trek* counterparts, now that we can't take for granted we're both interested in the same missions. I traveled there last week, as a matter of fact, and met with... uh... myself... and we basically agreed that mission goals no longer need to be identical. We can go there to accomplish some bit of research and they can come here to do the same, as long as a traveler first takes a mission outline to the program administrator of the other universe for approval..."

"Have you submitted this agreement to our attorneys for review?" Libby asked.

"Well, no," Marta said. "It's not as if we can write anything down—"

"Okay. What protection do we have then? What if they violate the agreement? What if you say they can't conduct a given mission and they simply ignore you and go ahead? What if they come and infringe on someone's patent or copyright—take some vital technological information back to their universe? What if they damage someone's property? What recourse do we have?"

"That's not an issue, ma'am," Marta responded. "I'm dealing with myself here. And I guess I'm willing to take myself at my word."

"Your report indicates the universes are diverging, right?"

"Yes..."

"So how do you know the people running their program aren't plotting some kind of sinister design on our universe?"

"Congresswoman, *you* are the people running our program. Do *you* have a sinister design on *their* universe?"

"Ms. Hamilton, I don't appreciate—"

A disturbance at the back of the small room cut the Congresswoman short.

Marta turned to see the door swing open and a burly security agent quickly step to block any view of the room's interior.

"Back off there, young fella," a creaky voice came drifting from the hallway, "I'm just lookin' for the meeting, dontchaknow. I didn't mean to get folks all bent out of shape."

"Cecil?" Although Marta meant to say this to herself, the microphone on the table in front of her sent her voice reverberating through the chamber.

Sen. Mumford glanced quickly toward the back of the hearing room and rapped his gavel sharply.

"What's this?" he asked, gesturing with his gavel to Marta.

"Um, one moment, Senator. I think we may have another committee member present."

Marta hurried to the hallway.

Circumnavigating the security officer's bulk, she limited herself to a smile, but only because she figured giving Cecil a hug would be unparliamentary.

"Cecil, what are you doing here? You should have told us—"

"The whole thing was kinda last minute, dontchaknow," Cecil reached to shake Marta's hand. "With the hurricane season winding down and all, I figured Raul and Fidel could look after things for a couple a days."

Marta heard Mumford's gavel rap again. She pulled Cecil past the guard and into the hearing room.

"It's okay," Marta said. "He's got clearance."

"I'm sorry," the guard said, "without the proper credentials, I can't—"

"Please, Billy," Sen. Mumford called out, "let the gentleman enter for the moment while we sort this through."

"Yes, sir." The guard nodded as he whispered to Marta, "Are you sure about this? I think he just mentioned a couple of Communists."

"Who?" Marta asked, then understood. "Oh, you mean Raul and Fidel? They aren't Communists. They're cats."

Marta watched Cecil stroll forward and could only imagine what the committee members must be thinking. What they saw was an impossibly old man, wearing a *Doc Ford's Rum Bar and Grill* T-shirt and crisply ironed cargo pants, shuffling up the aisle. He wore flip-flops on sockless feet and had a small hoop dangling from a piercing in his left earlobe.

Cecil removed his Seattle Mariners baseball cap as he stepped into the room. He shook out a mane of thinning hair that hung over his collar. Marta noticed he'd shaved sometime during the past couple of days.

"Am I correct to assume," Sen. Mumford said, "that you, sir, are the mysterious Mr. Cecil?"

"Well, it's just Cecil, and I wasn't aware I was mysterious, but yes, I guess it's me."

Several committee members, including Libby Pinch, shuffled through folders on the long, curved surface of their shared desk. Marta did the same, turning to the biographies of committee members. Cecil's profile was sparse. Marta wasn't sure what they'd make of the vague notation listing him as President and Chief Operating Officer of Cecil's Margin Service, a "specialized printing operation including a subsidiary interfacing with the veterinary industry as it relates to felines."

"Welcome, sir," Mumford said. "And please join us."

He pointed to a seat at the end of the committee table. "I'll be glad to see that chair occupied."

"Oh, no. I didn't mean to intrude. I just wanted to say hi, dontchaknow. I'll just sit down back here."

"Nonsense. You are an advisory member to this committee and, as such, have every right to engage in the discussion. Please, come forward."

As Cecil tentatively made his way to an empty chair at the far end of the committee's table, Libby bristled. One more bit of evidence of a program operating without accountability. Here was a committee member, privy to some of the most highly classified secrets of the American government, dressed like someone who lived under a bridge. Clearly, the man had no sense of decorum. His inclusion had to be a mistake and a capable administrator should have corrected that error.

"I, too, am pleased to welcome Mr. Cecil," she said,

taking advantage of the technicality that she still had the floor. "I see your business has to do with cats. That's interesting. I have a cat of my own. While I have seen references to lemmings and pigs as test subjects during the early days of time travel experimentation, I don't recall any mention of cats."

"Nah," Cecil said as he lowered himself into his chair on arthritic knees, "you try to send a cat back in time, you're just lookin' for trouble. Cats wouldn't sit still for it, dontchaknow."

"So that was not your company's connection to the program?" Now she *really* didn't understand. The only other reference in Cecil's biography was to a "specialty printing business," which made no sense. Federal facilities hadn't made large-scale use of printed materials for years.

"And what exactly is a margin service?"

"The margins on documents," Cecil said proudly. "We did the margins. There was a time when my little shop was regarded as the leader of the industry. That was years ago, though, when people put things down on paper, dontchaknow. Back before personal computers, before everything became bits and bytes and ... well, don't get me started. There's just no art to it anymore."

Libby joined the other committee members in exchanging puzzled glances. "Um ... if you don't mind my asking, Mr. Cecil, how old *are* you?"

"It's just Cecil, and no, I don't mind at all. I'll be a hundred and six come April."

This is what's wrong with the social security program, Libby thought. *With more and more people living into their hundreds, we've got to make some adjustments. We can't keep allowing them to start drawing benefits when they turn eighty.*

"To get ourselves back on track, Mr. . . . um . . . Cecil," Mumford intervened, "we are having a discussion regarding the apparent divergence of universes, if you've read the material concerning that particular issue?"

"Yep, I do enjoy readin' the reports, dontchaknow."

"So, Congresswoman Pinch was questioning Administrator Hamilton about the legal implications of the informal agreement she has formulated with the . . . ah . . . the *Star Trek* universe, which allows exchanges of missions after first receiving approval of the mission plan from the equivalent being of the reciprocating universe."

"Oh. Oh, well, okay."

"Congresswoman," Mumford said, "please proceed."

"Thank you, Mr. Chairman." Libby returned her attention to Marta. "What assurance of the trustworthiness of these individuals from this other universe do you have to offer us, Ms. Hamilton?"

"Well, none, other than during my limited experience as administrator, I've found no reason to distrust any of you. Michael Huxtable spoke highly of the subcommittee."

"I'm not talking about us. I'm talking about them."

"I realize that until you've actually experienced projection into the past of a parallel universe, this concept is difficult to grasp," Marta said.

"Do not condescend to me, Ms. Hamilton."

"Ma'am, I'm not doing that. Very honestly, we've had the same issues with members of our scientific and technical teams. They couldn't comprehend it's not a matter of 'we' and 'they'. It's just us. That becomes abundantly clear once you integrate with your past counterpart for the first time.

To trust and know yourself is to trust and know your counterpart from another universe."

"What about divergence?"

"Divergence may produce different experiences for you and your counterparts. And though it may alter you in subtle ways, you are still who you are. There are no *evil twins* as far as we can tell. Unless, of course, they're both evil."

Libby relayed her irritation with a squint. "I still don't see how we can allow an agreement of any kind without a legal review."

Mumford looked down the table to his left and saw Cecil with his hand raised.

"The chair recognizes Cecil."

Everyone stared at the old man.

"Um, and I recognize you too, Senator. I have a question."

"By all means," Mumford said through a chuckle.

"Why would you want to get lawyers involved?" he inquired of Congresswoman Pinch.

"I am an attorney myself, Mr. Cecil. And as such, I recognize the importance of exploring all legal aspects of a situation where we are dealing with public safety."

"So, if something goes wrong, you want to be sure there's someone to sue."

"Um . . . well, to recover damages . . ."

"How you gonna recover damages from another dimension? You think you can find a bank here that'd cash their check?"

The congresswoman, having no ready reply, cast a glare from Cecil to Marta and back to Cecil.

"Be that as it may," Mumford said, "Congresswoman

Pinch is correct to be concerned about our national—or I guess the correct term would be—*universal* security. What if someone from outside your group, someone who is not a person you know and trust, somehow gains access to the time machine? And what if that person or group *does* desire to do harm to our world or someone in it? Is that beyond the realm of possibility?"

A significant asset to Libby Pinch's political career was her innate ability to read body language. And Marta Hamilton dropped her eyes to the witness table and glanced quickly to the right before answering. *If she isn't lying*, Libby said to herself, *at the very least she's not telling us the whole truth*.

"No," Marta said quietly. "No, it's not."

"Then I think," Mumford said, "this committee should authorize a fact-finding mission to do a closer investigation regarding security at your facility as it relates to the issue of divergence. Would you have any objections to that, Madam Administrator?"

"No, sir." Marta crossed her arms. "None at all."

"In that case, the chair will appoint Congresswoman Pinch . . ."

"I will be glad to accept such an oversight role."

". . . and I will also prevail upon our most recently arrived member to assist you," Mumford added.

Pinch looked first at Cecil and back to Mumford.

"Mr. Chairman, I don't think that would be conducive to—"

"How about it, Cecil?" Mumford asked. "I know you said your plan had been to stop by and say hi. You would be doing this subcommittee a great service, though, if you would accept this assignment. Can you make time in your busy schedule?"

"Well, I suppose. I'll just have to call someone about takin' care of the cats, dontchaknow."

Libby's protest got no further than, "Mr. Chairman—" Mumford banged his gavel. "The committee will break for lunch."

Marta stood and walked to Cecil, where she offered the old man a nod of thanks. Before she could speak, though, Congresswoman Pinch inserted herself between them.

"I want you to know, Mr. Cecil, that I expect you to take this task seriously. And I want *you* to know, Ms. Hamilton, that I expect you to fully cooperate. Despite whatever you might think, my concern is not frivolous."

25

CECIL'S MARGIN SERVICE

SO, WHILE MARTA HADN'T sported an entourage when she traveled to Washington, D.C., she had one upon her return to Arizona.

Cecil said that while he figured Raul and Fidel could handle things for a few more days, he did want to get the trip over with. Congresswoman Pinch had been scheduled to conduct a fact-finding tour of the Bahamas and expressed reluctance to shirk that responsibility, so she asked to delay the Arizona excursion. Senator Mumford suggested strongly that she try her best to work with Cecil's schedule and journey to the Southwest with Marta the next day.

The evening before their departure, Marta prevailed upon her contacts at MI-6 to flesh out her sketchy background information concerning Cecil.

"There's not much," her former boss, Sir Rupert Fitzhugh, told her. "Nothing since a magazine article from the eighties, and a few references among the old Austin Powers movie credits."

Marta heard Fitzhugh's voice adopt a note of distaste. The British intelligence community did not care for Austin Powers movies.

"This gentleman has managed to live under the radar for many years, which, as you know, is not easy to do nowadays."

Marta accessed the information on her pocket computer and found an article from 1983 published in a trade magazine called *Footnotes & Margins*. Written by a man named Sean Brody, the story was headlined *The Mystic of Margins*, with the subhead, *At last, the true Cecil is revealed.*

Marta noted Mr. Brody's description of his first meeting with Cecil.

He emerged from the shadows of the back shop, followed an instant later by the mingled odors of printers' ink and pipe tobacco. He wore a clean white apron over jeans and a denim shirt with sleeves rolled to the elbows. His brown hair melded into a dark short beard dappled with gray. Thin arms tapered to artist's hands with long, elegant fingers that belied the strength of his handshake. He wore a green visor. He cast the aura of a man who took his small slice of the world quite seriously.

It seemed that Cecil had, indeed, built a business and a broad-ranging respect throughout the printing industry as a pioneering force in the field of margins. He was credited with inventing the two long red lines that defined the left hand-margin of legal pads.

"As he stepped back and considered those two lines, stark and bold and grave," Mr. Brody wrote, *"Cecil saw spaces that, given the serious legal context, begged for numerical specification. And that's where those numbers running down the left-hand side of legal transcripts originated."*

One of Cecil's major contracts was, first with Spokane County and subsequently with the State of Washington, to provide all the margin work for legal documents.

Marta found the article to be unusually contemplative for a trade magazine.

Even as a child, where others looked at a sheet of paper and saw a sheet of paper, Cecil saw margins. He saw borders symbolic of the limitations placed on common lives. Where others were satisfied to respect these borders, to leave them blank, Cecil saw lines of definition. He saw an invitation to something more. And the first time someone came to him, asking him if he could dress up an otherwise drab sheet of chartreuse stationery, the artistic side of Cecil found expression as well.

Mr. Brody described Cecil as *a man with an unwavering work ethic who mistrusts praise and dislikes excessive ego in others, although he realizes he suffers from that affliction himself. With a frank and honest self-assessment, he knows he is one of those mercurial few whose skill and accomplishments so transcend their contemporaries that a single name is sufficient to define them. Ichiro, Madonna, Cher, Pele . . . Cecil.*

If this was just an opinion, Mr. Brody wrote, the trait could be considered insufferable. *Cecil seems to be unanimously regarded, though, as a giant among his peers.*

Mr. Brody delved into the *metaphysical Cecil,* who *translated margins into the greater allegory of life.*

Cecil's margins embrace both the strict borders that give so many people comfort, and yet trumpet the free blank space urging them to reach for hidden potential if they would just venture beyond those borders and dare to paint on that virgin palate.

The article concluded with Mr. Brody's insight that,

despite all of his accomplishments, *there is a sadness about Cecil, for he understands that in his single-minded dedication to margins, he is himself trapped just inside those two long red vertical lines. Like Moses, while he can see the Promised Land, he cannot cross over.*"

"Wow," Marta said aloud as she read through the article a second time.

The only other thing the electronic file included was a snippet from the end of one of the Austin Powers movies. She missed it completely the first time the credits flew up and off her computer screen. When she slowed the replay to a crawl, though, there it was.

Cat-waxing by Cecil.

Cecil and Marta sat side by side in the squished-together cheap section for the return flight to Phoenix. Libby Pinch flew first class. Which was fine with Marta. She was anxious to talk to Cecil. Being elderly, he napped through parts of the long plane ride. During his waking moments, though, she learned more about his remarkable life.

"You didn't just *happen* to show up at the committee meeting, did you?" she asked him.

He smiled a wrinkled smile. "No. No, I was a bit concerned about your last phone call. You were a little down. I thought you might need some moral support."

Marta smiled. "I read about the margins."

"Oh, yeah." He shook his head. "That one article in *the Footnotes & Margins*. I wish he wouldn't have done that."

"Who? And done what?"

"Sean Brody. He was a good man. I even sponsored his

baseball team. I wouldn't have let him give the story to the *Footnotes & Margins* people if he'd asked. They probably badgered him, though, when they saw what he wrote for the *Spokane Chronicle*. Short thing, about eight inches. He said it was picked apart by some meddling assistant city editor. He called it a 'little mongrel of a story.' He was embarrassed by it. They ran it somewhere way in the back of the paper."

Marta was glad she'd read the whole article, because otherwise, she would have likely said that, all this time, she thought books and paper just *came* with margins. And Mr. Brody had recorded Cecil's response to *that* observation.

People who think that paper just comes with margins are the same people who think food comes from grocery stores, he had quoted Cecil. *They don't have the sense God gave a brick.*

The plane bumped through a pocket of turbulent air. Marta placed a reassuring hand on Cecil's arm.

"That story nearly sunk me, dontchaknow."

"I thought it was flattering," Marta said. "What happened?"

"A bunch of investors from the coast read it. So, they came to me and asked me to throw in with 'em. Wanted to build a big new printing plant west of Spokane, near the airport. And I was tempted, dontchaknow. I thought about it a long time. The only thing was, they were mostly footnote people, footnotes, as you know, being a lot more profitable than margins. I wasn't up to date with all the subtleties of footnotes like I was with margins. Then I remembered, when you get too big for your britches is when you get yourself in trouble. So, I told 'em no."

"That investment would have been bad for you?"

"Everything was changing, and us old-timers didn't see

it coming. The personal computer. And all of a sudden, everyone was doing their own footnotes and margins. Not with any real art or style, mind you. I guess it turns out a whole lot of people just aren't that particular, dontchaknow."

He sighed. "Within a year, maybe less, the whole thing would have gone bust and I'd have lost everything. Been like Mark Twain, having to take up the lecture circuit in my old age to pay off my debts."

Cecil smiled at a flight attendant, who scouted along the aisle for trash.

"And the margin service . . ." Marta probed gently.

"Didn't last much beyond another year and a half. And I don't mind admitting to you that for a while there I was lost. You have to understand, until then my whole life had been the margin service. The only distraction I allowed was baseball, and even at that I only listened to the games on the radio. Then, in the wink of an eye, everything was gone."

Marta could hear the bitterness.

"Those damn computers grabbed my business by the shoulders and shook the snot out of it."

"So, what happened?"

"Sean Brody, that same fellow who wrote the magazine article. I told you I sponsored his baseball team? Well, he gave me a present that Christmas. A Jimmy Buffet album. And just from sheer boredom, one day, I put it on this old portable record player I had. And the first song I heard was *A Pirate Looks at Forty*. Do you know it?"

Marta shrugged and nodded. Growing up in the Islands, she was familiar with Jimmy Buffet.

Cecil paused and enjoyed the sunlight reflecting off a veil of clouds below them, then turned back to her. "Well, you know the line that goes, ' ... *my occupational hazard being, my occupation's just not around...*'? That got my attention, dontchaknow, so I listened to the rest of it. And right there and then I realized, even during the best of times, the margin service was a world cast in shades of gray. The world this Buffett fella sang about, though, my goodness. It was bright blues and reds and yellows, rich teals and deep purples.

"That very day, I closed my savings account, put the building up for sale, and took the Greyhound to Miami. I hitch-hiked all the way down to the Keys and bought a sailboat—my old thirty-seven-foot ketch-rigged Tayana. The yacht broker tried to sell me something newer, something faster. I told him I didn't plan on bein' in a hurry. I changed the boat's name from *Dreamcatcher* to *Somewhere Over China*. Then I headed to the Caribbean, and never regretted it for a minute."

"You just dropped everything and left when you heard a Jimmy Buffet album?" Marta asked with a tiny bit of envy. Practically every step of Marta's life had been calculated. She was a foreigner to spontaneity, with the notable exception of some of her sexual encounters. And based on that limited experience, she had to admit, spontaneity intrigued her.

"Yep. Of course, everything had pretty much already dropped me. I'd lived a fairly focused and limited life to that point, and I guess I just sorta went overboard, dontchaknow."

Marta glanced past Cecil and down on mid-America spread below them.

"I went to a Jimmy Buffet concert just before I entered the GRC program," she said. "The experience was ... strange. The people were strange ..."

"What about the music?"

"I liked the music. It made me... I don't know... happy, I guess. Of course, it reminded me of home, the good parts of home."

"He's doing his hundredth birthday concert on St. Bart's this December. I'm gonna' sail over. You should go with me. Jimmy forgets the words more than he used to, but them Coral Reefers still put on a good show."

26

WAXING THE CAT

MARTA SAT QUIETLY WHILE Cecil napped again. He woke when the flight attendant came by offering another round of watery drinks.

"So, what's the deal with the cats?" Marta asked.

"Well," he said, smiling at the memory, "for the first year or so, I just sailed."

He said he taught himself seamanship. He breathed in the islands and the ocean. He took up diving, both scuba and snorkel. He discovered rum. He explored a hundred bays and a hundred reefs. He met drifters and scoundrels. He met some of the finest people he could imagine.

"Eventually, though, the whole thing began to smack too much of vacation. My people raised me with the belief that folks were not put on this earth to loll about, dontchaknow."

The life of a vagabond sailor, he explained, revolves around the marina community.

"You can't be bound for a new port every day. So, you sail into a harbor, find a place you like, and tie up for a week or two, or a month or two, or even a season. You meet the people and you join the community."

He said he noticed that many members of this society served their neighborhood with a specific purpose.

"Diesel mechanics fix engines. Sail makers mend sails. Others clean hulls or paint trim or catch fish. So, I came to need a purpose, something useful I could share, dontcha-know, and not a single person I came across expressed any urgent dissatisfaction with their margins."

"Hard to believe," Marta said.

He told Marta he was pondering his destiny over a rum punch at a dock in Martinique late one afternoon when a sixty-foot motor yacht tied up nearby. He heard yelling coming from someplace below and an angry-looking woman wearing shorts and a tank top jumped to the dock and stomped past him.

"I saw she was covered with cat hair."

Being native to the Caribbean, Marta knew that boats have boat cats. Sometimes they are an indulgence. Usually, though, they are working cats who help control vermin that slip aboard from the docks. And given the humid climate, cat hair adheres epoxy-like to clothing, furniture and sails.

Day after day, Cecil said he watched the big boats tie up. He saw the women with their tell-tail tufts of fur here and there, many of them at their wits end.

"So, one day, this woman gets off her boat, all in a snit and muttering to herself. So just on an impulse I stood up and said, 'Hey, Lady, ya' want me to wax your cat?'

"And the whole thing just sort of took off."

Cecil waxed the one cat, and then another. The happy boat wives told their friends, and one morning, Cecil said, he stepped onto the deck of *Somewhere Over China* and saw a whole bunch of folks lined back along the dock. And within a year or two, hairless felines were on display all over the Caribbean.

A voice from the plane's intercom system interrupted as the captain announced they would be landing in twenty minutes.

"So, you . . . you like cat waxing?"

"I do. I enjoy the aesthetics of it. There's something about a clean, hairless cat, like they were just waiting for someone to come along and remove the camouflage so you can finally see what a cat's all about. Of course, we give 'em a bottle of sunscreen on their way out. SPF fifty. A sunburned cat is a pretty sorry sight, dontchaknow."

Although Marta had never seen a sunburned cat, she nodded agreement.

"And I'll tell you another thing I like about it. I think this business is safe from the march of civilization. It'll be a cold day in hell before you find a computer can wax a cat, dontchaknow."

Marta laughed. "So, how'd the movie thing happen?"

"A big Hollywood producer and his wife brought their boat to the Caribbean, and the wife heard about my work. She was all in a tizzy to get her cat waxed. The producer was away for the day and knew nothing about it.

"Well, you can imagine his surprise when he came aboard that night and was confronted by a naked cat," Cecil said. "Like a lot of people, he was unnerved by it at first. The more he stared at that bald kitty, though, the more he was intrigued by the possibilities. So, he hired me to come out to California. I wouldn't have done it except I was running low on funds."

As Marta suspected, Cecil confessed he didn't tolerate the Hollywood lifestyle for long.

"I thought the Hollywood folks were too full of themselves. Caribbean cats were getting waxed for a good, functional reason, dontchaknow. With the Hollywood cats, though, it was all for show. I found I didn't care for the promiscuous waxing of cats. So mostly now, I just stay home."

"You still call your business Cecil's Margin Service," Marta noted.

"I owe a lot to the margin service. And besides, Cecil's Cat-Waxing Service just sounds silly."

27

SECRETS UNRAVEL

MARSHALL DECIDED TO SURPRISE Marta at Phoenix's Sky Harbor Airport. He was taking a chance, he knew, but he'd missed her so much. He could only hope she'd felt the same. If she didn't, though, he had a fallback position to excuse himself.

He waited just outside baggage claim, scanning the crowds. She'd shared a flight with the Arizona State University basketball team, and, as she was a short person, he almost missed her completely among the gargantuan human beings. He didn't see her until he felt a tug at his arm.

"Marshall. What are you doing here?"

Marshall had intended to be more restrained. He hadn't meant to put her on the spot. He found, though, he couldn't help himself.

"I come with good tidings and a new list of demands from Dr. Doonaughty." Marshall reached to scoop her into a hug.

Marta held up a hand of warning that stopped him mid-reach and made his heart sink.

"Congresswoman Pinch," Marta said quickly, turning

to a severe-looking woman wearing a business suit, "this is Marshall Grissom. One of our travelers."

Marshall offered the congresswoman an awkward handshake.

"Ah, yes. Mr. Grissom. I've read of your exploits. I have to say I'm intrigued to learn more. Now what of these demands? From some doctor? Is the scientific team trying to organize? I can get someone from the National Labor Relations Board involved if—"

"Um . . . no. No. Nothing like that. Just a guy who really likes . . . um . . . pie. And hasn't had any for a while because we've been out . . . of pie . . . So he was sort of looking for some extra . . . pie . . . and I hoped Marta could . . . um . . . help him out."

"Ms. Hamilton," Libby turned to Marta, "while this is a much smaller operation than it used to be, as administrator, you can't bog yourself down with minutia. You need to delegate someone else to see that this doctor whatever gets his pie."

"The Congresswoman is here to observe our operation," Marta told Marshall with a stern glance.

Marshall felt the flow of people around him but saw only Marta wearing her frown.

"Oh, good. That's just . . . good."

"And there's someone else, too," Marta said more brightly. "Someone you know."

Marshall followed Marta's gaze back into the crowd.

"Cecil!" Marshall raised his hand in a wave.

Cecil waved back and continued his mosey.

"I hope he didn't bring any rum with him," Marshall said from the side of his mouth.

"I beg your pardon?" asked the congresswoman.

"Oh, nothing," Marta said. "Just a little Caribbean joke."

They retrieved their luggage and paid a skycap to assist them to the parking garage's eighth floor. Marshall opened the car's back door so Libby could climb in. He put Cecil up front. As Marta walked back to tip the skycap, Marshall followed her.

"Sorry about that," Marta said. "I guess I should have called and let everyone know what was going on."

"No problem," Marshall said. Despite his disappointment, he could not suppress an excited grin. "As soon as you get back, though, you need to go see Elvin. He thinks he's found something."

The drive east into the desert became a special sort of torture.

Despite her best intentions, Marta had wanted to accept Marshall's hug. She'd wanted to drag him off into an elevator or a bathroom and comply with whatever Dr. Doonaughty demanded. And if Libby Pinch hadn't been there, she might have done it. Continuing to press Marshall into sexual servitude, though, was wrong when she knew he wanted more than she was willing to give.

And what is this about Elvin finding something?

Marta kept glancing from the back seat to Marshall's face reflected by the rear-view mirror. She implored with her eyes. With Cecil and the Congresswoman right there next to them, though, all Marshall could do was shrug an apology.

The farther they got from Phoenix the more uncomfortable Libby Pinch seemed to be.

Marta made an effort at polite conversation. "Ever spent any time in the desert?" she asked Libby, who sat beside her in the rear seat.

"Hardly. I pictured rolling sand dunes. These plants look like something Dr. Seuss would make up."

"Different kind of desert. The Sonoran Desert is really quite beautiful when you get to know it."

"I'll leave that to the camels and snakes and . . . and . . ."

Libby seemed to be grasping for a third example of unique desert fauna, so Marshall offered over his shoulder, ". . . Gila monsters?"

Libby turned a little pale. "You people have creatures here that are actually called monsters? That's their real name?"

"Well, yes . . ."

"My native habitat is a nice paved street with stop lights and restaurants and the occasional tree growing out of a large pot. Squirrels are pretty, but I don't want to pet one."

"Gila monsters are sort of the same," Marta said. "Pretty. And you definitely don't want to pet one—although a few tourists make the attempt. We see relatively little of the desert, though. We spend most of our time underground."

Libby appeared relieved.

A long line of fences rose on the horizon. Heavy chain link loomed ten feet tall. Razor wire curled around the top rail. The only break in this barrier that seemed to stretch from horizon to horizon was a dual set of gates with a guard station in between. The soldier peering into the back seat spent a little extra time with Cecil's passport.

Another security station in the main building's lobby

passed them along toward a bank of elevators. A few minutes later, they stepped into the cool underground corridors of the Historical Research Initiative complex.

"We'll have someone show you two to your quarters," Marta said quickly as they arrived at the reception area. "I know you're both tired, especially with the change in time zones. So, let's delay our initial tour until morning. This is Betty. If you want something to eat or drink, just call the reception desk and let her know. We'll have something delivered to your room."

"Do you have bathtubs?" Libby asked.

"I am sorry. I'm afraid all they built were showers."

Libby sighed as she and Cecil climbed onto a golf cart that would take them to the housing wings on the other side of the complex.

"Again, if you need anything, call Betty." Marta waved.

As soon as the golf cart disappeared into an adjacent corridor, Marshall urged Marta in the opposite direction. "Elvin should be at the projection lab. Hurry."

Marta carefully stepped over the lip forming the base of the airlock. She nearly tripped anyway when she saw Gretchen seated alongside Elvin, both staring intently at his bank of computer monitors.

The physicists studied confusing backgrounds consisting of a pulsating array of vaguely colored lines. The lines varied from relatively defined squiggly strings to fat, fuzzy blurs that gained and lost definition with an uncertain rhythm.

"Okay, here it comes again," said Elvin. "Now see if you can refine the timeline . . ."

"Damn," Gretchen said. "It's still too fast. Can we slow it down even more?"

"We'll lose all resolution if we go any slower. Let's try again."

"So . . . what are you two working on?" Marta asked tentatively as both Elvin and Gretchen waved to acknowledge her arrival.

"Didn't Marshall—?" Elvin began.

"No. A couple of people from the oversight subcommittee flew back with me and are going to be here a few days. So, we didn't have a chance to talk."

"Are we having maintenance issues with the wormhole again?" Gretchen asked, her tone scolding.

"We'll have to play that by ear," Marta said. "What's going on here?"

Elvin stood at his computer monitor and indulged himself with a long stretch of his arms and back. He slipped his glasses onto his forehead and massaged his eyes.

"Okay, well, I came across an uncatalogued recording of one of the missions . . ." he said.

"Uncatalogued?" Marta asked, and added without thinking, "How could that . . . ?"

Elvin's eyes darted to Gretchen as he quickly continued, ". . . and we discovered a very . . . unexplainable . . . phenomenon. I brought it to Gretchen's attention, because I needed some help in interpreting the data."

"That's right," Gretchen added. "Since the recording was uncatalogued, I wanted to be sure it was added properly in sequence, which it turns out we have still not been able to do. We don't know when this particular projection took place. Then I looked closely at the feedback data from the parallel universe—this is *The Lawrence Welk Show* universe we're dealing with—and found something unbelievable."

Elvin, standing beyond Gretchen's field of vision, gave Marta a cryptic frown and an almost imperceptible shrug. "It seems," he said, "that whomever, or whatever, was projected was sent back almost eighty years."

"To either 1967 or 1968," Gretchen said.

"Um . . . that can't be right," Marta said. "We've never—"

"That's what I thought at first," Gretchen said. "That the data was scrambled somehow, and the readings are incorrect. We've been going through this for hours, though, and I'm convinced the data is accurate."

"One of the animal test subjects, then," Marta suggested.

"No. The lifeline data is unique to each individual, be it animal or human. The animal markings are completely different. This is human. And given some time to compare with other projection records, I think we can determine which human—if it's someone who has traveled before."

Marta didn't like the sound of that. "You really think you can do that?"

"Since the lifeline is a depiction of data unique to each individual, yes, I think we probably can," Elvin said, adding another shrug. "Besides Marshall, we've decided not to tell anyone. For now."

"I think that's a good idea," Marta said.

"Well, sooner or later," Gretchen said, "we have to involve security. Maybe even that Mr. Wishcamper from the oversight subcommittee. I mean, don't you understand the implications here? In all likelihood someone was killed—sent back to a time before his or her birth. How did that happen without us knowing?"

Gretchen's voice dripped with accusation, and the accompanying expression reeked of suspicion.

"So, your conclusion is that this traveler, whoever he or she was, didn't survive?" Marta asked.

Marshall, who'd been standing quietly at the periphery of the conversation, said with excitement in his voice, "They found evidence that the traveler *did* survive."

Marta turned back to Elvin and Gretchen.

"We found *something*," Elvin said, then quickly qualified, "at least, I think we found something. Come here and see."

Marta stepped to Elvin's computer screen.

"As you know," he instructed, "the time that passes here during a projection is pretty much irrelevant to what happens in the limbo and the destination universe. And we know that the limbo time, as measured here—from the start of projection to insertion into the past universe—is exactly ninety-seven seconds. As far as sound goes, we pick up the *I Love Lucy* theme song when the ninety-seven seconds starts. And at the end of the ninety-seven seconds, we hear the theme song of the target universe. In this case, it's *The Lawrence Welk Show* . . ."

"Right, right." Marta made a rolling motion with her hands to move him along.

"Okay, watch."

He increased the speed so the whole recording took just under thirty seconds to play out. The monitor showed the same set of wavering and shifting bands of light that had been on Elvin's and Gretchen's machines a few moments ago. This time, though, smack in the middle of the monitor was an unwavering red thread—the lifeline—dividing the monitor vertically.

"So up to this point," Marta said, "she ... uh ... this person ... is fine, right? The lifeline isn't wavering or deviating at all ..."

"Yes, well, here it comes," Elvin said.

At the precise instant that Sheila would have transitioned from the limbo into the past of *Lawrence Welk*, Marta saw the red line fall like a guillotine from the top of the monitor to the bottom. As the recording continued, it did not reappear.

"Okay," Elvin said. "I've been dissecting the tracking data going into the destination universe. I started with one minute, and then two minutes and so on. I didn't see anything. Until I analyzed the third minute into the mission ... well I don't know how I saw it at first. I look now and half the time it doesn't even register at normal speed. Just watch."

Again, the same scene, absent the red line, shimmered and crackled before them. Marta stared intently.

"Wait," she said at three minutes into the recording. "I thought ..."

"Yeah," Elvin smiled, "I thought so, too. So, I slowed it down, way down. So slow that I'll have to isolate that point on the tape or we'll be here all night."

Again, Marta stared intently.

"And right ... here."

Distinctly Marta saw the flash of a thin red line bisect the monitor and then disappear.

"What can that mean?" Marta asked. "When my lifeline wavered during my difficulties, it was because the past being was overriding my consciousness and I was losing awareness of my future self. How could that happen so quickly?"

Elvin only shrugged.

"Does it reappear anywhere else?" Marta asked.

"No. We've analyzed another half hour and it doesn't show up again."

"I'm sorry, Marta," Elvin said. "I was working late with the Sheila video and I dozed off. Gretchen walked in and looked over my shoulder while I was asleep. She asked what I was looking at, so I told her I'd found an uncatalogued mission video."

"That's okay," Marta said, "because we need to tell Gretchen and Naomi the whole story."

When Gretchen excused herself to attend to other duties, Marta had taken Marshall and Elvin to her office and summoned Gillis to join them.

"That's what I said before," Marshall protested, "and you said—"

"I know, Marshall. You were right."

"And if they go to the authorities?" Gillis asked.

"I think they'll go to the authorities pretty soon if we *don't* tell them."

Elvin sat heavily on Marta's sofa and nodded agreement. "I've been keeping the tape from Gretchen, saying I need to finish my analysis first. As soon as she spends a little time with it, though, she'll know it's Sheila."

"That's only one of the reasons we have to tell them," Marta said. "The other is that we need their help to look into this any further."

"Yessss." Marshall added a fist pump.

"You believe she could have survived?" Gillis asked,

shaking his head to make evident his own skepticism.

"I still think this is a long shot," Marta said. "But we owe it to Sheila to at least try and find out."

28

THE EXPANDING CONSPIRACY

"THIS IS ABSURD," said Libby Pinch. "I'm just supposed to take your word? This is like one of those séances where bereaved relatives are supposed to take on faith that a medium is passing along messages from their deceased loved ones."

"Tell me, then," Marta asked. "What is my—our—incentive for lying?"

"To maintain control of your own little kingdom."

Both Marta's future and present self stared at the congresswoman without any idea how to proceed.

Libby had asked to speak with a representative from the *Star Trek* universe. Marta had agreed. And during naptime of the day following the fact-finders' arrival, Libby, Cecil, Marta, Marshall, Naomi, Gretchen, Gillis, Macy, and Leonard sat in the conference room and waited.

"So how do we inform them we are requesting a meeting?" Libby asked.

Libby had made a point to sit apart at the oak table's far end. She had motioned for Cecil to join her there, but he politely ignored her and stood off to the side.

"We can't," Gretchen said. "The only means of communicating between universes is to send a traveler."

"Then how will they know?"

"The laws of parallelism," Gretchen said. "Prior to the initiation of time travel, we believe events occurring in all of the different universes unfolded on nearly identical tracks. Certainly, the significant historical events. And while each visitation of a traveler from one universe to another upsets this parallelism to some degree, we can still expect the major historical events to take place similarly. Anything to do directly with this program, we believe, tends to fall into that category."

"So, they just know?"

"They are making the same plans and sharing the same concerns we are. It's just a matter of who takes the initiative to travel. Recently, the Marta from *Star Trek's* future has been the one—"

"Speaking of which," Marta said, "she's here. Congresswoman Pinch, what would you like to ask?"

This was the point at which Libby Pinch suggested she was being made the victim of a hoax.

"*Don't feel bad,*" future-Marta conveyed silently to present Marta. "*This princess is a royal pain in the ass in our universe, too. And she's not buying this, either. She wants some kind of proof.*"

"*Well, then,*" present Marta thought to her future self, "*I can think of only one way of convincing her. Give us twenty-four hours.*"

"For all the proof this provides," Libby said, "you could have dreamed this whole place up to siphon off billions of dollars while pretending to be sending yourselves all over the—"

"You think we're making this up?" Naomi asked, sitting taller and leaning forward on her elbows.

Libby did not answer the question directly. "If you wanted to manufacture a visitation here and there to satisfy naïve politicians or financial supporters, doing so would be easy."

"Okay," Marta said. "Here's what we'll do, Congresswoman. Please accompany Marshall, Gillis and Macy. They'll give you a crash course in time travel. Tomorrow, you'll meet the *Star Trek* version of yourself."

"Whoa, wait a minute. There's no way I'll—"

"Say, there," interrupted Cecil as he slipped into an empty chair. "Can I go, too? Sounds like a hoot, dontchaknow."

"Surely," Libby protested to Marta, "you won't allow an elderly man to undergo the rigors of such a journey?"

"While projection into the past can be challenging mentally," Marta said, "physically not so much. Cecil is in good health and as long as—"

"Mr. Cecil," Libby admonished, "there's no reason for you to take such a risk."

"They told us to come here and investigate. And this seems to be the only means of investigating. I don't want to go back to those ladies and gentlemen on the subcommittee and tell 'em we had the chance to go have a look and we didn't."

With satisfaction, Marta watched Libby's air of defiance deflate to one of uncertainty before settling into downright dismay. The congresswoman drummed her fingers on the table. She had talked herself into a corner.

"And you're willing to do this?" Libby asked Cecil.

"Wouldn't miss it."

"You're sure it's safe?" she appealed to Marta.

"As safe as we can make it. This is time travel, though, and the realities of physics make time travel a hazardous undertaking. If it makes you feel any better, I will accompany you. So, if anything bad happens, it will probably happen to all of us."

"Will I survive?" Libby asked weakly.

"Yes," Elvin called from across the room.

"Probably," Marta said.

Libby Pinch sighed once, seemed to come to some understanding within herself, and resurrected that expression of defiance.

"Then fine. What do we do first?"

Marta felt impressed. Maybe there was more to this woman than she thought. *Okay. We'll see how she handles the next part.*

"First," Marta said, "we need to ask you about your breasts."

"My . . . what?"

"I can handle this part if you want me to, Marta," Elvin said with the hint of a leer.

The defiance melted again. Libby looked slightly frantic, casting her eyes toward the door as if planning to make a run for it.

"Elvin, go away," Marta said. "Naomi, will you please deal with this?"

"I'm the chief of our medical and psychological division." Naomi stood and offered a comforting smile of greeting.

Stepping around the conference table, she took Libby's hand and led her into the projection lab. "I know you're confused, and I can explain. Nonorganic material can't be projected through time, so if you've had breast implants, or any other implants, for that matter . . ."

They passed into the corridor.

Marta and Marshall hurried through the lab and carefully peered around the corner. They wanted to be sure they didn't miss the next part. Naomi's soothing and forthright manner worked its magic, Libby Pinch's gradual relaxation made apparent by an easing of tension in her shoulders and the more casual pace of her stride as the two women conversed while strolling away.

"Any second now," Marta whispered to Marshall.

"Yep."

"Here it comes . . ."

In the distant glare of the corridor lighting, Congress-woman Pinch halted in her tracks and grabbed Naomi by the shoulders. Her piercing voice carried back along the hallway. "What do you mean, naked?"

Sometimes, Marshall thought, Marta's whole life seemed to revolve around that oak conference table occupying the big room adjacent to her office. Except, of course, for all the other rooms they used for . . . well . . . even that part of their lives hadn't escaped the oak table. Dr. Doonaughty's threats had forced them there a couple of times.

This meeting, though, could not take place anywhere near Marta's office. For this meeting, Marta instructed Gillis to find a space someplace among the unused areas and be sure no one could eavesdrop electronically on the discussion.

When Marta told him about the meeting, Marshall said, "Ooooh, this is spy stuff, isn't it?"

She smiled.

"I thought you weren't supposed to do spy stuff anymore," Marshall said.

When Marta applied to become administrator, British intelligence had to come clean with the oversight subcommittee concerning her role as an espionage agent. Technically, the subcommittee already knew about most of the spies, including Marta, because *their* spies had told them. They understood the interest of the various governments in having unfiltered reports of the technological accomplishments. So long as the agents behaved themselves, that was fine. An administrator, though, needed to be above all that, so Marta was told to cease and desist. The British government happily agreed. They would rather have an administrator on the scene than a spy.

"I'm not supposed to," Marta replied to Marshall, "so I leave the spy stuff to Gillis. He lets me know what's happening."

The room Gillis chose was one of many along a host of empty corridors. Back when the complex was full of people, this space had been used for storage of, among other things, folding chairs. So, everyone had a place to sit.

Late that evening, they trooped in. Marshall and Marta arrived first. Gillis brought the rest: Gretchen, Naomi, Elvin and Leonard Rose.

"I suppose you're wondering—" Marta began.

"I'm assuming by the clandestine nature of this gathering," interrupted Naomi, "you are considering doing something that could get us all in trouble." She swiped at her dusty chair with the sleeve of her lab coat before sitting down.

"Well—"

This time, an angry Gretchen Allen did the interrupting.

"This is about Sheila, isn't it? That recording we've been going over and over . . . that's Sheila. Somehow, when she tried to help you, Marshall . . ."

Marshall felt Gretchen's anger grow with every word until she stood and shouted her accusations.

". . . somehow she ended up eighty years into the past and you all have been lying about it. What did you do to her?" Gretchen kicked at her chair to emphasize her wrath. It clattered loudly onto its side.

Marshall withered under Gretchen's unexpected rage. "I . . . I didn't—"

"Marshall didn't do anything except save my life and Elvin's and probably Leonard's, too," Marta said, carefully parrying Gretchen's anger with a note of calm. "The reasons for not telling you were completely justified at the time. Politically, though, things are evolving quickly here, and I'm afraid if we have any chance of finding Sheila, we have little time left to act."

"What are you talking about?" gasped Naomi. "Are you saying Sheila's alive? How could . . ."

Marshall only listened as the others related the whole story of that awful night for Gretchen and Naomi. Leonard Rose joined Marshall's silence. When the story ended, Gretchen and Naomi stared cold daggers at Leonard.

He held their gaze for a few seconds, then looked back at his hands.

"Leonard?" Marta prodded.

Rose met their eyes again, cleared his throat and said, "There's nothing I can say I haven't already said to Marta, Marshall, Elvin and Gillis. I've said I'm sorry, and I am. I've told them how much I regret my involvement, and I do. I've said how thankful I am they chose to give me a . . . pardon of sorts. And I've done my best to contribute here ever since . . . but I don't think any of you believe that. So, there's no point going over it again."

Rose closed his eyes to the harsh, exposed lighting that exaggerated shadows on the walls of the crowded room.

"Naomi, Gretchen," Marta said, "you must make a decision about your involvement from now on. We are at your mercy. You could go to the authorities and turn us in. Legally, that's probably the smartest thing you could do. But I know how you both feel about Sheila, and I'm hoping you will be willing to risk helping us. I won't ask you for a decision right now . . ."

Naomi raised her hand in an offer to speak, but Marta didn't allow it.

"No. I don't want an answer now. The two of you need to talk this over and be sure what you want to do. Besides, we have other things to discuss."

"The congress lady and the old guy?" Elvin asked.

"Correct. My strategy of stonewalling the committee on the details of our operation here is out the window. We must project the congresswoman to the past so maybe she'll understand the relationship among universes. But realistically, it's only a matter of time before the oversight subcommittee starts restricting our activities. Congresswoman Pinch has a stick up her butt about unauthorized intrusions from one universe to another. She's worried about the effects of visitations from other universes on our world."

"Well, so are we . . ." Naomi said.

"But she thinks she can write regulations that will govern the laws of physics."

"Does she know that we—in effect, you—have established a working relationship with the *Star Trek* universe?" Gretchen asked. "And that we've already agreed not to send missions to each other's world without prior consent?"

"Yes. These are politicians, though, and that will hardly be sufficient. They'll want inspectors and regulation manuals and grievance procedures and... some kind of interuniversal treaty formally spelling out what will be allowed."

"And the final authority..." Naomi wondered aloud.

"Certainly not us," Marta said. "Depending on what Libby Pinch and Cecil see and do here over the next couple of days, our lives will become a lot more complicated."

Gillis sighed. "Ah, well, it was fun while it lasted."

Marshall could no longer sit patiently.

"What about Sheila? What are we going to do? Doesn't the appearance of the lifeline, however brief, mean she survived the transition from the limbo into that other universe?"

"And then the lifeline was gone..." Gretchen pointed out.

"I'm sorry, Marshall," Elvin said, "I think the brief appearance of a lifeline and then its absence is evidence of death rather than survival."

Marshall couldn't believe that the others weren't seeing it. "There *was* a lifeline, no matter how brief, so there *had* to be a host, didn't there?"

"Okay, here's the hole in that argument," Elvin said. "They sent Sheila to the 1960s, at least thirty years before she was born. There would be no past version of herself."

"That's the issue I can't get beyond," Gretchen agreed.

Marshall scanned from face to face, desperate for support. *We are so close.*

"I'm not so sure," Marta said. She touched his hand and turned to him. "I'm sorry, Marshall," she said. "I'm sorry I kept this from you. I just didn't want to get your hopes up if there wasn't some rational seed of optimism."

Marshall didn't understand. *What was she saying?*

"I asked Gillis to do a genealogy search regarding Sheila's family. He learned that her grandmother was a woman named Amanda Page, who attended high school in a small Eastern New Mexico town called Portales during the years 1966, 1967 and 1968."

Marshall riveted her with his eyes.

"And . . ." he asked, his heart racing.

"Gillis was able to find Amanda's senior yearbook photo. Gillis, if you would?"

Gillis set his pocket computer on the table and called up its virtual three-dimensional screen. His fingers manipulated a floating keyboard. An image appeared. Although the name below the picture was Amanda Page, they were looking at Sheila Schuler.

"Well, let's think about this for a moment."

Everyone turned to Naomi, who, with apparent indifference to this debate, had been staring absently at the slick, gray wall next to her. Now she stood and stepped into the virtual image floating ethereally in the gloom. From Marshall's angle of observation, Amanda Page's face seemed eerily imposed on Naomi's body.

"We know from animal testing that when the lifeline disappeared," she said, almost as if speaking to herself, "we were unable to recover the test subjects."

She frowned and stared intently into the stream of light, then seemed to finally acknowledge the presence of the others.

"We are simply assuming the inability to recover them meant the death of the projected being. During a couple of missions, though," she said as she nodded to Marta, "we witnessed disruptions of your lifeline."

"Yes. They seemed to coincide with my loss of awareness of my future self. The past being was absorbing my consciousness."

"In your debriefing following the Flagstaff mission, you told us you felt the only thing keeping you linked to your future self was Sheila's presence and her constant reminders of your mission."

"Right."

"So, does that mean, if you had lost your conscious connection with the future, your future self would have ceased to exist? Or would your future self sit there in a dormant state? And could you be *revived* by someone reminding you of your future and your mission?"

Elvin started to speak, but Naomi raised her hand, commanding silence while she thought another moment. Then, she continued. "And what defines an equivalent being? We've assumed it's DNA, or the combination of magnetic field, electric charge and aura. Clearly, though, your equivalent being doesn't have to be an exact biological copy. Consider the biological variations we've encountered. In one universe, Marshall had reptilian characteristics. In another, Frank was a cockroach."

She retreated another step, so she could again see

Amanda Page's floating apparition. "What if your equivalent being only needs to be a close match? Genetically, I mean? What if there's some element of organic reality even more basic than DNA that we don't know about?"

29

THE NAKED REPRESENTATIVE

"Only if there is no video."

Less than twenty-four hours after Gretchen and Naomi were drawn into the Sheila conspiracy, Congresswoman Libby Pinch stood at the projection platform, clutching a robe around herself so tightly her knuckles turned white.

"We always record projections," Naomi explained one more time. "It's important to have a visual record to coordinate with other data regarding the projection just . . ."

Naomi caught herself. She almost said *just in case something goes wrong*, but she thought Libby didn't need to hear that particular phrase right now.

Naomi thought they'd settled this yesterday. After breaking the news about the requisite nudity, Naomi had fended off Libby's objections with clinical explanations of its necessity. She promised the atmosphere would be as professional and nonsexual as possible.

"Sort of like going to your gynecologist," Naomi said. "I think we'd all choose to do that with our pants on, but we just can't."

Naomi hoped no one had told Libby about Elvin's betting pools.

"Members of Congress do not allow themselves to be photographed naked," Libby said emphatically. She pointed at a bank of video recorders staring at her from across the platform. "I want those cameras removed. I have to run for re-election next year."

"This program is secret. All its data is secret. Nobody will see the video," Naomi said.

"And if you believe that, you know nothing about major league politics."

"What about it, Naomi?" Marta asked with a sigh. "This one time, can we get by without the cameras?"

Naomi pulled Marta aside.

"We run the video for a very good reason. If something goes wrong, the visual images could offer critical clues as to what happened. If a traveler gets shipped off to some place we don't know about, or if we have tracking problems with the lifeline, Elvin needs every bit of data available to try and find them."

"We're going back only a few days to the *Star Trek* universe. This is as routine as time travel gets . . ."

"I'm surprised at you," Naomi said. "Nothing about this will ever be routine."

"Yes, you're right. Just go along with me on this, okay?"

Naomi answered the expectant stares of everyone awaiting the outcome of this whispered conversation. "Remove the video equipment."

Elvin stood to protest. Marta silenced him with her glare.

The three robed travelers took their places near the platform. As Naomi reached to take the congresswoman's robe, she heard Libby's whispered confession to Marta.

"I hoped you were going to stand your ground regarding the video cameras. Then I would have had a last-minute justification for withdrawing."

"You'll be fine," Marta whispered back.

Libby closed her eyes. Naomi saw facial muscles contort as Libby clinched her jaw.

"Let's proceed," Libby said.

Galen Postelwait stood at the control panel, ready to flip a switch and push a throttle forward. Elvin carefully calibrated three monitors.

Naomi stepped to his side.

"Don't worry about it," Elvin whispered to her. "I've got my secret backup video running."

Marta prided herself on her ability to objectively assess strength and weakness. When it came to self-examination, she gave no quarter. She knew she wasn't adept at time travel. She did not fear those journeys. In fact, she missed the adventure. Her retreat to the role of administrator left her with a certain sense of failure. She understood, though, that something about her physiological or psychological makeup did not tolerate the ordeal of integration into her past self.

She performed her quick jaunts to confer with herself in the *Star Trek* universe, because she considered it her duty as administrator, and because these were strictly routine solo missions so her weaknesses would not endanger other travelers. Being able to anticipate these visitations eased the trauma of integration.

With Libby and Cecil, though, Marta went along

because she wanted to guide them—and the oversight subcommittee—through the event. She'd chosen the subcommittee hearing room a week ago in D.C. as their destination.

Marta had been purposefully vague with both Libby and Cecil as to their past target. By her repeated description of the mission as *routine*, she'd conveyed an impression they'd be hopping back a couple of days when they were all here on campus.

Her only concern was that the distance between Arizona and Washington, D.C. would be by far the longest geographical span they'd attempted to negotiate. Elvin had expounded his theory, though, that just the number of years traversed made no difference in the ninety-seven second elapsed time between universes, the time projector would also be indifferent to physical distance. So, she reluctantly accepted this risk on behalf of Libby and Cecil.

Marta wanted to counter any suspicion Libby or the subcommittee might have concerning their parallel counterparts. She needed a graphic demonstration that she wasn't manufacturing these stories about conferring with her *Star Trek* twin.

Marta shed her robe and without a hint of self-consciousness, stepped onto the platform. Cecil disrobed. With a grin, he maneuvered a leathered and wiry body next to Marta.

Libby still clutched her robe closed, right hand at her breasts, left hand at her waist, knuckles of both hands white.

"Congresswoman," Marta said. "If you will please join us. It's cold, and we need to go."

Libby Pinch, a fiftyish woman who, in her single-minded devotion to the ego fulfillment of political office, had not done a single risqué thing for nearly twenty-five years, shuddered a little. Finally, with a grim stare that drilled every other set of eyes watching, she shrugged off her garment and faced them with defiance.

"I will not," she hissed to Marta while maintaining eye contact with the others, "let your gang of perverts intimidate me."

She held her chin high, put her hands on her hips and smiled a grim smile.

Spontaneous applause rolled through the projection lab, and the travelers were on their way.

30

HISTORICAL SIGNIFICANCE

One Week Earlier
Washington, D.C.

"DO NOT CONDESCEND TO ME, Ms. Hamilton," *Star Trek* Marta heard Congresswoman Pinch snap at her. Marta knew she must be careful here. She fought her instinct to snap back and put this buzzing mosquito of a woman in her place. Marta, though, no longer operated as a lone wolf answerable only to herself and a handful of superiors at MI-6. She oversaw an entire cast of players, who depended upon her to keep their time traveling carnival show thriving.

So, Marta bit her lip and, with a silent curse of frustration, reminded herself she was now a diplomat.

"Ma'am, I'm not doing that. Very honestly, we've had the same issues with members of our scientific and technical teams. They couldn't grasp that it's not a matter of 'we' and 'they.' It's all just us. That becomes abundantly clear once you integrate with yourself . . ."

And at that moment Marta was joined. She felt a slight wave of nausea as the familiar, yet unexpected presence of her future counterpart filled her mind. The thoughts of two beings tumbled and twisted together.

"Why are you here now?" past-Marta demanded mentally of her future counterpart. *"We agreed we wouldn't—"*

"Just hang on," future-Marta insisted, *"and watch this. You'll enjoy these next couple of minutes."*

Past-Marta had been interrupted mid-sentence during her response to Congresswoman Pinch.

A concerned Senator Mumford saw her momentary disorientation. "Ms. Hamilton, are you all right?"

Marta gathered her selves and pushed through the first uncomfortable moments of integration that made her want to jump up and run away.

"I'm fine, Senator. I'm not so sure about Congresswoman Pinch, though."

Libby Pinch leapt wide-eyed from her chair, knocking over a pitcher of water, and gave a little scream.

Oh my God, what's happening to me? she thought frantically.

She scanned left and right—consumed by panic—as if to discern the source of this assault on her . . . what? Her mind? Her soul? Her very being? She looked down and found herself, unaccountably, relieved to be wearing clothes. She realized she was standing with one arm clamped across her breasts and a hand over her crotch.

Her fellow subcommittee members came to her aid, reaching to try and steady her.

"Libby!" shouted Mumford. "Libby, what's wrong?"

He waved to the security officer. "Get the EMTs right now!"

"Please, Senator," Marta called over the turmoil. "Please don't do that. Let me handle this."

Marta stood and stepped from behind her microphone.

"Congresswoman." She walked toward the dais. "Libby. Listen to me. I want you to look at me and relax. Just relax and focus. You are hearing two distinct voices. You need to separate one from the other. Just take a couple of deep breaths and listen."

Through the mental turmoil, Libby saw Marta approach her as if she understood what was happening.

"You did this to me!" Libby shouted at Marta. "Whatever it is you're doing, stop right now or . . . or . . ."

"That's right," Marta said. "Just listen. You'll understand everything."

Gradually, Libby began to make sense of the muddle. She *was* able to discern two sets of thoughts fighting for attention. She stared with amazement at friends and colleagues now gathered around her. Through the mind of her future counterpart, she saw details of the next week unfold before her.

And as she learned the specifics of her amazing journey back to this point of time, she slowly sat and gave Marta a curt nod.

"Ladies and gentlemen," Marta announced, "I want you to meet a future counterpart of Libby Pinch from the *I Love Lucy* universe. And, by the way, my future self from that world is with us as well."

The subcommittee members regarded Libby and Marta in a state of communal astonishment. The spell was broken when the Congresswoman spoke.

"I understand now," she said. "I have indeed been joined by . . . by myself. I know everything she knows. She knows everything I know . . ."

"And," Marta added, "you'll find it impossible to keep

anything of significance from each other, anything that's readily accessible from either sets of memory."

Libby conferred with herself a moment and nodded her assent. Then she glared sharply at Marta. "That's not to say that we don't need to take precautions. Danger to both worlds exists here. And although you may not welcome more direct supervision from this subcommittee, our role is oversight. And we would be remiss in our duties to all the beings of both our planes of existence if we did not exercise that oversight."

"I realize that," Marta said. "What we needed, though, was a graphic demonstration of the trust you can place in your counterpart from an alternate universe. You literally are dealing with yourself. And if you can't trust yourself . . ."

"Yes. As I said, I understand."

Abruptly, both Libbys realized they hadn't heard from Cecil. She turned to see him sitting at the far end of the long semicircular dais. He was grinning.

"Cecil," Libby heard Marta say, "are you—?"

He leaned into his microphone. "This is *really* cool, dontchaknow."

Senator Mumford attempted to gavel down the bedlam that erupted as every subcommittee member dumped the pretext of decorum and shouted questions to Libby.

Finally, the sharp clap of Mumford's gavel striking its base plate restored them to their senses and shocked Marta from her concern over Cecil. Mumford indulged himself first.

"Libby, first let me ask whether you are certain what you

are experiencing is genuine and not some sort of hallucination?"

"I ... this is difficult to describe ... I don't think I've ever felt anything more genuine in my life. I am unquestionably experiencing the presence of another consciousness. Not a foreign presence, though. It's undoubtedly me ... a me that has experienced several extraordinary things that ... that I have not."

Mumford again tried to draw Cecil into the discussion.

"Can you give us your impressions, Mr.... uh ... Cecil?" he asked.

"This is waaaaaay better than rum," Cecil said, his grin magnified

"So, Congresswoman Pinch, your future counterpart has come here from about a week ahead?" asked another subcommittee member.

"That's correct."

"Tell us something of what will happen over the next few days."

Marta glanced at Libby, who seemed a little blank.

"It's not that simple," Marta said. "Our world at HRI is pretty insulated from outside events when we are preparing and executing a mission. Neither Cecil nor the Congresswoman will be here during the next week, because at the end of this hearing, Senator Mumford will appoint them to conduct a fact-finding tour at the HRI campus. They have been secluded there for several days."

"But if the three of you studied news reports of the past week before you were projected back here, you would have been able to tell us what global events occur over the next week?" the Congressman persisted.

"We could tell you what happened in *our* universe—the *I Love Lucy* universe—over the next week," Marta said.

"Wouldn't the events be the same?"

"Generally, I suspect they would be," Marta said carefully, "though not necessarily. The visitations to the pasts of both of our worlds have been frequent enough to upset the parallelism. So, we couldn't be—"

"We could be forewarned of anything significant that will happen, and we could take steps to mitigate—"

"This is where it gets tricky, Congressman. In order to be forewarned, you would have to be visited by a traveler *from* the future. That means you are being forewarned of an event that, from the perspective of that traveler, has already occurred. And it is our experience and our belief that significant past events cannot be changed."

"How can that be?" the Congressman persisted. "Suppose you could tell me where I'm going to . . . to have dinner on Wednesday, say. What happens if, forewarned, I simply decide to go somewhere else?"

"I think, Congressman," Marta said, her diplomacy slipping, "you overestimate the historical significance of your choosing where to have dinner."

The congressman scowled at her and a new wave of questions directed toward Libby Pinch washed toward the shore.

"Ladies and gentlemen," Marta shouted over them, "I'm afraid you'll have to interview the Congresswoman later. We only have a few minutes here, and right now, Libby needs to be allowed to sit quietly and have a conversation with herself."

Senator Mumford banged his gavel a few more times.

"Upon advice of the administrator, I will ask for silence."

Still appearing confused, Libby put her hands to her head and appealed to Marta, "This is difficult. This is the most unsettling sensation. I'm not sure I can—"

"Believe me, I understand. Just sit. Relax and close your eyes. Do your best mentally to put aside these new 'memories' and simply have a conversation with your future self. Ask the questions you feel you need to ask. Answer the questions she asks you."

Everyone watched as Libby sat, leaned back and closed her eyes. The silence lasted almost five minutes, which in any setting involving people who have been elected to office is an absolute eternity. Finally, Libby sagged deeper into her chair and her eyes snapped open. She took a deep, relaxing breath and said, "I'm . . . she's gone."

Marta turned to Cecil.

"Man," he beamed, "that was really, *really* cool."

31

THE GUY

MARTA, LIBBY AND CECIL flashed back into being in the *I Love Lucy* universe roughly three hours after their departure. Marta and Cecil stepped forward to accept offered robes. Libby, though, stood silently on the projection platform, mouth agape, eyes wide and staring into the receding memory of her experience.

Released from the responsibility of his monitors, Elvin had stepped to the platform and was indulging himself with an appraisal of the only member of congress he'd ever seen naked.

"Elvin, go away," Marta said. "Um, Congresswoman Pinch? Libby? May I remind you, you're still nude?"

Libby seemed to snap into awareness of her surroundings. She scrunched down and assumed the same pose she'd displayed when transitioning into the consciousness of past Libby, one arm clamped across her breasts, and one hand over her tuft of pubic hair.

"Oh, my," she said. "That was . . . that was . . ."

"Your robe?" Marta stepped forward and extended the garment at arm's length.

"Thank you." Libby jumped to take the robe and folded herself into it.

"And now," Marta said, "you will please accompany Naomi and Gretchen to your debriefing while you still have some memory of what just happened."

As they watched Libby march away, Marta turned to Cecil.

"So, what did you think?"

"That was just so . . . so . . ."

"Cool?"

"Especially that thing in between."

"That thing? You mean the limbo? The eternity?"

"Eternity? Well, it did tend to go on. That guy was pretty interesting, though. We had a nice discussion about baseball and religion. And I'll tell you what, he was really impressed with your friend Sheila, dontchaknow."

Marta listened to Cecil with only a fraction of her attention. Mostly her mind raced through a list of ways Libby Pinch and the oversight subcommittee would now complicate their lives. It took a couple of beats for her to do a quick rewind and process what Cecil had just told her.

"Wait." She pulled Cecil around to face her. "A guy? What guy? There's not a guy . . ."

"Oh, yeah, that's right. He explained that. We're being shunned."

Marta's predisposition to cynicism took over. She stared hard at Cecil, trying to figure what kind of angle the old man might be working. Then she was struck with sadness because she had liked Cecil so much and now, he was up to . . . what? As she searched for deceit, though, she found only a peculiar old fellow with no sense of guile.

"And this . . . guy," she said slowly and softly, steering Cecil away from the milling lab techs and scientists who might otherwise overhear their conversation. "What did he look like?"

"I couldn't see him," Cecil said.

"But he spoke to you? Like words coming through a loudspeaker or something?"

"No. He just spoke to me."

"Like telepathy?"

"Nope. I talked to him, and he talked back."

"So why haven't any of the rest of us ever seen or heard this guy?"

"Well, he's not one to intrude. Until you get him goin', I mean. Once I got him started, he had plenty to say, believe me."

"Okay, so let me be sure I understand. You initiated this conversation? What did you say?"

"As near as I can recall, after I got into all that blank space, I took it in for a while and then I said, 'Wow, this is really cool.' And he said something like, *I beg your pardon*, and the way he said it, I thought maybe I was trespassing or something. So, I introduced myself, and we went on from there."

"And none of the rest of us have ever heard of this guy, because we're being shunned?" Marta couldn't grasp the gist of Cecil's story.

"They don't like the designated hitter rule."

"The . . . what?"

"Baseball. The American League. The designated hitter?"

Marta was only vaguely familiar with baseball. "He answered *you*," she pointed out.

"Well, he's not rude."

Marta guided Cecil into her office. She closed the blinds over the big windows looking out at the lab and sat him down.

"Cecil, if anyone else comes in here, I don't want you to say a thing to them about any of this. I'll only be gone a couple of minutes."

"No sweat." Cecil smiled.

Libby Pinch repeated her account of time travel for the third time. Details were drifting.

"I'm ... I'm sorry," she kept saying to Naomi with greater and greater distress. "I'm usually very good at ..."

"Not to worry, Congresswoman. You've done very well. We've recorded your statement, and I—"

Marta rapped once, hard, on the door and pushed it open, giving Naomi a start. Nobody ever interrupted a debriefing.

"Naomi," Marta said urgently, "let's have Jolene finish here, please. We have an issue with Cecil."

Naomi had decided to focus initially on Libby, assuming her recollections would be the most critical, and that at his advanced age, Cecil would have less to offer. So, her first notion upon hearing Marta's anxious request was that Cecil had suffered some sort of post-projection trauma.

"Oh, dear," said Libby, "I hope he's all right ..."

"Yes, well, I apologize for the interruption. I think we need Naomi to look at him right away."

Appearing puzzled, Naomi accompanied Marta. As they entered the projection lab, Marta saw Elvin and Gretchen replaying some data on their monitors while

Marshall relaxed at a desk next to them.

"All of you." Marta ordered, "Come with us."

They crowded into her office. Marta closed the door behind them.

She asked Cecil, "Do you still remember?"

"Well, I think so." Cecil added a twinkle of a smile. "But if I forgot, how would I know?"

Marta rolled her eyes. "Just tell them."

And Cecil recounted his experience, leaving nothing out.

"The designated hitter?" Naomi asked.

"And steroids. That's a whole other thing, though," Cecil said.

Marta turned to Naomi. "What do you think?"

Naomi used a tiny flashlight and probed Cecil's eyes.

"I'd like to take a look at his blood pressure."

"Hallucination?" Gretchen asked.

"We can't rule that out. Remember, there's so much about the limbo we don't understand . . ."

"Now let me ask you this," Cecil said. "If it was a hallucination, how did I know about your friend, Sheila? None of you have mentioned—"

"Okay," Marshall said eagerly, "let's talk about Sheila. What did the voice say about her?"

"Like I said, he really likes her. Thought she was sharp. So, he was sad she wouldn't get to go on."

"Go on? What did he mean by, *go on?*"

"He didn't say. He told me she was bright and funny, even though she was scared. Oh, yeah, and he said at first, he thought I might be Marshall, because Sheila told him Marshall would be along and they could talk about baseball.

So, he and I talked about baseball, too."

"This is crazy," said Marta. "How many times now have travelers gone to the past? And every one of them occupied that interminable limbo. And not one ever came back talking about hearing any voices."

Naomi cleared her throat and glanced at Marshall.

"Um . . . that's not exactly true," Naomi said.

"What?" Marta demanded.

"I have had the report of one traveler experiencing an encounter with another being in the limbo."

"Who? And why don't the rest of us know about this?"

"I spoke with this person in a doctor-patient relationship. And that person's account of this encounter was the subject of that privileged session."

"Me," Marshall said with a broad grin. "I heard the voice."

Astonished, Marta turned to Marshall. *How could you not have told me*? She felt a wave of disappointment and a little anger. "You heard this . . . guy?"

"No. I heard Samantha. I was in the limbo, and she spoke to me. Just as Cecil said, a disembodied voice. I knew immediately I was talking to Samantha, though."

"And what did she—?"

Naomi cut Marta off.

"I don't believe we should require Marshall to reveal any details. The voice he heard said nothing that had any bearing on our missions or this program. The message was quite personal, and until now, I considered it very likely an illusion."

"You know what the message was, though?" Marta asked.

"I know what Marshall told me it was. And he told me in the confidence of a doctor-patient relationship."

Marta looked back at a grinning Marshall. "So, we think this is real?"

"No question in my mind," Cecil said.

"Absolutely," Marshall said triumphantly.

Naomi shrugged.

"Marshall," Marta said, "you come with me."

Marta left Cecil with Naomi and pulled Marshall through the corridors to her apartment.

She closed the door after them, then impetuously pulled Marshall's face level to her own and kissed him. His enthusiasm was evident as he returned the kiss and slid his hands down to her bottom.

She pulled away.

"Hold on there, cowboy. We have some things to talk about."

"Like why I didn't say anything?"

"Like why you could tell Naomi and you couldn't tell me?" She failed to keep her voice from displaying a genuine hurt.

"I didn't *tell* Naomi. Not for the longest time. And I didn't tell you because of what you all were thinking."

"And what were we thinking?"

"Everyone thought I was on the edge of some kind of breakdown, because I couldn't save Samantha and because of Sheila. You and Naomi took me off travel status. If I'd told anyone I'd heard voices in the limbo, it would have been a sure sign that . . . that . . . my dinghy had sprung a leak."

Marta stepped away from Marshall and berated herself for kissing him. She needed to stop sending such mixed messages. She did enjoy the kiss, though.

She crossed her arms over her chest. "I was never worried about your... dinghy. And I never thought you were too emotionally fragile to travel. I just think it's too dangerous."

"You're still worried about Elvin's theory? I've already told you I don't believe that stuff. He's just..."

Marta raised a hand, gesturing Marshall to stop. She clasped his hands and guided him to her couch.

"So, what's the big secret?" she asked as they sat. "About what she told you?"

"Secret? There's no secret. I think Naomi just didn't want me to have to go into it with so many people listening."

"So..."

"Samantha said to me, 'Marshall, it turns out you were my only real friend. And I promise you, I'm going to be all right now.' And I felt so good for her. I knew with absolute certainty that she *was* okay. Then I got back here and learned she'd died. And I was angry at her. I felt completely betrayed, and I just didn't know how to reconcile those feelings with my grief."

Marta watched Marshall's face spread into a wide grin as he spoke.

"Well, you're not seeming so angry now."

"No. Don't you see? I think I understand. Cecil said the guy was sad because Sheila didn't get to *go on*. That implies there's someplace else to go."

"What," Marta said, not hiding her skepticism, "you mean like heaven?"

"I don't know. But I think that Samantha got to go on. And that she *is* okay. And it means something else. Samantha waited. She waited to talk to me before she went . . . wherever. Sheila could be waiting for us right now. I need to go. I need to get back to the limbo and find out—"

"Okay," Marta said, "I don't know if I believe accounts of disembodied *guys*, and I'm sure I don't believe in heaven. If this works for you, though, it's fine with me. You get ready. I'll tell Elvin and soon as everything's programmed, we'll send you on a quick trip back into the *Star Trek* universe. We'll see if either Sheila or this *guy* shows up in the limbo."

32

CALIBRATING THE DOOHICKEY

"AND WHAT IS THE PURPOSE of the mission?" Libby Pinch asked Marta.

Bollocks. Marta thought as the Congresswoman strolled into her office. In their haste to prepare for Marshall's journey, she had overlooked Libby Pinch.

"Um . . . feeling better?" Marta asked.

"Yes, I think so," Libby said. "Though I have to say that was a very unsettling experience. Not one I'd care to repeat. Um . . . how long does it take for the smell to go away?"

"Smell?" Marta asked.

"Aha," Marshall said. He stood near the projection platform, wearing his robe. "You smell it, too."

He walked to her, leaned down and sniffed her hair.

Libby shrank away and looked to Marta for help.

"Marshall," Marta said, "you have to stop smelling people."

Marshall seemed puzzled. "Yours is different than mine," he said. "Mine's like . . . damn, I just can't place it. But yours is . . . like . . ."

"Like the rain," said Libby.

"Yeah. In the desert. Like the rain in the desert."

Marshall snapped his fingers. "Smell her, Marta. Go ahead."

"I'll . . . I'll take your word for it. But, Libby, this isn't some perfume you wear, or soap or . . ."

"I'm allergic to perfume. And I seem to have gotten a pedicure."

"Ha!" Marshall said again. "Sheila's toes. Please, Congresswoman, don't go anywhere. I want you to smell me when I get back."

Which was the dumbest thing Marta thought he could possibly say.

She didn't want Libby hanging around.

Like many first-time travelers, Libby had suffered hangover-ish symptoms that cropped up a few hours after her return. She'd completed debriefings and medical exams, then returned to her quarters for a nap.

Now, with just about the worst timing Marta could imagine, here she was, smelling like rain in the desert, and watching Elvin, Gretchen, Gillis Kerg, Naomi and a few other key staff make final preparations for the impending projection.

"Well, we won't schedule you for a return to the past any time soon . . ." Marta said, attempting a jocular tone that fell short.

"This mission?" Libby asked again. "You indicated to me earlier you had nothing else planned."

"Oh, this one just sort of . . . came up. Out of the blue, you know . . . That happens . . . sometimes . . ."

Marta and the others who knew about Sheila hadn't made any explanations to the technical staff concerning Marshall's sudden journey. The support staff seldom questioned the details. Libby Pinch, though, required an explanation, and she could not know the truth.

"Out of the blue? Is there some sort of emergency?"

"No. No emergencies. Just ... routine ... sort of a ... calibration ... Yes. Every so often, the um ... the tuning mechanism of the projector ... um ... that's the instrument that allows Elvin to accurately locate the targeted universes ... it has to be ... calibrated. It tends to wander. So we send someone to the *Star Trek* universe for just a quick fifteen-minute bump into the past while Elvin and ... and Elvin—the *Star-Trek*-Elvin, I mean—get a base-line reading from a very close and familiar universe, which allows them to—"

Libby did her best to feign understanding and interest as Marta stumbled through her fictional explanation. Finally, she interrupted. "Can it wait?"

"Can what wait?"

"This calibration mission. Can it wait? Before we risk any more time travel, I think we need to establish a mission profile approval process just to be sure that the oversight subcommittee is adequately informed of—"

Marta recognized this as the moment everything changed.

"No. No, we can't delay the mission. It's scheduled to go in just a few minutes. And ... and they are expecting us. I received a visitation from my *Star Trek*-self, and they have a problem and really need to ... uh ... calibrate. So, we can't just stand them up. They might think something had gone wrong and ... Marshall has to go and be ... calibrated."

"Who is going with him?"

"With him?"

"Yes. You've explained the rules requiring at least two travelers."

"That's except for the . . . the calibration missions. You can only calibrate with one traveler . . . because—"

"And that's another thing," Libby said. "We need to forge some sort of authorization agreement with the oversight subcommittee in this other universe. Now that I understand what's happening here, I think we'll be uncomfortable with the ability of people from another world to cross into our word without authorization."

"I can't imagine how we could—"

"We've spent decades trying to figure out what to do about aliens illegally crossing the border from Mexico. I don't think we want to open that whole can of worms on the parallel universe front, do we?"

"Um . . . well, I don't think we can build a fence." Marta felt dismayed that Libby's journey back to the past had only seemed to fortify her regulatory resolve.

"Okay," Libby said, "if we can't delay the mission, I'd like to start getting a bit of an education regarding how things work. Since the point of this mission is instrument calibration, perhaps Mr. Detwyler would be so good as to walk me through that process as it occurs."

"Oh, I'm not sure about that. Elvin needs to be pretty focused and undistracted during a mission."

"One of the other physicists, then? I can just look over Mr. Detwyler's shoulder and have someone else explain . . ."

Marta felt herself sinking deeper into the muck of her deception. Then she thought of Marshall and there glimmered the bright seed of a plan.

"Okay. I'll see what we can work out." She continued to improvise. "Um . . . Libby, have you seen our periscope?"

In the program's early days, Marta's predecessor, Michael

Huxtable, had been upset when he saw the time projector's finished control panel. It consisted only of a flat metal plate with a throttle-like device, a dial and a couple of buttons. For the sake of the investors, Huxtable ordered the control panel to be upgraded with useless gauges and strobe lights and a blaring siren to enhance its appearance of complexity.

"Believe me," he had said, "you invest a billion dollars, you want to see something more complicated than an on/off switch."

And as a part of that ruse, Huxtable ordered the installation of a periscope. He had one shipped from a surplus U.S. Navy submarine. It rotated and slid up and down to reveal a dark and murky cluster of pipes and ducts and cables filling the narrow attic crawl space above the projection lab. Huxtable decreed that any time an investor's representative— either government or business—was present to observe a projection, a member of the technical staff would be manning the periscope.

Since the investors had fled, Huxtable's periscope just sat there off in its corner, even more absent of purpose than before. Now, though, Marta needed a distraction.

She guided Libby toward the monitors. "Gretchen, while we're making our last-minute mission preparations, I think you might take a moment and brief the Congress-woman on the periscope. She hasn't seen that yet."

Standing behind Libby, Marta gave the congresswoman a nudge toward the project's chief physicist.

"The periscope?" Gretchen displayed her bewilderment.

Out of the range of Libby's vision, Marta adopted a desperate expression and with an imploring shrug silently mouthed, "Help me out here."

"Of... of course." Gretchen took Libby by the arm. "Of course. The periscope... is right over here. Let's go right over here."

"And what is this device used for?" Libby asked as they crossed the room.

Gretchen, being a theoretical physicist rather than a spy by trade like Marta, was completely unskilled in the art of extemporaneous deception. Marta cringed as she saw panic creep into Gretchen's face and heard her answer, "Well, nothing."

Bollocks, Marta said to herself. *No bloody way is Gretchen devious enough to figure out what we need to...*

Miraculously, though, Libby volunteered to be deceived.

"Ah, Ms. Hamilton briefed us on that at last week's subcommittee meeting regarding quantum mechanics... So, this is Evlin Detwyler's infamous *nothing*?"

"Um... um... okay."

One of Marta's reports to the subcommittee had discussed the physical concept of nothing. For physicists, *nothing* was not *nothing*, for *nothing*—the theory goes—cannot exist. Because, Marta had tried to explain, once you label *something* as *nothing*, it has become *something*. So, *nothing* is a difficult concept which has been the subject of many a drunken late-night physics debate. When the subcommittee read, though, that the physics staff of the HRI was preparing a major effort to research *nothing*, they suspected someone was making a sarcastic comment on federal employees. Marta filed several more reports to make things clear and was still not sure she had succeeded.

Libby tugged the periscope down to her eye level and clamped her forehead to the eyepiece. She slowly did a full

360-degree revolution as she peered into the vague and spectral realm revealed there.

She gasped a couple of times and—eyes still glued to the instrument—asked, her voice tinged with awe, "Is this an actual glimpse into the quantum world?"

Marta feared that Gretchen's answer would be, "No, it's a glimpse of the attic."

Gretchen saw Marta's frantic gestures, though, including the universal hand signals for "keep going, stretch this out," so Gretchen cleared her throat and said, "Yes. Yes, it is. The quantum world. Right there in our ... periscope. Now just have a nice long look and tell me what you see."

Marta quickly switched her focus to Marshall, who had removed himself again to the proximity of the projection platform. She waved for his attention. For a moment, she considered dashing to Marshall's side for a quick explanation. But she feared Libby might glance away from the periscope at any time, so she mouthed to him, "You need to get hard."

Bewildered, Marshall squinted at Marta and mouthed back, "What?"

"You ... need ... to ... get ... hard." she mouthed even more fiercely and pointed toward her crotch.

He shrugged his inability to comprehend.

Marta made a dismissive motion with her hands and searched desperately. Standing only a couple of feet away, she saw Betty the receptionist, Macy Gardner, Naomi Hu, Jolene the medical tech and Cecil gathered at Elvin's monitors. They, too, wore puzzled looks as they watched this scene unfold.

Marta stepped to the group and whispered fiercely to the women, "Quick, all of you. Show Marshall your breasts."

The women regarded Marta with varying degrees of shock and uncertainty.

While Marta's demand didn't produce immediate compliance from the ladies, it certainly got Elvin's attention.

"Tits," Elvin whispered just as fiercely as Marta had. "The boss wants you to show us your tits."

"Show *Marshall* your tits . . . uh . . . breasts," Marta hissed again with a glare at Elvin that could have cut steel.

They were still a little stunned. Marta's order had been so absolute in its intensity, though, they snapped to it.

Marshall exhibited an expression of helpless horror as the four women lifted their shirts and bras.

The front of Marshall's robe jutted with an obscene thrust that he tried to hide by covering it with his hands.

Marta motioned for the women to cover up, and called to the Congresswoman, "All right, Libby, we're ready to go now. You'll want to come over here, right up front."

Libby made one more quick revolution of the periscope, and then strode toward the rest of the group.

As they walked, Marta turned and whispered to Elvin, "If she asks, the purpose of this mission is to calibrate your . . . your . . . your doohickey here."

Elvin smiled. "Oh, believe me, Marta, my doohickey is completely calibrated."

Marta scowled fiercely, then warped the scowl into an only slightly crooked smile as she turned to face Libby.

"Yes, now just stand right here," she said, "and we'll watch Marshall take his journey into the past."

Libby, her mind filled with the wonders of the microcosmic

world she'd just witnessed in the projection lab's attic, took her position next to Elvin's monitor.

"All right, Marshall," Marta called. "Let's go."

Marshall hung his head and shielded his eyes with one hand as he faced the bank of video cameras.

Libby could tell from his body language that Marshall was completely uncomfortable with the public nudity aspect of his job. She empathized. She'd felt the same way herself. So, she determined to look away and spare him at least some dignity.

But she didn't look away quickly enough.

Her eyes popped wide. Her jaw dropped and her knees buckled ever so slightly.

"Oh, my good Lord," she said just loud enough for the gathered scientists around her to hear.

Suddenly, Libby Pinch forgot all about things that were very small.

Marshall winked off the platform. Still, Libby stared.

"God, I love this job," Elvin said, shaking his head.

33

DID YOU SMELL THAT SMELL?

MARSHALL'S EMBARRASSMENT was eventually swallowed by the eternity of the limbo. A veteran Traveler, he relaxed and settled into its stark white calm. His physical self was . . . somewhere else. During his initial projections, he thought of his physical being as having been broken down into its tiniest components and scattered throughout the universe. While most other travelers, even the veterans of many missions, still fought moments of panic as this timeless sensation of physical separation between mind and body unfolded., Marshall felt comfortable here. He adapted almost instantaneously to this blank landscape.

This time, though, he needed to break away from his limbo routine. He couldn't help feeling just a bit foolish as he thought, Okay buddy, where are you?

No answer.

He tried a different tack.

Samantha, are you here? Sheila?

No answer.

Okay, so I must be doing it wrong.

He thought back over Cecil's story of his encounter with this being he called the Hall Monitor. Cecil said the guy's response came to a spoken observation. Marshall had never uttered a word here. He didn't even know whether he had a voice with which to speak. He commanded his vocal cords, and from somewhere, his physical body responded.

"Um . . . I'm trying to contact the . . . the Hall Monitor?" he said nervously.

He heard a heavy sigh.

"Hello?" Marshall tried again.

"I don't suppose you'll go away."

Marshall thought the voice sounded a little snooty. Just enough of an uppity condescending tone to make Marshall feel as if he was intruding into some sort of private club where he was still naked and everyone else wore tuxedos.

"Well, speak up, man."

Marshall fought off a wave of panic. "Well . . . um . . . I . . . I . . ."

"What's wrong with you?"

"Wrong with . . . Nothing, I guess. Except I'm allergic to anchovies."

"That's a benefit as far as I'm concerned. Are we finished with true confessions now? It's not as if I don't have other things to do."

"Um . . . no." At least this being had offered Marshall a starting point. "That's one of the things I wanted to ask. What exactly do you do? I wasn't aware there was anything to do."

"Oh, Lord, you people again? You don't have a pass, do you?"

"No. I'm sorry. Nobody's ever asked me for one. I don't even know where I'm supposed to get one."

"You're not authorized to be here. We handle enough traffic as it is without having to worry about you people. I told

them this would happen one of these days. One of these days, I said, a bunch of yahoos from some goofball dimension will stumble onto the physics of time travel long before they know enough to leave it alone . . . and here you are."

"I'm not a physicist. I really don't understand any of this. I just travel when they tell me to and . . . and . . ." He realized he was rambling. *"They said I'm supposed to apologize for the designated hitter rule."*

"Is this a sincere apology, or are you just kissing ass?"

"Well," Marshall mumbled. *"Well, I . . . you know, I really don't mind it. I guess I grew up being kind of an American League guy, and I think the complexity of making the double switch is way overrated. And what about Edgar Martinez? What would have happened to him?"*

"Well, there is that. Still, it's no excuse. You people knew nothing about Edgar Martinez or Harold Baines or Frank Thomas when this whole thing started. How could you have even conceived of this abomination?"

"It wasn't me. I didn't do it. I wasn't even born when—"

"Do you have any idea how many lame excuses we get here? 'I wasn't there. It's not my fault. I was just following orders.' Let me ask this. Have you risen up in protest?"

"Um . . . was I supposed to?"

"Of course, you were supposed to. Even if you don't create an abomination, you are equally guilty if you tolerate it."

"Okay, well, I'll rise up when I get back home, I promise. Right now, I really do have a couple of things I need to ask you about."

Another heavy sigh.

"First of all, tell me your name. I see now I'm not going to get out of this without checking the records."

"I'm Marshall. Marshall Grissom,"

"Whoa. Marshall? The Marshall? Well, this is a different sack of pickles altogether."

"Um . . . you keep pickles in sacks?"

"No, of course not," the Hall Monitor said. "It's an expression like . . . easy as clams. I must say, you have some lovely friends. That delightful young woman, Sheila. And Cecil? How can one not be intrigued by a man who waxes cats?"

Marshall heard a chuckle.

"They told me about you. I should have known. And Naomi. They told me about Naomi. What's her last name again?"

"Hu," Marshall said. "Naomi Hu."

"That's what I'm asking you. What's Naomi's last name?"

"Hu."

"Naomi."

The most infective peal of laughter Marshall had ever heard filled the limbo. The laughter thundered for a while, until finally the being said between gasps of breath, "Oh, my. Oh, forgive me. I just couldn't resist. I've been waiting so long to do that. Or would have been if time existed here."

"Oooookay." Marshall offered a polite pause before steering the conversation in a different direction. "I have another friend who came through here, I think. And I want—actually, I think I need—to know about her."

"Another of your time traveling interlopers?"

"No, I don't think so. Her name is Samantha Kennedy, and she . . ."

"Whoa again. You're Samantha's Marshall? You're Sheila's Marshall and Samantha's Marshall?"

"I . . . I suppose so. About Samantha. During one of my . . . my journeys through your corridor, I heard her speak to me. I heard her tell me she would be okay. Then, when I got back, she was dead and—"

"She waited for you, Marshall. She delayed going on just so she could give you her message. I didn't encourage it. Well, at first, I didn't speak to her at all. You know, the whole shunning thing. But she just wouldn't go on. So finally, I warned her you would probably misunderstand. Expressing her gratitude was very important to her, though."

Marshall felt deep emotion swell into his consciousness and his voice broke as he said, "Her gratitude?"

"Perspective changes when you get here—for those of you who are supposed to be here. Things about your previous stop become clear. You taught Samantha a profound lesson of friendship. You helped her to recognize the difference between people who want you in their lives simply for their own gratification, and people who genuinely want the best for you. You helped Samantha a great deal."

"And she's gone . . . on?"

"Yes."

"And she's okay?"

"That's largely up to her."

"So, she's in . . . in heaven?"

"Heaven, indeed," the Hall Monitor said with a tone of amusement. "She's at her next stop. And believe me, it's a good deal more challenging than the last one."

"So, there's no heaven?"

"How would I know? How can anyone know for sure?"

"So, there's no God?"

"Same answer."

"I guess . . . I guess I just assumed that you are a . . . a superior being. And that superior beings would have all the answers."

"Oh, good. Religion. I can't tell you how much I enjoy the philosophy of religion. Tell me, Marshall, are you a religious man?"

"There were stages of my life when I tried to be. Mostly, though, I don't get it. I guess you'd have to say I'm a skeptic."

"Me, too. I applaud those for whom religion brings a genuine comfort and who sincerely seek to be better people according to their beliefs. What bothers me about religious people—and we see a lot of this here when these people go on—is they think fear of the unknown territory ahead is a betrayal of faith. So, they get here and think now they'll know for sure, and are disappointed, even angry, when they still have to guess. They want relief from the burdens of faith. As far as I know, you don't ever get to know for sure.

"And since you brought it up, let's talk about God for a moment. You'd be shocked to know just how many planes of existence there are, each with its own concept of the Almighty. And I must admit, I find yours to be fairly implausible."

"Um . . . you do?"

"Why do you people insist on investing your God with so many human characteristics? Why do you presume God must have a human face? Why is this being jealous or mean? Why would He create you as thoughtful, sentient beings, and then demand that you wreak vengeance on those who exercise these same marvelous gifts, but come to different conclusions than your own?"

"Well, I wouldn't believe in that kind of God. I would believe that God must be compassionate and understanding . . ."

"More human traits," the Hall Monitor said. "Why compassionate? Why not indifferent?"

"Um . . . okay," Marshall said, *"But we're getting a little far afield here."*

"Yes, of course. Forgive me. I do love a good philosophical exercise. You had other questions?"

"You say we're misusing time travel. Sheila thought the same thing. Are you saying she was right? Should we stop?"

"I'm sorry. I won't absolve you of the burden of that decision. You've gotten yourself into this, and now you have to sort your way out. I will tell you the worst thing I find about time travel, though. It tends to cheapen existence. It offers hope to go back and do it over. Do it better. And if time travel ever becomes widespread in your society, you will find it will just be another excuse for people to do the wrong thing. Because after all, they think they can go back and fix it."

"Well, I suppose it could—"

"Any perceptive being needs to understand that time is precious. No matter how many planes of existence there are, the time you have is limited. And you must spend this treasure carefully. If you can travel through time, you tend to lose sight of this very fundamental truth, this key to a useful and satisfying life. Now, you have other questions?"

Marshall had many questions. But the one that emerged was, *"Do I smell funny to you?"*

"I beg your pardon?"

"I come back from my time traveling missions with this smell . . . and the others say it must be soap or shampoo or . . . but I think it comes from . . . well . . . here."

"Ah," the hall monitor said. *"Another mystery revealed. You people are the ones running up bills in the parking garage."*

"I'm sorry, the parking garage?"

Another heavy sigh. *"Have you never wondered what*

happens to your corporeal being while you're in the corridor"

"My what?"

"Your body."

"Um, well, yeah. The physicists argue about that a lot."

"Your physicists are woefully lacking. I won't even try to get into the science of it all. Suffice it to say there's a parking garage where the bodies of beings who are authorized to use the corridor are stored during the journey."

"And this has what to do with the smells and the toes?"

"Detailing. It's a service we provide. Yours is New Car *smell."*

"That's it." Marshall said. "It's been driving me crazy because I couldn't... um... They do that even if we're not supposed to be there?"

"They don't know you're trespassing. The garage workers are only doing their jobs. They just think you're a bunch of really lousy tippers. Enough of this, though. You have a universe to catch—"

"Wait," Marshall said, "I wanted to talk to Sheila."

"I'm sorry. She's not here. Her universe arrived and, well, the physics can't be denied."

And that was it. Berating himself all the while for his meandering conversation with the Hall Monitor, Marshall felt himself join with his counterpart in the very near past of the Star Trek *universe. He vowed to try again. Did the Hall Monitor know the details of Sheila's fate? And if he did, would he tell Marshall?*

Congresswoman Libby Pinch hadn't wandered far. A mere ten minutes passed between Marshall's departure and

Elvin's announcement of Marshall's imminent return. She'd walked absently to the monitors, trying to formulate a question or two. She could not scour that image of Marshall from her mind.

Members of Congress were hardly exempt from lustful thoughts, and in acting, from time to time, on those thoughts. For Libby Pinch, however, eroticism hadn't reared its bawdy head for some time.

She was married, though her husband had his own career back home and their separations were long and frequent. Members of congress as a whole must be careful as to conduct of their sexual lives, particularly the extra-curricular, and given the timelessness of double standards, even a hint of sexual impropriety would be the immediate kiss of political death for a female lawmaker.

Other senators or congressmen had never been a temptation for Libby. Many of them were fat and old. And those who weren't were—like Libby—too full of themselves to tolerate that sort of sexual liaison. No bed in Washington was big enough to accommodate two such enormous egos.

She had long ago settled into a semi-monastic lifestyle that was only frustrated by the occasional distraction.

Like this one.

She had never seen anything like it.

And now, her absent meanderings around the projection lab kept her always within a few steps of that spot, front and center, where she could witness Marshall's return.

Marta sidled up to Libby. "Pretty impressive, huh?"

"I . . . what? I'm sure I don't . . ."

"Don't worry about it. It's happened to all of us. The

first time you see it, well, it just kind of takes your breath away."

Libby glanced at Marta and decided to abandon all pretense.

"None of the reports have ever said anything about . . . that." Her eyes remained wide with wonder.

"We try to keep Marshall's erectile problem to ourselves. He's embarrassed, and we're pretty much used to it by now. Back when we started, though, I had to stand next to him on the projection platform for every mission. And I couldn't be so obvious as to just turn and look, you know? So, I actually bought a computer program and started doing eye exercises to improve my peripheral vision."

They both faced the platform now. Libby felt the thrum of vibration through the floor as the two shining globes began to return to life.

Marta reached to the clothing rack behind her and handed Marshall's robe to Libby.

"Here he is."

Marshall winked onto the platform and, despite her best efforts to reclaim her Congressional comportment, Libby let her eyes linger just that split second too long.

"Um . . . Congresswoman," Marshall said. "Can I please have my robe now?"

He did not, however, renew his request to be smelled. Under the circumstances, he thought the question would be inappropriate.

34

COINCIDENTALLY . . .

"I CAN'T BELIEVE IT," Naomi said to Marta. "I just can't believe it. You pimped Marshall out to a member of Congress. You exploited an intensely personal problem to distract—"

"I'm sorry." Marta felt more than just a little guilt. "If I'd had more time to think of something else, I would have. It was all so spur of the moment, you know?"

Marta, Marshall, Elvin, Gretchen, Naomi, Gillis and Leonard were at the Time Warp. Tonight, Marta had ushered her colleagues into the bar and put a "closed" sign on the front door.

Naomi glared at Marta and continued her scolding. "Marshall, you have every right to feel mortified and used by such a—"

"Look," Marshall said, "I've spent so much time being mortified over the past couple of years that I just . . . Marta did it for Sheila. So, I guess I can stand being mortified one more time. And before we start casting stones here, what about you? Is that any way for a psychiatrist to behave? Can't psychiatrists get disbarred for showing patients their boobs?"

"Psychiatrists don't get disbarred," Marta pointed out. "Only lawyers get disbarred."

Naomi hung her head. "I . . . I was showing you my breasts in my capacity as your friend, not as your doctor. And you're right, Marshall. I've never done anything like that before. And I don't know why I did it. It's just . . . the situation, I guess. I just got caught up in the moment . . . as I suppose Marta did . . . I promise I'll never do it again."

"Never say never," Elvin said with a wink.

He stood and walked behind the bar to get a beer. He held the bottle high with eyebrows raised in a question mark. Both Marta and Naomi nodded yes.

"Well, you're not the only one," Gretchen said to Naomi while casting a frown at Marta. "I lied to a member of Congress. An entire Congressional subcommittee now thinks the quantum world resides in our attic. I could be arrested for perjury."

"You weren't under oath. But just in case Congress-woman Pinch tells anyone about that, we should probably dress the attic up a little. Make it look more . . . sciencey."

"Marta," Naomi cautioned, "listen to yourself. What's come over you? You're the one running the show now, and if you keep being this . . . I don't know . . . this reckless, you'll get into a lot of trouble. Michael Huxtable was in charge when you covered up the truth about Sheila's disappearance. If they discover what's happening now, the subcommittee will blame *you* for the deceptions."

Marta regarded those gathered there and saw questions on every face, each one painted with the neon tinge from glimmering beer signs.

"Okay, guys," she finally said. "I didn't have time to plan

anything today. I didn't have time to consider the consequences. And maybe this all will eventually come back to bite us—me—in the ass. I'll do better. Let me warn you, though, of what's about to happen. Libby Pinch is returning to the subcommittee, and they *will* establish a strict set of guidelines concerning how we operate. They will give themselves the power of approval over every mission, no matter how innocuous. They will establish pre-mission outlines. They'll try to restrict where we can go, and who can come to us. And they will be looking over our shoulders every step of the way." She scanned the faces around the table again. "I'm not worried about them finding out anything about today. At worst, I would get fired. No guidelines are in place. We haven't formally broken any rules—yet."

"This isn't Marta's fault," Marshall said. "Marta's doing this for me, and for Sheila. No matter what the rest of you believe, I *know* we can find her. The guy—the Hall Monitor—talked with her. He said *her universe arrived.* I think that means she got there."

"And I'll repeat," Marta continued, "whatever doubts I originally had, Marshall has convinced me we have to try. But everyone seated at this table needs to understand this oversight subcommittee won't approve a mission back to the 1960s to hunt for Sheila Schuler. We've painted ourselves into a corner with our deception. We can't tell them anything about it.

"I think they'll hit us with these new regulations long before we can put together a mission to find Sheila. So that's when we'll be breaking the rules. That's when we all—not just me and not just Marshall—stand to suffer a big pile of consequences. If there's any chance that Sheila's alive back there, Marshall and I will determine a way to find her. Anyone who doesn't want to be involved, say so now and I'll respect that."

"You're both overlooking one very important point," Naomi said. "You and Marshall *can't* do this. Perhaps a person *can* be sent back to a time beyond birth if they can find a close enough genetic match. Relatives share DNA patterns, and some of those patterns are more closely matched than others. It just depends on the individual. From the yearbook photo we saw, Amanda Page and Sheila Schuler could be twins. That would indicate to me the strong possibility that their genetic markers are very close. Not an exact match, of course, but maybe close enough to provide a host and allow Sheila to survive. Genetic matches like the one we're talking about are not common, though. The odds that any one of us would find a compatible host seventy-six years ago are astronomical."

"So," Marshall said, thinking aloud, "I have to find a ninety-something who lived somewhere near Portales, New Mexico, during the late 1960s, and convince that person that he or she should become a time traveler."

"And how," Gillis Kerg asked, "will we even begin to locate someone like that?"

Marta, Marshall and Gillis still puzzled over the probability of finding a traveler for a Sheila rescue mission as they filed into the nearly empty cafeteria in search of sandwiches. Only a scattered handful of people occupied a room originally built to serve hundreds. As they considered their options for seating, a figure waved from a distant table.

"Hey, there's Cecil," Marshall said, waving back.

Marta had hoped the three of them could quietly continue their conversation concerning the Sheila problem, but ignoring Cecil's invitation would be rude. Cecil sat with a half-empty cup of tea cooling before him. "I asked for a touch of rum to go with it." He laughed, pointing at the cup. "But I guess it's not on the menu."

"How are you feeling?" Marta asked. "Any hangover from the projection."

"Just tired."

Marshall elbowed Marta.

"Marshall, I will not."

"Is there a problem?" Cecil asked.

Marta rolled her eyes. "Marshall wants me to smell you."

"Haven't you noticed a smell since you got back?" Marshall asked.

"I have, dontchaknow," the old man said. "I was gonna ask someone what kind of soap you got in the showers here."

Reluctantly, Marta leaned over and sniffed at Cecil's neck. Surprised, she backed away. "Mmmmm, that is nice," she said.

"Like a new car, right?"

"No, Marshall. It's more like . . . an ocean breeze." She patted Cecil on the shoulder. "We'll go grab some soup and sandwiches and join you if that's okay?"

They walked to the cafeteria-style display, assembled their meals and were heading back to the table when Marta noticed that Cecil's chin had dropped to his chest, his eyes were closed, and his arms hung loosely at his side.

She stopped.

"Oh, no," she said to Marshall. "You don't think he's . . ." Her momentary panic eased as Cecil emitted a low snore. His chest rose and fell with the rhythm of his breathing.

Gillis whispered, "What do we do now that won't embarrass the old fellow?"

"Let's go sit down as if nothing happened," Marshall said. "And when he wakes up, carry on a conversation like we didn't notice he'd nodded off."

They quietly settled themselves at the table. Marta anticipated that the slight jostling of chairs and plates would rouse Cecil, but his snoring became more pronounced. As they ate, they returned to a whispered discussion of the dilemma they faced in finding someone to seek out Sheila in the distant past.

Finally, Gillis said a little too loudly, ". . . tell me how to even start, and I'll begin the search. But finding a 93- or 94-year-old who attended high school in a fly speck of a town in Eastern New Mexico? Even using the high school yearbooks, half of the candidates—the women—wouldn't even have the same name . . ."

And that's when Cecil said, "I know a guy."

Marta assumed the old man must have woven fragments of their conversation into whatever dream he might be having. "I beg your pardon?" she said.

Cecil yawned and glanced around the table. "A guy over ninety who grew up in Eastern New Mexico," Cecil said. "Remember the guy who wrote that magazine article about me and gave me the Jimmy Buffett album? We talked about him on the plane ride over."

Marta, still confused at Cecil's abrupt entry into the

discussion, thought back. *Magazine? The story about the Margin Service...?*

"Sean Brody. I sponsored his baseball team. He and I became pretty good friends, and we stayed in touch for a while after I moved away. He told me he was from Eastern New Mexico..."

Gillis withdrew his pocket computer again. Checking quickly around the expanse of empty tables to assure their privacy, he went through the process of calling up the old Portales High School yearbook that included Amanda Page's senior picture.

"This Brody guy could have gone to any one of dozens of high schools," Marta pointed out.

"It's a place to start," Marshall said.

Gillis ordered a search. A blur of photos resolved itself into a single photograph of Portales High School sophomore Sean Brody.

"I don't believe it," Marta said.

"I don't believe it, either," Gillis agreed.

"Why not?" Marshall asked. "There he is. How lucky could we be?"

"That's why I don't believe it," Marta answered. "Because luck like that doesn't just happen. Consider how improbable this all is. First, we've got Cecil, who should never have been a part of this program. And he happens to know maybe the one man in the world who can connect us to Amanda Page, who is..."

Marta glanced at Cecil and thought better of continuing.

"I'm sorry, Cecil," she said. "I hate to be this way, but this conversation has crossed over into an area beyond your security classification. I have to ask you not to repeat this to anyone and . . ."

Cecil smiled and stood stiffly. "Don't think a thing of it. Like I told you before, I know how to keep a secret. And I got things to go do. See you folks later."

He shuffled a few steps away before turning to add, "And I hope you find your friend, Sheila, dontchaknow."

"How could he know about Sheila?" Gillis asked as Cecil disappeared into the corridor. He cast a suspicious gaze on Marshall.

"Hey, I didn't tell him," Marshall said. "He talked to the Hall Monitor. It's not a hallucination."

"I'm not worried about Cecil," Marta said. "I'm worried about what else is happening here. This can't be just a series of random circumstances connected by coincidence. There's something going on here that we don't understand."

"Well," Marshall said, "whether we understand it or not, it's all pointing us to Sheila."

35

REGULATING THE UNREGULATED

"WE MUST PREPARE A REPORT," Libby said to Cecil as they waited together at Phoenix Sky Harbor Airport for their return flight to Washington, D.C.

"I plan to have a chat with Senator Mumford," Cecil said, "so I guess I'll just leave the formalities to you."

"Well, I will make the strongest recommendation possible that these people and this operation be reined in."

"I figured as much." Cecil knew his voice would never outweigh Libby's, and he expected any group of politicians would be predisposed to regulate the unregulated. "You just go ahead and do what you think is right."

Libby took her first-class seat. Cecil walked back to the coach section. When they landed at Reagan International, she offered him a ride. He declined.

His flight to Miami departed late morning the next day, so Cecil was waiting when Sen. Mumford's staff arrived to open the office. When finally ushered into the Senator's inner sanctum, Cecil beheld the historic furniture and the massive marble fireplace that dominated one wall.

"Some place you got here."

Mumford smiled and directed Cecil to the chair opposite his desk.

"Well, I stopped by to tell you what I think."

"Don't you want to make a formal recommendation to the subcommittee? I can certainly assign you a staff person to help you organize—"

"Nope. My report is pretty simple. You got some good people down there. You ought to trust 'em to do the right thing, dontchaknow. You ought to leave 'em alone and let 'em find out what there is to find out."

"I'll certainly pass that suggestion along. And when will we be seeing you again?"

"I doubt it'll be anytime soon. I think things have stacked up a bit back on the boat. I got the cats to deal with, and I'm realizing that at my age traveling is more difficult all the time. But if you need anything, I'll be glad to take your call."

Libby handed her report and recommendations to Mumford two days later.

"All missions should be approved by the oversight subcommittee," she summarized as she sat with Mumford on antique high-backed chairs facing the nonfunctional fireplace. "Simple missions—calibration missions and routine conferences between Ms. Hamilton and her *Star Trek* universe counterpart—should be granted a blanket approval unless they deviate from the routine."

She suggested that Marta ask *Star-Trek*-Marta to go to the oversight subcommittee there and make a formal request that they refrain from any travel to the *I Love Lucy* universe without specific approval of the *Lucy* oversight subcommittee, with the two previously stated exceptions. The two Martas were to be conduits for such requests.

"And I would like to see all future historical survey missions to the pasts of other parallel universes presented for approval to a subcommittee representative. This person would be assigned to the HRI campus and would act as a direct liaison to the subcommittee."

Libby pointed out that this person should not usurp authority of the HRI administrator with regard to operation of the program. However, the liaison would report his or her concerns about any given mission profile to the subcommittee.

For fear of repeating the *Joey Bishop Show* catastrophe, missions involving the exchange of travelers—each to accomplish the same desired result in the other universe—would be banned until Elvin and Gretchen could be more definitive about what exactly caused the *Joey Bishop Show* universe to deconstruct.

"I'm recommending that missions should generally be limited to observation of historical phenomenon or pursuit of more effective law enforcement," Libby said.

Finally, she proposed that the subcommittee direct scientists at HRI to begin work on a detection system that could be used to limit unauthorized intrusions into the past of our universe.

Mumford patted the inside breast pocket of his suit jacket and withdrew a black cigar roughly the size of a clarinet.

Libby blanched.

"Um . . . Senator, I don't think you can . . ."

"Oh, don't worry. I just chew on them a little every now and then. We haven't passed any laws against that . . . yet."

Out of deference to Libby, he placed the cigar on his chair's leather armrest. "I think our subcommittee will be anxious to adopt the specifics of your report with a minimum of amendments. I want your gut feeling, though. Do you trust these people?"

"Well," Libby said carefully, "that's a difficult question to answer. Like any agency, they think they know best how to conduct their business. And I've no doubt they will make every effort to skirt some of these regulations . . ." She paused, not sure how to continue.

"Am I hearing some qualifications here?" Mumford asked.

"Um . . . Senator, the time I spent in Arizona was . . . was the most bizarre experience of my life."

"You traveled through time."

"Well, besides that."

"Now you've got me worried. Obviously, you left some things out of your report. The subcommittee needs the whole picture here."

Mumford leaned forward in his chair and picked up the cigar again.

Libby said nothing for a moment. She thought about the periscope and her breasts. And the cigar, because it reminded her of Marshall.

"No, Senator," she finally said. "No, they don't. Let's just say I think the crew in Arizona would benefit from a little more supervision."

36

A SHOCKING DEVELOPMENT

March 2046

"I'M SENDING YOU TO WASHINGTON," Marta told Marshall as they shared dinner at her apartment. Marshall hoped the evening would lead to more. He didn't understand Marta's withdrawal of the past few weeks. They still slept together on occasion. Once the sex was done, though, Marta seemed to settle into some distant place she wouldn't allow him to share.

"By myself?"

"What, do you want Elvin to go with you?" Marta lifted her glass of wine and looked at Marshall over the rim.

"No, of course not. But why aren't you . . ."

"I'll be in Los Angeles," she said. "Sir Rupert Fitzhugh, my old boss at MI-6, and a few others from the agency are there for a conference. Sir Rupert asked me to provide a briefing."

"You can do that? Security-wise, I mean?"

"Oh, yes. Remember, Great Britain has a member on the subcommittee, and Sir Rupert gets regular reports. I think he just wants to see me. He was kind of my mentor there."

"Why me, and why now? Going to Washington, I mean?"

"Senator Mumford asked me to go there tomorrow and meet with the subcommittee the day after. I told him about my scheduling conflict, and he allowed me to send a stand-in. You are the senior traveler. You are who I trust to handle this."

Marshall smiled and raised his glass to acknowledge her compliment. "What's it all about?"

"The senator didn't say, but I'm sure it's to formally give us the details of what Libby Pinch is recommending, and to tell us who they will send here to keep an eye on things."

"Already? I thought we'd have more time. To put together a plan for Sheila." Suddenly, a thought occurred to Marshall that made the pit of his stomach fall away. "Marta, does it bother you that I want so badly to bring Sheila home? You know, because of . . . us?"

Marshall saw that his question took Marta by surprise. She hesitated a little too long before answering.

"Marshall, I know how you felt about Sheila—"

Marshall had his courage up now, and he plowed ahead.

"Something's been wrong for weeks. Something's changed, and I don't know what I've done. I . . . I . . . I'm sorry. That question was just so . . . so presumptuous. I would never just presume your feelings for me."

Marta pressed a fingertip to his lips and her eyes softened.

"Marshall, I know how deeply you care about Sheila. She was an extraordinary woman and friend. I want her to come home just as badly as you do, and maybe it does bother me just a little. But your concern . . . that's just who you are. I know that."

She did not, however, address the larger question and an awkward silence occupied the space between them.

"Um . . ." Marshall finally dared, "when you go to Los Angeles. Will that guy Nigel Smythe be there? The MI-6 spy you said you have sex with a couple times a year?"

Marta's eyes regained their steel. "Yes, he is."

"Well . . . are you . . ."

"Marshall, you and I never made any commitments to each other. We've never put any conditions on what . . . what we've shared. My job is . . . it requires that I . . ."

She shook her head and Marshall detected a well of emotion in her voice.

The moment passed, though. When she spoke again, her tone sounded flat, factual. "No. No. I'm not going to have sex with Nigel Smythe."

"You're right," Marshall said. "We never . . . and I shouldn't . . . Um . . . when do I leave for Washington?"

"Betty booked you on a 9 a.m. flight."

"Okay, then I'd better get some sleep."

Senator Josiah Mumford didn't mind working late.

Divorced years ago, no one waited for him at home—an apartment where, as far as his cat was concerned, Mumford was just the guy with the food.

In this office, though, he was a By God United States Senator.

His seniority earned him one of the larger office suites on the third floor of the Russell Senate Office Building. Describing it as plush would not do it justice. His mostly uncluttered desk, a magnificent relic circa 1910, had previously belonged to Warren Magnuson, and John Nance Garner before him. The heavy oak chairs were all antiques.

The marble mantled fireplace that dominated one interior wall was nonfunctional, but Mumford's staff still had wood piled high behind ancient brass andirons as if just waiting for a match, and a small stack of split tamarack, fragrant with sap, occupied a wood box beside the hearth.

Heavy drapes were drawn back from the windows, offering a view of the U.S. Supreme Court building across Constitution Avenue. The Russell Building dated to the early 1900s. When, in 1976, a new building—the Hart Senate Office Building—was complete, the Senate Rules Committee couldn't find enough Senators who wanted to move there. Office choice is based on seniority, and most senior senators didn't want to abandon the elegance of antiquity.

Senator John Chafee, a Republican representing Rhode Island, called the Hart building "a palatial monstrosity."

Mumford stood and stretched expansively. Stepping carefully because his knees rebelled at being asked to perform after sitting in committee hearings for much of the afternoon, he walked to a fully-stocked bar next to the fireplace and poured himself two fingers of smoky bourbon from a distant era, to which he added a pair of ice cubes.

Mumford swirled the amber liquid twice, then raised his glass. He took a sip, felt the gentle bite of the whisky, and rolled it momentarily over his tongue. He savored its warmth as he swallowed and settled into an antique chair with a high curved back that embraced his bulk. He'd positioned his chair to face the window so he could look down on all that history.

So, now they would send a representative to Arizona and keep an eye on the time travel project. And if the program could just muddle along without any disasters or any investigative journalists discovering what they'd concocted beneath the desert, Mumford would be done with it. If a historical debacle waited, as he feared it might, the calamity would occur on somebody else's watch.

Mumford hadn't told anyone—not even his chief of staff who had loyally run this office for twenty-eight years—that he would not run again. She would be devastated. Although they'd never spoken of it, Edna Hargrove loved him. He knew it. Had known it for the better part of a decade. This would be like a second divorce.

Goddammit, though, he was eighty years old. He wanted to retire. He'd been a good senator. Not a giant. Not in the same league as the previous owner of his desk, Warren Magnuson, or Robert Taft, or Henry Jackson, or Ted Kennedy, or John McCain, or . . . But he was close.

Time to go. Not to Delaware, though. Between Washington, D.C. and Delaware, he was tired of shitty weather. A new place. Somewhere unsullied and warm. Florida? No, half the people he knew fled to Florida in winter. Maybe Arizona, though?

Behind him, a distinctive click of the latching mechanism on the door separating his inner sanctum from an outer office surprised him only a little. He'd sent the staff home a couple of hours ago. Security people were stationed in the hallways, but he'd given Marshall a pass that would allow him access.

Mumford closed his eyes and savored another sip of bourbon. He would miss the sound of that click as much as anything. Modern doors and locks didn't make that noise. That sound was completely unique to the old latch mechanisms built into these doors more than two centuries ago, with their springs and levers and tension coils so carefully oiled and maintained. The outer office had all the modern security devices you could want. The lock on this heavy door, though, still opened with a skeleton key.

Marshall Grissom had sat patiently before the subcommittee and listened to criticism from Libby Pinch. Before Marshall flew back west tomorrow, Mumford wanted to soften the edges. So, he'd invited Marshall over for a drink and a friendly 'hang-in-there' kind of discussion.

"Mr. Grissom," he called over his shoulder, "so glad you could stop by."

"No, Senator," said a voice he didn't recognize. A man's voice thick and quavering.

Mumford tried to stand, but the chair was soft and deep. With the glass of bourbon still in his right hand, his left arm and shoulder failed to achieve the task. He surrendered back into his seat. The man stepped around and faced him from five feet away. His eyes were red-rimmed and moist.

"What's wrong?" Mumford asked.

He recognized this man, had seen him around. Didn't know him. Probably worked in one of the committee offices. Not budget. Something in defense? The identification card hanging from a lanyard around his neck said . . . Victor Franz? Worry over details like where the man worked evaporated as Mumford studied him more closely. The man's face was drawn with grief, his eyes puffy, complexion pale. His hands trembled.

Mumford's first thought was something must have happened to Edna or one of the other staff members and this Victor Franz brought news of tragedy.

"What is it?" he asked with foreboding.

"They're forcing me to do this," the man said, his voice husky. "I'm sorry. I guess this makes me the worst kind of coward, but I just don't know what else to do."

Mumford, still more confused than frightened, had yet to make sense of this scene. "Someone is making you do something you don't wish to do?"

The man nodded and stared at his shoes.

"Tell me who. I'll call the FBI director—"

"No! No calls to anyone."

The man turned with a panicked look and walked to Mumford's desk. The senator leaned forward beyond the curve of the chair's high back to watch him.

Victor Franz closed his eyes, clasped his hands to his head, and said painfully, "I don't see a letter opener."

"You need a letter opener?" Mumford asked.

Clearly the man suffered a perilous psychological state. Mumford began to understand he could pose a threat.

"In the drawer?" the man asked some unseen presence. He hurried around to the front of the desk, tugged open a drawer and pawed through it. "Which drawer? There are seven drawers."

He nodded to himself and pulled open the top left drawer. His hand trembling, he withdrew a heavy, stiletto-like letter opener—a gift to Mumford from the Mexican Ambassador many years earlier.

Franz returned to face the still-seated Mumford. Franz raised the stiletto high, his arm stiff. Mumford knew the man intended to stab him. Franz froze in this awkward position, though, apparently unable to will further movement. Eyes closed tight, he grimaced as tears seeped from beneath his eyelids.

Mumford sank deeper into the chair.

Again, came the doorknob's soft click, followed by a whoosh of the door skimming across deep carpet.

"Senator? What's going on here?" a new voice asked, its tone displaying alarm.

The man holding the stiletto opened his eyes, growing even more distraught.

"Get over here." the man demanded of the newcomer in a voice bordering on a growl. "Close the door and get over here, or I'll kill him right now."

Mumford heard the soft snick of the door latch.

"Senator?"

Marshall entered Mumford's field of vision. "I'm . . . I'm here, Mr. Grissom. I would suggest you leave."

"No. Over here. Get over here, by the curtains. Move."

Marshall, his face ashen, took careful steps. "What . . . what's going on here?"

"Don't talk." The letter opener's gleaming tip followed Marshall's movement.

"Please, sir," Mumford said in an effort to wrest the man's attention from Marshall, "What do you intend here?"

Mumford's question seemed to startle Victor Franz. He closed his eyes and took a deep breath. "I'm supposed to kill you."

"But why . . ." Mumford's voice trembled.

"They have my family. They know everything about me. I *have* to do this."

"You don't have to do anything. If they've got your family, the FBI can—"

"The FBI can't be involved. They'll know. The minute I think something, they know."

"How could they possibly—"

"They've planted a . . . a device of some kind in my head. They know . . . everything I'm thinking."

Marshall understood.

Voices that knew this would-be killer's every thought.

My God, someone is manipulating this poor man from the future. Someone from the future is trying to kill Senator Mumford!

Naomi had developed a theory about the complex relationship between the traveler from the future and his or her past self. The wracking disorientation that took place when a future being integrated unexpectedly with his or her past self often created a blind terror in the unwitting past being. But this relationship evolved. The future entity tried to make his or her past counterpart understand what was happening. Eventually, things settled down. The past being would comprehend and share all the future being's thoughts and emotions. Sooner or later, though, a past being could subjugate and even banish the intruder. A past being's initial reaction, though, was one of panic, of total bewilderment, and often, complete submission.

Standing in the corner by the curtain, Marshall raised his hand like a second grader, and cleared his throat. "Um . . . If you don't want to do this, they can't make you. You just have to tell them that you won't."

"Shut up. Now that you've shown up, they'll probably make me kill you, too."

"Did you contact your family?" Marshall asked. "Do you know for certain they've been taken?"

"No. They forbade me."

"But you don't *want* to kill me," Mumford entered the exchange.

"Oh, my God, no. I have no choice. They'll take everything—"

"Go to the phone on the Senator's desk," Marshall said. "Call your wife. See if she's all right."

"They say no."

"Give me the number. I'll call."

"They'll kill them if you do."

"Okay," Marshall said. "Let's try something else."

Marshall relied on experience while interacting with his past selves. *They are not copies or evil twins or clones. They are you. And just as they have access to all your emotions and memories, you have access to theirs if you can get past the confusion and fear. Relax and search your mind. Your future self could not keep the truth from you. He might divert the information for a while, but ultimately, the past being had as much access to the future being's thoughts and memories as he did to yours.*

"This voice in your head," Marshall said, "just ask it if that's true."

"If what's true?"

"If they, in fact, have your family, here in this world—be very specific about that. Ask if your family in this universe is really in any jeopardy."

"This universe? What are you talking about?"

"Just ask—specifically. And then listen for the answer."

The quivering subsided. Franz perspired heavily. He squinted his eyes closed and became quiet. Marshall watched the muscles of his face and neck relax. The deep wrinkles that formed as he squeezed his eyes so tightly eased and disappeared. He almost smiled. The tension leached from his arm and hand. The letter opener fell to the floor. He exhaled a long, cleansing breath.

But then his eyes popped open and darted wildly back and forth. He put his hands to his head and moaned.

"What?" Marshall asked.

"Now he's scared. He says if I don't do what they say, they'll leave him here in my . . . my head. And he'll, he'll—"

"I can fix that," Marshall said.

And he hoped he could. He didn't know if the person operating the time machine from the future of another universe realized that Elvin had programmed an automatic response to the "panic button" travelers used to indicate they were in trouble and needed to be returned to the future. Travelers were advised to locate tasers when they arrived at their past destination and jolt themselves, or convince someone else to do it, if anything went awry. The taser's zap disrupted a lifeline, which clung to a combination of aura, magnetic field and slight electrical charge unique to every person.

The physics teams watched the lifeline display—a thin red line bisecting vertically the monitor assigned to each traveler. If it wavered due to a sudden surge in the electrical component, the traveler would be extracted as quickly as possible.

Elvin decided that relying on someone to monitor the lifelines was a little slipshod, so he wrote a program to automate the return. The wavering lifeline would automatically result in the initiation of the return protocol. With any luck, those manipulating this poor man from the future didn't know about this update—unless, of course, Elvin or Gretchen happened to be the culprits. Marshall couldn't believe that.

"Senator, you don't have a taser handy, do you?" Marshall asked.

"What are . . ." Franz glanced down at his abandoned letter opener. "I won't let you—"

"If I could call one of the security guards," Mumford said, "he would have one."

"No." the would-be murderer said. "Please."

"I have to agree, Senator," Marshall said. "We can't involve security. This man has done nothing wrong. He doesn't deserve to be punished. How could we explain to anyone else that he's being manipulated from the future via a time-travel program nobody is supposed to know about?"

"Yes, I see your point."

Marshall noted the lamp on Mumford's desk.

He helped Mumford from the chair and stepped around the would-be assassin.

"He's very frightened now," the man said of his future counterpart. "He's ordering me to—"

"Ignore him."

Marshall switched the lamp on and unscrewed its lightbulb.

"Okay," Marshall said. "You have to trust me here. I want you to stick your finger in this light socket."

"You want me to do what?"

"Stick your finger in this light socket."

"I may be a little crazy, but I'm not stupid. And he, by the way, doesn't think it's a good idea, either."

"Look, it's not like I'm telling you to do it with your

tongue. It's only going to be a little jolt . . ."

"Okay, then you stick *your* finger in the light socket."

"I'm not the one trying to get rid of voices. Besides, if my idea succeeds as it's supposed to, this will probably only work once. A circuit breaker will trip, and the power will be off until someone resets it."

"What do you mean, *if it succeeds as it's supposed to*?" the man asked, clamped his hands to his head and squeezed his eyes shut again. Then he peeked back at Marshall. "And this will make the voice go away?"

Marshall nodded.

Franz tentatively approached Mumford's desk and pointed his right index finger. He looked first to Mumford, then to Marshall, who nodded again. With deliberation, the man extended his finger toward the open socket. Eyes closed, he turned his head turned away.

Franz stiffened as a jolt of electrons leaped through his body to the floor. Somewhere a circuit breaker tripped. Mumford's office went dark.

Marshall heard the thump of a body hitting the carpet. A groan. A scrabbling sound. A red, battery-operated security light popped on, bathing the scene with an eerie crimson glow. Franz was on his hands and knees. When Marshall touched his shoulder, Franz rolled onto his back. The mask of excruciation slowly melted into a relieved smile.

"He's gone."

"And if he ever comes back and commands you to do something you don't want to do," Marshall instructed, "just tell him no. And then push him away. In a couple of days, he'll leave on his own."

37

GUNSMOKE

"HERE," MUMFORD SAID, "Let me get you some water."

Someone took care of the circuit breaker and lights tripped back on. Mumford walked to a mini fridge in the bar across the room, drawing Marshall with him.

"Now what do we do?" he whispered. "I agree we can't get security involved. Of course, I could call Mr. Wishcamper . . ."

"We don't have time for that." Marshall glanced over his shoulder at Franz, who now sat in the high-backed chair. "This guy will quickly lose any memory he has of his mental interaction with his future self. We have to talk to him right now. Then, we just let him go. As I said, he hasn't done anything wrong. He was manipulated in a way no one else could understand. And he won't tell anyone anything he might remember of this, because he knows they'll think he's crazy."

"Someone within your group wants me dead? Why?"

"I don't know. I find it hard to believe anyone on our team would do this. And the implications of *that* are even more frightening. That would mean someone outside the current program knows about and has gotten access to the time projector."

Marshall dragged a second, identical chair close to Franz and sat facing him.

"My name is Marshall, by the way. Please do your very best to answer my questions . . ."

"Victor is my first name. I'm a senior staffer with the Ways and Means Committee."

"Mr. Franz—Victor—if you help us, I think the senator will be willing to overlook all this and you won't be arrested. No one else need ever know this happened."

Franz looked from Marshall to the Mumford and nodded his head.

"Okay," Marshall said. "The voice was you . . . um . . . another version of you who resides in a parallel universe."

"A what? Oh, come on . . ."

"We can't go into detailed explanations right now. We don't have time. Just tell me, how did they get him to threaten you that way. You have to know this. He wouldn't have been able to hide it from you after you started questioning him."

"I don't know. He didn't say anything about . . ."

Franz stopped and his expression of frustration shifted to amazement.

"You're right," he said. "They paid him. A lot of money. He . . . he didn't care what would happen to me."

"Who paid him?"

"A man . . . a man named Jones. John Jones. But that's not true. He knew that wasn't his real name. He didn't care."

"What did this Jones look like?"

"I . . . I can't see him anymore. I had an image but it's . . . I'm sorry I just . . ."

"It's already fading." Marshall turned to Mumford, who paced in front of his desk.

The senator stopped. "Why did they want to kill me?"

"I don't think he knew." Franz shook his head with frustration. "It's all becoming a blur. I can't see it anymore."

Desperately, Marshall demanded, "Concentrate. What year did he come from?"

"Year? I don't . . . wait . . . this year. Now."

"Anything?" Marshall pressed. "Any images? Any impressions at all . . ."

"Just . . . just, no that's dumb."

"What?"

"I have a mental picture of an old actor. From a long time ago. I can't think of his name, though. A big guy with a cowboy hat. Holding a gun . . . standing in some Old West town . . ."

"*Gunsmoke*," Marshall said, almost to himself.

"James Arness?" Mumford asked. "He's talking about James Arness. He played Matt Dillion on *Gunsmoke*."

"That's right." Franz said. "That's the guy."

"Gunsmoke," Marta said. "That makes sense."

"Why does it make sense?" asked Sheldon Wishcamper.

Wishcamper had joined Marshall in Mumford's office as they gathered around a speakerphone. Marta shared the conversation from her Los Angeles hotel room. Without explanation, she'd chosen not to engage 3-D video. Wishcamper had questioned Franz before they allowed the man to go on his way. By the time Wishcamper arrived, though, Franz's recollection of why he threatened Senator Mumford was gone.

"Among all the parallel universes with which we've had contact," Marta's voice carried through the phone, "the *Gunsmoke* universe is considered something of a ... pariah. A rogue universe, if you will."

"Why? Are they evil?" Wishcamper asked.

"No. It's really not their fault."

Marshall said to Mumford and Wishcamper, "Do you recall the basic issue of divergence among parallel histories?"

"Ms. Hamilton has told the subcommittee," Mumford said, "that each time a time traveler goes to the past of a given universe, historic paths of these universes diverge slightly."

"That's correct," Marta's disembodied voice made Marshall wonder if she was alone.

"Back before we learned to target universes," she explained, "the universe a traveler reached on a journey to the past was completely random. And by pure happenstance, or more likely some quirk of physics we don't yet understand, the *Gunsmoke* universe received of a disproportionate number of these indiscriminate visits from the futures of other universes.

"Elvin and Gretchen say this statistical anomaly caused *Gunsmoke* to stagger off on a divergent historical path significantly different from the rest of us. So, if someone wanted to manipulate the past of a specific universe and not be detected in his own universe, *Gunsmoke* would be the platform from which to do it."

"Because ..." Wishcamper prompted.

"Okay," Marta said. "Before we instigated time travel, the theory goes, all histories of all universes, at least where significant historical events are concerned, were in lockstep.

Minor details might vary, but larger historical facts remained the same. So, if I, for example, wanted to plot the murder of Senator Mumford, my counterparts from other universes would be doing the same.

"In the *Gunsmoke* universe, though, someone might be able to carry out this plot independent of the other universes historical track. The others wouldn't know. They couldn't follow clues and find the culprits in their own universe."

"Oh, boy," said Wishcamper. "So, let's take a look at who would have to be involved to pull off something like this."

"Someone familiar with my office," the senator said. "Mr. Franz had to be told where to find my letter opener."

"Someone who knows about the time travel program and someone who knows how to operate the projector," Marshall said.

"Doesn't narrow it down much." Marta's voice crackled via the speaker phone. "We've got hundreds of scientists and technicians and support staff who left when we downsized."

"And you've also got everyone on the subcommittee," Mumford said. "They don't know how to operate a time machine, but they certainly know about this program. Most of them have visited my office many times."

"And we can't send someone to the future of the *Gunsmoke* universe to see what's going on, because the projector was not constructed to send people to the future," Wishcamper recalled.

Marshall stepped to the window, his mind conjuring images of Marta and Nygel Smythe.

"That's correct," Marta said.

Silence settled over the office for a few moments.

"How difficult is it for people from this *Gunsmoke* universe to trade information back and forth with people in our universe?" Wishcamper asked.

"Very difficult," Marta said. "The only way to communicate is for them to send a traveler to the past of this universe with a message. If we can get the *Gunsmoke* people to beef up security around their projector soon enough, there's no way they can learn whether or not the murder attempt succeeded."

"Unless," Wishcamper said, "you or another key member of your team is behind this, from that other universe, I mean. You can use the projector any time you want, right?"

"Mr. Wishcamper," Marta's voice sparked with a hint of impatience, "as I've tried to explain before, my *Gunsmoke* counterpart is me, and I am her. Divergence or not, she will not do anything out of character. Nor would Marshall or any of the others. I'm confident of that."

"Mr. Franz's counterpart apparently accepted a bribe and left his twin here to take the fall for murder," Wishcamper said.

"What that means," Marta replied, "is that the Mr. Franz of both worlds is a man of questionable character. Our Mr. Franz didn't want to kill a man here. He didn't want to see his family harmed. That doesn't mean he wouldn't take a bribe. I'd watch him if I were you."

Alone again after his return to the projection platform of the *Gunsmoke* universe, the Victor Franz native to that world poked along, trapped by rush hour traffic on Interstate Seventeen. He checked the dashboard time display of his rental car for the tenth time in the last five minutes.

"Shit," he muttered. "I should have followed Jones's advice and cut across Northern to Highway 51. I'll miss my damn flight if traffic doesn't thin out here pretty soon."

The afternoon Phoenix traffic showed no sign of diminishing, though.

Franz had ridden a roller-coaster of emotions for three days. First came an unbelievable revelation of time travel. When he'd accepted Jones's money, he thought his task would be something simple, like turning over some classified files or spying on some of the Ways and Means Committee members.

They'd flown him to Phoenix, though. Driven him through the desert in the middle of the night, snuck him into tunnels making up a weird underground fortress, then introduced him to an honest-to-God time machine.

He would have bailed when Jones told him to take off his clothes, but Jones was clearly the type of person you didn't disappoint. Jones told Victor he would enter the mind of... himself, at a place called the *I Love Lucy* universe. There he was to order this other... him... to kill Senator Josiah Mumford. Jones assured Victor he would not care for the outcome if he failed. When this other him refused at the last second to commit the murder, the real him feared these guys would kill him the instant he returned to his own world.

They seemed surprised when, after several minutes, Victor had not forgotten the whole thing. When he realized they took it for granted he would forget, he feigned loss of memory. Perhaps being gripped by terror kept events of the other world fresh in his mind. Then it occurred to Victor that they might not have any idea whether he'd done it or not. He'd gone to another universe, right? What means did they have to check up on him? So, he lied. He told them the other him had stabbed Mumford and security had come and arrested this other Victor and hauled him away.

Jones seemed pleased. Jones pushed some buttons on his computer keyboard and while Victor watched, five million dollars were transferred to a foreign bank account. Jones gave Victor the account information and, right there on the spot, Victor transferred it to a second account. And now the money waited for him, banked on an island paradise. He would call the moving vans as soon as he got back to D.C.

First, however, he needed to get to the damn airport, return this damn rental car and catch his damn plane.

He glanced enviously across three lanes of traffic where the HOV lane hummed along. The next time traffic forced him to a halt, he scanned carefully for any sign of police motorcycles and saw none.

"Fuck it," he said, and to a cacophony of horns, began to force his way through the creeping lines of cars and trucks toward his left.

When he finally found an opening that just barely allowed him to accelerate into the HOV lane, a pickup truck zooming up behind him blared its horn as its driver protested the inconvenience of having to slow down. The angry driver settled just a few feet from Franz's bumper as they moved along at fifty-five miles per hour.

Franz raised his right hand high and extended his middle finger, hoping the pickup driver could see it. He laughed and thought, *So what if I'm driving alone in the*

HOV lane? How severe could the penalty be? After all, I've got five million dollars.

That's when Victor Franz's rental car blew up, obliterating Victor Franz and, in a flash of karma, the pickup tailgating him.

"So how do we proceed from here," asked Mumford. "Should I inform the subcommittee . . ."

"I'd rather you didn't, Senator," Wishcamper said. "If a subcommittee member is involved, I don't want that person to know the plan failed. We'll increase your security, have you lay low for a while, and I'll start looking around. Ms. Hamilton, is there anything your people can do?"

"I'll call Elvin and Gillis," Marta said. "I'm in Los Angeles, so I can't do this myself. We'll send Gillis back one day to the *Gunsmoke* universe immediately. Hopefully that Marta will be at the complex. He'll find me and let me know what's going on. Maybe we can stop this, or at the very least, identify who's behind it."

38

MEANWHILE, BACK AT THE RANCH

MARTA CLOSED HER PHONE and pulled open the bathroom door.

"Okay," she said to Nigel Smythe, "you can turn off the shower and come out."

"Marta, you only had to tell me the call was a matter of security. I wouldn't have tried to eavesdrop," the handsome older man with ice blue eyes told her. "You didn't have to send me to the loo."

She saw he'd taken his tie off and opened the first few buttons of his shirt.

"I'm sorry, Nigel," she said. "I've got a few more calls to make. And you know me. I'm just not that much of a trusting soul."

"All right," Nigel answered. "I'll wait in the bar."

She turned her back to him. He embraced her from behind, his hands brushing across her breasts.

"Later then?" he asked, kissing the nape of her neck.

Marta closed her eyes as his fingers found the hard outline of her nipples through her blouse. The thought of a night of unencumbered, unemotional sex with a wonderfully skilled lover seemed very appealing.

She turned in his arms, put both hands on his chest and looked into those remarkable eyes. She wanted to say yes. She intended to say yes. But what she heard herself say was, "Nigel I . . . I'm sorry. But I just . . . I just can't. Not yet."

Gillis Kerg snapped into the consciousness of the *Gunsmoke* version of himself, at once amazed at the foreign aspect of this unique world.

Gillis had probably made more routine projections, quick jumps going back only a day or two, than any other traveler. These were typically scientific missions during which Elvin and Gretchen gathered data regarding the limbo's physical nature, the wormhole, or the past world, the time being traversed so brief that integration of the past and future entities felt comfortable. A future being brought only twenty-four hours' worth of experience his past counterpart had not yet shared. And that's how this projection should have been. Gillis traveled back a single day.

Here in *Gunsmoke*, though, the two Gillis's memories did not track at all. Their lives had continued along broadly similar paths. But the variations here were significant. For one thing, at the moment of his arrival, Gillis from *I Love Lucy* was startled to find *Gunsmoke* Gillis staring with unbridled lust at a topless Marta Hamilton.

They were in Marta's apartment. She'd just taken off her shirt and was smiling a most seductive smile.

"Oh, my goodness," was the thought *Lucy*-Gillis sent ringing through *Gunsmoke*-Gillis's mind.

"*Oh, fuck,*" the other Gillis responded mentally. "*What in the bloody hell are you doing here? After all this time,*

Marta is finally going to . . . and you drop in from . . . I Love Lucy? Okay. Just back off and be quiet . . . "

"*Um . . . I can't,*" future-Gillis responded. "*We have a situation. There is some urgency involved.*"

Gillis threw his arms into the air and issued an exasperated, "Aaaaaaghhh!"

Marta's smile changed to an expression of uncertainty. She covered her breasts with her hands. "Gee, Gillis, that's not exactly the response I'd hoped for."

Gillis stepped to her, pulled her hands away and replaced them with his own.

"*Hey,*" the second voice shouted in his head. "*I said we have a situation.*"

"Oh, for God's sake!" Gillis yelled as he shook his fists at the ceiling.

"Gillis?" Marta's voice now carried a note of alarm.

"I can't believe this," Gillis told her. "I've been joined. *I Love Lucy*. From one day in the future. They say . . . what? How is that possible?"

"What are you talking about?" Marta asked as she turned to retrieve her shirt from the couch behind her.

"He says someone from our universe has attempted to murder Senator Mumford."

"How could . . . when?"

"Not sure. Very soon, if it hasn't already occurred. Your counterpart wants you to see if you can stop it."

"Let's go." Marta went to her bedroom and tucked her pistol into the waistband of her pants."

"Do they know who?" she asked as they hurried through the concrete corridors.

"A man named Victor Franz," Gillis told her, sharing

future Gillis's memory track. "He works at the capitol building in D.C."

"So, they would have to bring him all the way out here? And somehow get access to the projector. Is the senator all right?"

"Yes. Their Marshall disrupted the attempt."

"Marshall?" Marta said with a wistful sigh. "You still have him there?"

Future-Gillis took over the conversation.

"Yes, but Elvin thinks it's only a matter of time. You haven't said anything—the you back there, I mean. We've all seen it, though. I don't think the *Lucy* Marta is handling Marshall's impending death very well."

Gillis and Marta hurried through tunnels and came to a stop at the projection lab entrance. Marta engaged a lever releasing the airlock.

"I guess we should start bolting the door," she said.

"I'm afraid locks are nothing more than a nuisance to someone who really wants to get in," Gillis said.

Entering the darkened lab, Gillis knew immediately they were too late. Two giant metal orbs flanking the platform still glowed with remnants of a plasma-like substance produced during a projection.

Marta approached a bank of computers alongside the platform. She pointed to the coordinates glowing on one of the readouts. "When we get Elvin down here, he'll tell us this is the setting for the *I Love Lucy* universe. Will it do us any good to look at security tapes?"

"Not the official tapes. They won't have gone to the considerable trouble of getting in and out of here just to be caught by the video system."

"What about your worm?" Marta asked.

Gillis smiled. Months ago, he had hacked into the security system and installed his own backup. When any security cameras were switched off, Gillis's system switched them back on, and diverted their feed to his hidden server. Back in the days when the complex bustled with a thousand people, security guards switched off cameras scanning certain areas with some frequency. They were covering for their colleagues who snuck away for unauthorized breaks or clandestine sex.

"I should have a digital record of whatever happened," Gillis said.

Marta sighed. "I don't think there's anything else we can do here. Judging from the look of things, they've been gone at least an hour or so. What we'll find somewhere in the desert—in one direction or another along the main road— is an abandoned car, probably stolen. And some tracks where a helicopter landed. I'll send security teams to search, but I'm not hopeful."

When they arrived at Gillis's apartment Marta called security and had them post a guard at the entrance to the projection lab. She dispatched two teams to search the desert road.

Gillis's recordings showed that four culprits entered the facility using many of the same techniques Gillis had employed to sneak out during the program's early days when security was more stringent. Back then, everyone was supposed to be confined to the campus for the five-year terms of their contracts. Gillis, though, used his technological skills and devices to occasionally slip off to the town of Superior for recreation.

Trusting that the cameras tracking them were shut down, the intruders made their way through a remote gate and crossed a no-man's land between fences, using reflective shields to divert motion-sensitive laser blasts. They defeated the locking mechanisms on a remote storage building and used a small equipment elevator to reach the lower labyrinth.

Projection lab cameras showed one man disrobing while two others attended to the machine. A fourth man, wearing a black wide-brimmed fedora that cast deep shadows across his face, looked on. The scene played silently as Gillis's worm didn't include an audio stream from the primary system.

"I've been procrastinating about tapping into the audio feed," Gillis apologized to Marta.

The process from projection to recovery took less than an hour.

"They've got some balls, these guys," Marta said.

"Oh, they took a risk," Gillis said. "But think about it. We don't have nearly enough security staff to cover the acres of tunnels and empty offices and labs since the downsizing. And clearly the staff we have is susceptible to bribery."

"Tough to be honest if the bad guys are willing to throw enough money at you," Marta said. "Do any of these guys look familiar?"

Gillis leaned into the glow of the 3-D video projection hovering over his desk. "Obviously, the one they projected is this Victor Franz. I can't really see the big guy in back. But I know I've seen these two running the equipment. They were probably victims of downsizing. We'll run facial recognition and have their identities soon enough."

"Too bad they didn't bother with the platform spotlights."

Marta and the combined Gillises watched a blur of faces comprise an eerie parade before them until, like rolls on a slot machine, first one, and then the other face matching the interlopers clicked into place.

"And they are..." Gillis waited for the personnel records to come up, "... Charles Buck, a computer technician and member of the mathematics team, and Scott Milton of the physics group."

"I don't think I ever met Charles Buck," Marta said. "I remember Milton, though. He was a whiney, self-important twit who came and yelled at me one day because I dared to question one of his group's conclusions. It'll be fun having him arrested."

"We can't involve police," Gillis said.

"Of course, not. I'll contact Wishcamper. Now that we know who they are, he won't have any trouble finding them. And then, who knows where they'll end up. But I'm sure Wishcamper will persuade them to talk. They can tell us who the fourth man is."

"That's assuming Mr. Milton and Mr. Buck live long enough to be arrested."

"Yeah, I hadn't thought of that. We don't know how desperate the masterminds behind this will be to cover their tracks."

"Let's run the recording again and see if there's any way we can put a face on the fourth guy."

Projection lab images again skittered across the screen. Gillis watched carefully. He found an instant where the fourth man, apparently reacting to some sound, glanced quickly behind him. As he did, the shadows under the brim of his hat softened.

"Maybe this is what we need." Gillis tapped commands into his virtual keyboard. The effort produced a muddy, grainy image on which only a few facial features could be called distinct.

"That's not much," Marta said.

"If we're lucky, we don't need much. The recognition program may be able to extrapolate from what little we have here."

Again, a torrent of facial images flew through the three-dimensional holographic frame floating above Gillis's tiny computer. It jerked to a stop, stuttered, flashed forward, stuttered again, and finally resolved itself into a face.

The face meant nothing to *Gunsmoke* Gillis, but his *I Love Lucy* counterpart pushed his way into the conversation with the mental exclamation. *Something's wrong with your recognition software. This isn't possible. This man is dead.*

Flashing below the holographic face was a personnel record identifying the fourth man as Jason Pratt, a pre-downsizing member of the janitorial staff.

"What do you mean dead?" *Gunsmoke* Gillis said aloud.

"Who's dead?" Marta asked.

"He—the other me—says this guy is dead. He says Marshall killed him."

Marta studied the face and personnel record. "Marshall? This guy's a janitor. I've never even heard Marshall raise his voice to anyone, much less . . . why would Marshall kill a janitor?"

"What? Okay, okay, just wait a minute," Gillis said to the air above him. Then he shook his head at Marta. "I have to step aside and let him talk, okay?"

Marta nodded.

"Are you telling me Marshall didn't shoot Jason Pratt on the night Sheila was murdered?" the *Lucy* Gillis asked her.

"No. Marshall was already dead in our world. And this Jason Pratt wasn't there when I finally got to the lab. I've always suspected that at least one more person was involved that night. I mean, I didn't believe Rose and that Gormly guy could handle Sheila by themselves . . ."

"What about Gormly? What happened to Gormly?"

Marta raised her eyebrows in a *what do you think happened to him* look, and the answer came through *Gunsmoke* Gillis's memory.

"You shot Gormly."

"Yes, I did," Marta said. "I stood him on the projection platform and made him admit that he and Rose had sent Sheila to a point prior to her birth. He tried to bribe his way out of it. I shot him. Elvin used the time projector to clean things up."

Gillis answered her unabashed confession with his crooked smile and nodded his approval.

"Why?" she asked. "What did you guys do with Gormly?"

"We sent him a few years into the past of Marshall's lizard world. Marshall wouldn't let you kill him."

"Lord, I do miss Marshall," Marta said softly.

"On that night in our world, though," the *Lucy*-Gillis told her, "Leonard Rose said Pratt knew how to operate the time machine. Elvin said he probably learned the basics just by watching or talking to technicians. Why would he need to involve Milton and Buck this time?"

"Because Pratt sent Sheila to a random time and place. He didn't need to pinpoint a specific universe or date. Getting Franz back to the *I Love Lucy* universe on the right day is much more complicated. He needed technical help."

Gillis stood and clicked off his computer. The floating image of Jason Pratt dissolved with a flutter of glittering light particles.

Marta put her hand on Gillis's shoulder and stared at him with cold eyes.

"And you say Jason Pratt is the one who killed Sheila?"

Gillis nodded.

"He tased her, stripped her of her clothing, carried her to the projection platform, and announced he was sending her to the 1960's. And he smiled when he did it."

"I won't let Wishcamper have him." Marta's voice resonated like a frigid wind emanating from a deep cave. "I'll deal with him myself."

39

ELVIN DRAWS THE SHORT STRAW

"YOU CAN'T DO THAT," Elvin said, "because Gillis is already here."

"So what?" the *Gunsmoke* Marta asked with exasperation.

Marta had summoned Elvin Detwyler and Gretchen Allen to meet with her and the Gillises at her office.

Elvin wore a tattered bathrobe and slippers shaped like ducks. What little hair he had remaining formed tufts and wisps, half a halo around the sides and back of his head. Gretchen's robe wrapped around a pair of men's pajamas. Her long, auburn hair, which she usually wore in a braid, cascaded loosely behind her shoulders and down to her waist.

"Let me be sure I have this straight," Gretchen said. "You want to send our Gillis, who is presently inhabited by Gillis from *I Love Lucy,* back to that universe so he can tell them to send him back to us again, but a few hours ago, so he can observe the break-in."

"Yes."

"We can't do that," Elvin said. "We have no idea what would happen if we projected a traveler, who is currently hosting a traveler, back to occupy that same traveler in the past."

"What?" Gillis asked.

"Okay, okay, okay," said Marta, her frustration multiplying. "Suppose the *I Love Lucy* Gillis does the panic button thing and returns there before we send our Gillis back."

"You're forgetting," said Gretchen, "that the event you want to observe would then be in the future of the *I Love Lucy* world. And we can't send travelers to the future."

"We'll tell them to wait a day before they do it."

"Ah," said Elvin, "but then the traveler," and he pointed at Gillis, "the *I Love Lucy* Gillis, would be crossing this moment of time. Us. Here. Right now. On the same path between the same two universes. Again, we have no idea what might happen. I think we'd just be asking for trouble."

Marta drummed her fingers on her desk. "Why don't we try it, just this once?"

"I will remind you," Elvin said, "that I am presently disdained among the universes—or so the travelers tell me—because I am blamed for blowing up the entire *Joey Bishop* world. Once, okay. We can call it a mistake. Twice? I don't think so."

"Both Gillises will stay here, then. We'll use different travelers."

"And once more I remind you," Elvin said, "no one outside our little conspiracy knows the details of Sheila's death and your execution of Andrew Gormly. Are you sure you want to rouse anyone else's curiosity by involving them—"

He stopped midsentence.

"You're smiling," he said. "You've got that evil gleam . . . No! No way. Not again."

"Oh, come on, Elvin. You've been through this before.

We have no other choice."

"No fucking way. Send Gretchen."

Gretchen Allen sat up very straight. "Are you crazy?" she demanded.

"Why not?" Elvin asked. "I took my turn, back when we were trying to save the *Joey Bishop Show* guys. It's someone else's turn. Gretchen should do it just for . . . just for the . . . opportunity to observe . . ."

"I will not," Gretchen said with a voice that chilled Elvin, "take off my clothes in front of this bunch of yahoos."

"Yahoos?" asked Gillis.

"Look it up," said Gretchen.

"Gretchen, please," Marta said, "this is the man who killed Sheila."

Gretchen's lower lip quivered. She briefly hesitated before shaking her head no.

Gillis leaned and whispered into Marta's ear, "She won't do it, because she has a happy face tattooed on her boob."

"What?" Marta said and turned to him with a jerk.

Again, Gillis whispered. "A happy face. On her left breast. The other Gillis says he's seen it. In the *I Love Lucy* universe."

Marta's mouth fell open. She looked from Gretchen to Gillis and back again. She sighed. "Sorry, Elvin. It's you."

"Send Macy," Elvin said.

"As you just reminded us, Macy is not a member of our conspiracy," Marta said. "Besides, I gave her a couple days off. She's in Phoenix. It's got to be you, Elvin."

"No. And you can't make me."

Marta smiled a dangerous smile. "Do you really want to stand by that position? Because I'm pretty sure I can."

Ten minutes later, a naked Elvin Detwyler stood scrubbed and shivering as the blobs of plasma began to crawl across gleaming metal globes and soft vibrations tickled his feet.

"Remember," Marta called to him, "find the *Lucy* version of me. Tell me to wait one day and then project myself back to a few hours ago."

"Wait, wait, wait," past-Gillis said. "That won't work. Our Marta—the *Lucy* Marta—is in Los Angeles. We can't project her if she's in Los Angeles."

"So, who else . . ." asked Marta.

"Not Elvin," Gillis said, "because if we send him now, we'd have that whole same traveler crossing the same time point between the same two universes thing going on."

"You're damn right, *not* Elvin," Elvin said.

"Macy," said Gillis. "Macy would be available. I'm afraid she's our last option. We don't have to tell her everything. She just has to deliver a message."

"I thought Macy was in Phoenix," Elvin said.

"Your Macy is in Phoenix, but our Macy is here . . . or she was when I left, and I'd have known if she planned to go anywhere."

Elvin seethed. "Fucking divergence."

"So, you're up, Elvin," Marta said.

"Yeah, yeah." He offered a dismissive wave

"And don't screw it up."

"Fuck you," Elvin said under his breath.

"You wish," Marta replied.

A pale Elvin Detwyler knocked at the door of Gretchen Allen's office door.

Sweat beaded on his forehead. He gasped for breath as if he'd sprinted here. Gretchen could not envision Elvin sprinting anywhere under any circumstance.

"Elvin, are you okay?"

"No."

"What's wrong?"

Elvin held one hand up, a call for time out. He closed his eyes until his breathing slowed. "Marta's gone, right?"

"Her flight to Los Angeles departed early this morning," Gretchen said.

"Okay . . . Marshall . . . ?"

"You missed him by a couple of hours. His plane to Washington is probably already in the air."

"The fuckers did it again."

"Which fuckers are those?"

"The *Gunsmoke* guys. They made their Elvin come back here again, and you're not going to believe this."

Gretchen listened carefully, then interrupted Elvin's explanation. "Jason Pratt is dead," she said. "And we've checked other universes, as well."

"Not in *Gunsmoke,* he isn't," Elvin said. "We're supposed to wait a few hours and then send Macy back with a message for Marta . . ."

"Remember, Marta's in Los Angeles," Gretchen said.

"Not in the *Gunsmoke* universe. And in the *Gunsmoke* universe, Macy's in Phoenix and Marta's here."

Gretchen hesitated. The divergence between the two universes was clearly growing more dramatic and with the disparities came greater risk. "We need to call Marta."

Marta's cell phone rang as she stared into the mirror. She stood in her bra and panties, debating her "look." How much makeup? And the red lipstick? The red lipstick was something of a message to Nigel Smythe. A midthigh dress that covered her shoulders? Or the button-up blouse and the short skirt that Nigel Smyth had told her, on more than one occasion, really got him going?

But what did she truly seek in this mirror? She faced a decision. She must decide who the woman reflected to her would be. And her choice, she realized, must be made before she walked into the hotel restaurant for dinner with Nigel and her former colleagues from MI-6.

The ringing of her cell phone shocked her from this reverie.

"Marta, thank goodness we caught you . . ." Gretchen said.

"Jason Pratt is not dead?" Marta gasped following Elvin's summary of the *Gunsmoke* universe events. "And he's trying to kill Senator Mumford in our world? Has someone alerted D.C. security?"

"No need," Elvin said. "The attempt doesn't succeed. Marshall talked the would-be assassin out of it . . ."

"Marshall?" Marta shook her head. *Jesus. How many more ways would Marshall keep digging at her guilt, nagging by his example, urging her to become someone she couldn't be.*

"The thing is," Gretchen said after taking the phone from Elvin, "we need to send someone back prior to the attempt on Senator Mumford's life and explain this to the *Gunsmoke* version of you so something can be done about Jason Pratt.

He's a rogue operative, now. Unless he's stopped, he can use the *Gunsmoke* time projector to create all kinds of havoc. And we have to learn who's directing him. It's not Gormly, because the *Gunsmoke* Marta killed that Gormly."

At least there's one version of me who still has some balls, Marta thought, remembering that Marshall dissuaded her from executing Gormley in the *Lucy* world.

". . . so, do you want us to wait until you get back and send you, or should we send Macy now?" Leonard continued.

"We can't afford to wait. We still don't understand the space-time distortions. If we wait twenty-four hours, we don't know how that affects the timeline. Send Macy. Tell her exactly what to say to the *Gunsmoke* me. Offer no explanations. We'll deal with that issue later."

"Okay," Gretchen said. "Anything else?"

"Only a reminder that *Gunsmoke* is one very cocked-up universe. The divergence is apparently a lot more pronounced than we've thought. We must be very careful when we deal with them.

"But Jason Pratt . . ." Marta thought of the video that showed Pratt leering as he dropped Sheila onto the projection platform and ran his hands over her body. ". . . this we have to do."

She closed her phone and stared into the mirror again. She should call the airline, get a flight back to Phoenix as quickly as she could.

That's what she ought to do.

Instead, she stared into her bathroom mirror and applied the red lipstick.

Macy Gardner flashed into her past *Gunsmoke* counterpart, who relaxed in a North Phoenix movie theater. The integration was easy, as both Macys were experienced travelers and only a few hours separated past and future. Macy whispered to her sister that she needed to go to the bathroom. She walked to the theater lobby and placed a phone call to Marta.

40

A NEST OF VIPERS

GUNSMOKE MARTA SAT IN THE driver's seat of a small all-terrain vehicle, tucked away from the road behind a stand of cactus. She'd located the intruders' vehicles, a dark SUV and a small Jeep hidden fifty yards away.

Marta donned night vision goggles and, peering through the saguaros, watched four figures approach the cars. She heard doors opening and closing. A single figure got into the Jeep and drove east further into the desert. Three men entered the SUV and turned west toward Superior.

Marta had considered confronting the intruders at the projection platform. Future Macy told her though, that the assassination mission had failed. Victor Franz had not killed the *I Love Lucy* version of Josiah Mumford.

So, a better plan would be to follow Pratt and learn who directed him in a world where Andrew Gormley no longer existed.

But Marta hadn't counted on two cars. Which should she follow?

The lone man in the Jeep didn't look big enough to be Pratt so Marta focused on the SUV. Though she drove without lights, she tracked the other vehicle easily through a thick plume of dust it kicked up along the dirty paved surface.

When brake lights flared a quarter mile ahead, she backed off the throttle and came to a stop.

A full moon cast its light, creating long shadows among the prickly giants. Marta was glad for her vehicle's black paint and the tight black slacks and shirt she wore. The cuffs of her slacks were tucked into heavy black tactical boots. She pushed her ATV off the road. Angling into the desert, she crept forward to get a better view of her quarry. Through the green glow of her night vision apparatus, she found the SUV next to another car. Three men stood alongside.

She needed to get closer to hear the conversation.

As she moved, an angry buzz emanated from a mesquite bush a couple of yards to her left. Marta froze. She stepped carefully away, only to have another buzz erupt from her right.

She remained still as a post and summoned her logical mind to force a wary calm. She reminded herself that boots protected her feet and ankles. She steadied her breathing and looked carefully about. Even her night vision apparatus did not reveal the snakes. They were tucked away under their rocks and bushes.

Rattlesnakes will do everything they can to avoid you, she said to herself, mentally reciting her reading on the subject. *They don't want to strike if they don't have to. Leave them alone, and they will leave you alone. Okay guys, I'm going to do my very best to follow those instructions. You just have to do your part.*

She searched for bare patches of sand and rock along the

desert floor and carefully picked her way forward, rousing more buzzing as she went, though the snakes remained hidden.

She focused on the terrain ahead until distant voices became distinct.

She searched for what she hoped would be a safe place to stop and saw a broad patch of bare rock only about twenty yards from the vehicles. She stepped to it quickly, and lacking cover, squatted to lower her profile in the moonlight. The buzzing quieted.

A large man, who must be Pratt, exchanged handshakes with the two smaller men. The smaller men got into a sedan.

Pratt returned to his SUV, then made a show of snapping his fingers and retracing his steps, as if he'd forgotten something. He made a motion with his left hand for the driver to roll down his window. A flare of light bloomed painfully in Marta's night vision goggles accompanied by a boom that resonated across the desert. Marta tore the goggles from her eyes as a second gunshot sounded. She fumbled the goggles, sending them skittering across the rock surface.

Still blinded by a muzzle flash magnified through the goggles' optics, Marta froze. Seconds plodded by as she waited for her eyes to dilate, then gather enough light to see again.

Gradually the two vehicles reappeared through the moonlight. The men were gone, though. *No, wait.* Now she could make a pair of heads just above the seatback. They didn't move.

Carefully, she reached to the holster on her hip and withdrew her pistol. She began a slow turn when a voice to her right said, "Put down your gun or you're dead where you stand."

Although she suspected she was dead anyway, Marta complied. The automatic bounced onto the rock next to the goggles.

Pratt approached carefully, eyes fixed on Marta, shuffling his feet along the uneven desert floor. He got within a scant five yards when he stopped and stared.

"You're Marta Hamilton."

"And you're Jason Pratt."

Pratt seemed surprised to be recognized but recovered quickly.

"Your presence is inconvenient," he said. "It does add an element of amusement, though. I need to be sure you aren't concealing any other weapons. Take off that shirt."

He gestured with the gun for emphasis.

"Raping me would be a mistake," Marta said. "You'll leave too much evidence, too much DNA on the body."

Pratt laughed. "There won't be a body to find. I've rigged that car over there so the hydrogen tank will explode."

Marta understood Pratt's plan. With all the safety precautions and regulations, hydrogen explosions were rare. When they did occur, though, very little was left to analyze. The authorities could probably conclude there were three victims, but there wouldn't be enough remaining to identify them.

"Now, this can be as rough or as easy as you want," Pratt said.

"If you want this shirt off me, you'll have to get it yourself," Marta said, her voice cold with anger.

Pratt was a big man, a foot taller than Marta and

probably a hundred and twenty pounds heavier. She needed to get him close, though, so she could at least try to fight.

"No. You take it off. I know what you're thinking. You need me to come close enough so you at least have a chance. I could just shoot you and you'd have no chance at all."

Marta glared into his eyes and yanked the shirt over her head.

"And the bra. Then you'll get your chance."

Marta peeled off her exercise bra and faced him with defiance.

"Very nice," Pratt said. "On your knees."

Marta glanced at the rock surface beneath her and slowly complied. In the shadows at her feet rested a loose rock, about the size of a softball.

Which of us lives and dies, she thought, *will come down to where the snakes are.*

Pratt took a step forward and the buzzing began.

First to his left, then to his right. A mesquite bush only a yard from where Marta knelt took up the chorus. Pratt froze, one foot suspended a few inches off the ground, his other foot perilously close to a buzzing tumbleweed.

"Snakes," he said, eyes still fixed on Marta.

"And they're pissed off." She looked cryptically down to Pratt's right foot, opposite the tumbleweed. She smiled.

Still not daring to move or look away from Marta, Pratt said, "What is it?"

"Nothing," Marta answered, her grin getting bigger.

The voice of an angry desert surrounded them as more snakes reflected their companions' sense of danger.

Marta continued to cast her gaze down, waiting for her chance.

She made a show of opening her eyes wide and gasped with a sudden intake of breath. Reflexively, Pratt succumbed with a quick peek, seeking the snake he feared was there.

In one motion, Marta scooped up the rock, flipped it onto the tumbleweed next to Pratt. She fell prone onto the hard, bare surface.

Pratt's shot whistled above her as a snake in the tumbleweed next to him struck.

At the same time Marta felt a hard thump at the top of *her* left boot.

"Aaaaaahhhhhh!" Pratt howled.

More gunshots erupted as he fired time and again at the ground around him. His leg gave way, and he fell hard.

Marta rolled away from a buzzing bush and, rising to her hands and knees, stared into the cold eyes of the snake that had hit her. The reptile sat coiled, ready to strike again.

While Pratt writhed and screamed, Marta remained as still as she could. She fought against panic. Adrenaline coursing through her body demanded she scramble away. Still, she remained motionless. Marta and the snake stared at each other for a twenty-second eternity before it withdrew to the underbrush. Carefully, Marta stood. She found her night vision apparatus and saw snakes in eerie shades of green as they slithered their retreat.

Marta began to shake. She removed the night vision device and, ignoring the thrashing and screaming coming from Pratt a few yards away, looked quickly at her ankle. She didn't feel pain, but her skin-tight pants were torn and a wound just above her boot was leaking.

The surge of adrenaline must be masking the pain of the snake bite.

Hand still trembling, Marta found her pistol and approached Pratt. "How many times did you get bit?"

"My legs," he groaned. "My . . . my hand."

Pratt's left hand and arm were already swollen grotesquely.

"I'm going to get your belt," she said, assuring herself that Pratt's weapon rested a safe distance from his injured arm. "For a tourniquet."

"Okay. Hurry. Hurry."

Marta reached cautiously, unbuckled Pratt's belt, and pulled it away.

She stood and stepped back.

"Thanks." She wrapped the belt around her calf just above her wound, pulled it tight and tied it off.

Pratt raised his head and snarled but did not beg for her assistance. She approached again and saw evidence of at least three other bites.

"Who are you working for?" she asked.

"Help . . . help me," he wheezed.

"Give me a name. Then I'll call in a helicopter medevac unit."

In a move that must have required every ounce of his waning strength, Pratt rolled so he could reach Marta's leg with his uninjured arm. Marta felt his hand clamp onto her ankle.

"I'll take that as a no." She stomped down hard with her free leg. She heard the crack of a bone breaking in Pratt's wrist.

He screamed again.

As her adrenaline flow eased, a desert breeze blew across her bare breasts, reminding her she should find her shirt. She saw it and the bra in the middle of the rocky patch. She stepped carefully to the shirt and pulled it on, stuffing the bra into the waistband of her pants.

Pratt's moans didn't subside. The humane thing to do, she thought, would be to shoot him. She couldn't imagine the agony he must be suffering. Her own leg throbbed under the tourniquet's pressure. A gunshot wound would only complicate things if Pratt's body was found, though. While individual rattlesnake bites were seldom fatal, she suspected four or five would be more than enough to do the job.

Carefully navigating the uneven terrain, Marta made her way to the cars. In the SUV's glove compartment, she found a remote detonator. She stared at the two bodies, both men executed with gunshots to the head, and felt better about leaving Pratt to the snakes and coyotes.

She walked unsteadily to her four-wheeler, drove a safe distance away, and pushed the detonator button. The car disintegrated with a roar and a flash of fire, taking Pratt's SUV with it. She steered the ATV forward and flipped on its headlights. The blast hadn't reached Pratt, but he was no longer moving.

Marta drove toward the complex, stopping to wipe the detonator clean of any fingerprints and heave it as far as she could into the desert.

She was only a little upset they would not be able to track down those from whom Jason Pratt had been taking his orders.

"So, we've done everything we can for now?" Gillis asked.

They were in Marta's apartment.

She'd returned to the complex and gone immediately to Naomi.

"It's not a snake bite," Naomi told her. "You just scratched your ankle on a cactus or something."

"You're kidding."

"Nice tourniquet, though."

Marta stood. "Ha, Ha."

"If you want, I can cut a couple of exes in your leg and we can find someone to come and suck on it."

"Greetings, Marta Hamilton," her apartment said.

Marta sighed. "Not tonight. I'm too tired to yell at you."

"I only wanted to point out that you have a bra hanging from the back of your pants."

"Duly noted. I'm going to take a shower. In a few minutes, a man will come through that door. And I am finally going to get laid. If you make even the slightest noise, I will tell all the other apartments that you have an electron deficiency and you only shoot neutrons."

The apartment gasped. "That would be a lie. You would be a liar. Um ... for future reference, what is this 'getting laid?'"

"It's what will never happen to you if all the others think you are electron deficient. So shut the fuck up."

Marta's doorbell chimed. The scene unfolded just as Marta recalled. Gillis waited in the hallway. Marta invited him in. And as before, she'd removed her shirt when Gillis's counterpart from *I Love Lucy* interrupted them.

The Gillises relayed their message of urgency.

"Don't worry," she said. "It's been taken care of. Everyone can stand down and go home."

"You're sure?" The crooked smile bloomed across Gillis's face.

"You're leering," Marta said.

"Yes, I am."

She felt his eyes caress her.

"You have no idea how long we've waited . . ." Gillis said as he reached for her.

Marta stepped back.

"We? What do you mean . . . *we*?"

"I'm sorry," Gillis whispered as he pulled her to him and nuzzled her neck. "I misspoke . . ."

"Gillis, you tell me the truth. Is he still here?"

"Well . . . yes. He won't intrude. He just wants to watch."

"Oh, man, I . . . no. No, I can't. I don't have many qualms when it comes to sex. But this is just . . . it's just creepy. What would the *Lucy*-Marta think?"

Shit, Gunsmoke Gillis said to himself.

Shit, the Gillis from *I Love Lucy* agreed.

When they'd gone, the apartment said, "So, that was getting laid? Which was the laying part?"

While *Gunsmoke* Elvin complained adamantly about being impressed into time travel duty, he relished the limbo's liberation. Here, the power of his mind seemed unlimited. Complex theories became clear, their proofs or refutations almost elementary. His inability to retain many of the details upon his return frustrated him, although following his previous journey, tantalizing tidbits of knowledge had remained with him long enough to make a few skeletal notes and a few more bits of the time-travel puzzle were locked into place.

In the limbo, he could cast his mind to the farthest reaches of imagination. He sensed not only the raw almost frightening power of his intellect, but an increasing strength of perception as well.

And right now, he perceived a presence. The snooty Hall Monitor? No . . . No, something different. Someone . . .

"Marshall?" he said aloud.

"Elvin?" inquired a disembodied voice. "What are you doing here?"

41

RESURRECTION

MARTA HAMILTON WOKE TO a shrieking alarm clock in her Los Angeles hotel. She'd been up late, waiting for Gillis's report upon his return from the *Gunsmoke* universe. When she returned to Arizona, she would ask Wishcamper take a close look at the *Lucy* counterparts of the culprits— Buck and Milton—who had been identified there. He would evaluate whether the former GRC employees of this universe represented a threat.

In any other case, she would act on an assumption that the two men in question would soon accept bribes in this universe, as well. Such assumptions were problematic, though, where *Gunsmoke* was involved.

Marta had a breakfast meeting scheduled with Sir Rupert. She'd enjoyed seeing the guys from MI-6 yesterday. Mostly, it had been a social occasion. Sir Rupert asked how she was doing and encouraged her in her new administrative role.

She indulged herself in a luxuriant stretch, then made her way to the shower. She closed her eyes against the stream of warm water, remaining surprised, and a bit regretful, that she'd rejected Nigel. This whole Marshall thing was out of hand.

Standing there, she felt herself grow drowsy and drift

into a dream. About Marshall. *Dammit. Who else?*

In her dream, Marshall hovered someplace . . . above her? No, around her. A desert, or sea or . . . the limbo. Marshall floated in the timeless limbo that divided the dimensions of separate universes. Then Marta laughed, overcome by a sensation of giddy carelessness. Like the time she shared with Marshall in the Caribbean.

From the mists of this dream came a proclamation. "Marshall's not dead."

When she shook her head and opened her eyes, though, the jubilant voice remained. Marta from *Gunsmoke*. "*That's right. Come on. Figure out what's happening here. We found him. He's alive!*"

The *I Love Lucy* Marta had never before received an unanticipated visitation from the future. She required a moment to process the experience. First, she felt confused. Then, she recognized the sense of mental overcrowding, two trains of thought colliding one with the other.

"*Gunsmoke?*" she demanded. "*What is this? Is this about the people who tried to kill Senator Mumford?*"

"*Whoa,*" future-Marta said as she intercepted those thoughts, "*I only came because I thought you deserved to know—*"

"Know what?" Marta said aloud. "Oh, wait, that wasn't a dream? Marshall?"

Marta stepped from the shower and sat heavily on the toilet lid. Her heart hammered. She felt short of breath. The room spun for a moment. Water dripped from her body and puddled on the floor.

"Your Marshall's alive? He survived the—?"

"Jeez, I thought you'd handle this better," Gunsmoke Marta said. *"I thought at least you'd be happy ... I was ... hey, wait a minute. You're falling in love with the guy? How did that happen?"*

"I'm not in love with ..." Marta began, when the other half of her brain countered, *"Don't get hostile. I'm only reacting to what you are thinking ... and feeling. You might be able to deny it to yourself, but you can't deny it to me."*

Suddenly, scene after scene of unbridled, incredible sex bombarded *Gunsmoke* Marta's consciousness. Now, *she* felt lighthearted and out of breath, too.

"Oh, my," she said.

"So, you and Marshall have never—?"

"No, he's been missing for almost eight months. When we found him and he arrived on the platform, I hugged him and, well, kissed him and, um ... the kiss did get a little involved ..."

"So, you'll be following up?"

"Yes, yes, I think I see the wisdom in that. Before I go, though, you guys need to understand this."

So, the Marta from *Lucy* closed her eyes and absorbed information from her future self.

On the horrible day *The Joey Bishop Show* universe was blown into oblivion, Marshall and Carla O'Neill were being projected to the past of that universe from the *Gunsmoke* universe. The plan was an exchange of travelers between the two universes with each set of travelers attempting to alter the past of the destination universe at the request of their counterparts from the foreign world.

By pure happenstance, though, the timing of the exchange was precise. *Gunsmoke* Carla left the limbo between universal dimensions at exactly the instant *Joey Bishop* Carla crossed into the limbo.

While the physics of the disaster remained unclear, the meeting of the two Carlas caused a cataclysm. *Gunsmoke* Elvin believed that event sparked a phase shift that rearranged the *Joey Bishop Show* atoms into a swirling cloud of cosmic dust.

"So how did Marshall survive?"

"Marshall was just behind Carla, still in the limbo when everything blew up. The limbo protected him. But interference from the blast—some kind of shock wave, we think—masked the signals passing through the wormhole. And though Marshall was there the whole time, we had no way of knowing."

"How did you find him?"

"Elvin. We sent Elvin to your world so he could tell you about . . . well, you know all that. Anyway, Elvin says he and Marshall had a conversation in the limbo. Marshall was waiting. He didn't know anything had happened. Time doesn't exist there. Five minutes or eight months were all the same as far as Marshall was concerned.

"And when Elvin got back, we activated Marshall's monitor and there he was—lifeline and all. We brought him home as if nothing had happened."

"So, Elvin was the hero?"

"Sort of—I guess. His heroism was kind of lost in his panic when he went to put on his slippers and started screaming that someone had painted his toenails green."

"Is your Elvin searching for Sheila, as well?" the *Lucy*-Marta asked, wondering if Sheila could be hidden somewhere in the limbo, too.

"No," Marta's future self said. Future-Marta saw, through

her counterpart's memory, Marshall's obsessive prodding not to give up hope where Sheila was concerned. "I'm sorry to say that, without our Marshall being there to remind us, we have not maintained that search."

Present-Marta felt herself enveloped by a shroud of depression and a cold stoicism as she absorbed her future counterpart's sense of helplessness at the loss of her friends. With Marshall as a support, the *Lucy*-Marta had been able to do a decent job of suppressing her grief and anger at Sheila's death. Through the bared sentiments of her *Gunsmoke* counterpart, though, Marta saw that emotional solitude is a cold and lonely tomb.

"You need to open up a little," Marta advised her future counterpart. *"I know it's hard, but I can recommend it."*

"Well, I almost started a thing with Gillis, just out of loneliness, you know? And while I'm sure he wouldn't mind, I feel terrible about . . . about using someone that way."

"I understand. Gillis has always been sort of intriguing."

"Yes," her future self said. *"But mostly, Gillis is . . . safe."*

Present-Marta's first instinct was to find someone to tell the good news, but she was alone in Los Angeles. Instead, she sat at the small desk in the hotel room and punched up her virtual computer display. For as long as her memory allowed, she typed furiously, hoping to record every word her future self had conveyed, until she realized the words were not important.

When her mother had left for good, Marta began construction of a wall shielding her from emotion. Her father's death reinforced the wall. As she immersed herself in her career, she carefully added to it, brick by brick. Then came Marshall, stumbling along, dislodging bits and pieces

as he went, until he'd visited upon her the curse of introspection. The curse of *feeling*.

Her future counterpart was right, though. What each
could deny to themselves couldn't be hidden from the
other. A masterpiece of irony.

Marta surrendered and let her future counterpart's
emotions flow through her in a torrent of grief and
loneliness. Over the span of a lifetime, grief and loneliness
could not be denied. Happiness, though, lay hidden in the
moments.

She booked an early return flight to Phoenix and
hurried to catch her plane. She knew Sir Rupert would
understand.

42

DR. DOONAUGHTY STRIKES AGAIN

AS HE DEPLANED INTO the oven-like jetway leading into Terminal Four at Phoenix's Sky Harbor Airport, Marshall dreaded his three-hour drive back to the HRI facility. He found his luggage, walked into the superheated shade at the north curb and searched for a shuttle that would take him to the long-term parking lot. From there, he'd have to fight afternoon traffic on 202 and . . .

He barely had time to drop his bag and brace for impact when he saw her. Marta Hamilton homing in on him at practically a dead run—a petite black missile leaping the last three yards.

Marshall just managed to remain standing as he caught her upon impact.

A dozen passers-by offered grins as she put her arms around his neck and wrapped her legs around his skimpy waist. She clamped her mouth to his lips like a leach.

"Um . . . hello," Marshall said working his way around her tongue. "Glad to see you, too. But, um . . . is this any way for a federal government administrator to behave in public?"

He glanced sheepishly at the amused stares of pedestrians rushing around them as she clung with tenacity.

"We missed you."

"Well, do I have to go through this scene with everyone?"

"I missed you the most."

"What are you doing here? I thought you were in Los Angeles."

"We're leaving your car here. I got another one. We'll send someone from security to pick yours up. I have some things I couldn't wait to talk with you about."

The surrounding rush of people began to seem less and less significant to Marshall as he found a warmth that had been missing for weeks in Marta's eyes. He felt the unrelenting and suggestive pressure of her body against his.

"Um . . . I don't suppose the evil Dr. Dingus Doonaughty had anything to do with forcing you to change your plans, did he?"

Marta adopted a quizzical expression for only an instant. "Now that you mention it, yes. Yes, he did. I do have some demands that must be met lest he destroy civilization as we know it."

"Well, quickly then," Marshall said.

As they rode to the eighth floor of the attached parking garage, Marshall hoped they'd have the elevator to themselves. When a small group boarded at the fifth level, he held his bag strategically in front of himself to hide evidence of his enthusiasm. He remained undiscovered until a woman to his right dropped her wallet while fumbling with her purse. She and Marshall reached simultaneously for it, and nearly bumped heads on the way down.

"Pardon me," she said.

"Here, let me get that," Marshall replied as he swung his

small bag toward the floor and reached for the wallet with his other hand. The woman's eyes followed his hand as he retrieved the wallet, brought it to waist level and extended it to her.

As she accepted her wallet, she did a double take of which Marshall was uncomfortably aware. She glanced quickly to his eyes and could not restrain a fleeting third glance. Embarrassment showing, she next peeked at Marta, who by now had laced her fingers together with Marshall's. Marta gave the woman a smile and a wink.

The elevator doors opened, and Marshall hurried into the cavernous garage, towing Marta with him.

They separated from the other passengers, who dispersed through the vast structure. As they passed among rows of vehicles, Marta stopped and pulled Marshall to her.

"Marta, they have security cameras here, too."

She quickly glanced at the girders and network of pipes crisscrossing the ceiling. The angles of light left barely visible black spots of shadow where, indeed, surveillance cameras probably nestled.

"Hmmm. You're right. Still, the evil doctor insists."

She turned, and grasping his hand, hauled him after her as she darted across the bright driveway between the rows of vehicles and back into the shadows where her rental car waited.

"Now that that's out of the way," she said ten minutes later, "we can talk."

"We could have talked before." Marshall glanced anxiously around the garage for any foot traffic. "Someday you'll get us caught. I'm sure the U.S. Postal Service has rules against its administrators fooling around with employees in parking lots."

"I've checked the regulation manual and they don't address the issue specifically. Although . . . if you want, we can constrain ourselves to the . . . more formal and socially accepted forms of greeting."

Marshall thought back to the first frenzied night they'd made love, both of them breaking a long and arid abstinence imposed by the circumstances of their lives. He thought of the recent drought. He knew sex between them would not always be so spontaneous and urgent. He had enough married acquaintances to realize that eventually, people settle into a calmer and more conventional sexual routine. Out of sheer exhaustion if nothing else. Right now, though, he was making up for lost time and reveling in their carnal adventures.

"No. Of course, not. You just . . . I'm just not used to someone finding me this . . . this . . . compelling."

"Well, learn to live with it." She leaned across the seat to peck him on the cheek.

"Okay, what's so important that you had to come all the way here to pick me up?"

She raised a sarcastic eyebrow.

"I mean besides . . ."

"I wanted to be the first to tell you. You're not dead."

"Oh," he said with a note of uncertainty. "I think . . . I think I knew that."

"The *Gunsmoke* universe." She pulled him to her. "The explosion didn't kill *Gunsmoke* Marshall. He was lost in the limbo and they got him . . . you . . . back."

As Marta's story unfolded, Marshall again marveled at everything they still did not understand. Here was more evidence of what little control they had over this process, as well as the threat that now-diverging histories of the universes might represent.

"This is why we have to keep looking for Sheila," Marshall told her. "We don't know enough just to assume she's dead."

"Elvin and Gretchen are coming around," Marta said. "They agree, we have to try harder."

Marshall grinned. "I like not being dead. And I'm glad you came all the way here to tell me."

"It's more than that," Marta said in a wavering whisper. "I came because I had to remind myself that our life together is real."

She raised her eyes to his. In them, Marshall saw softness and depth new to him.

"The *Gunsmoke* Marta, every time we integrated ourselves, I felt something about her I didn't like. And because I couldn't pin it down, it scared me."

Marshall reached across the car seat and put his hand on hers.

"Then when she came into my consciousness to tell me they'd found you, I understood what it was. She was so... so buried inside herself. Even though she was thrilled to have you back, she still couldn't admit to the feelings she has for you. Seeing me the way I used to be is such a gift! My life was never bad, you understand. I'm proud of the life I've built, the professional success, what we've done here... But with you, every day is interesting in a way it never was before..."

Marshall gave her a lecherous grin.

"...and, no, it's not just the sex...it's being able to relax and let someone else close to me...Anyway, thanks for hanging in there."

Marta told him of the trauma her *Gunsmoke* counterpart endured while losing both Sheila and Marshall. With both her friends gone, she approached her duties with an even colder and more isolated persona than ever. She stayed with the program, because her friends had left a legacy she wanted to protect from the manipulative greed that killed them.

They were beyond the city now, driving east, the setting sun at their backs, Marshall at the wheel. Finally, Marta lapsed into a long silence as she stared out the window. Marshall left the silence in place. He was patient. He understood the silence.

"The scariest thing," she said finally, "was that I decided if you were back on active travel status, I'd have to stay away from you. Sexually, I mean. And emotionally. That's what the last few weeks have been about."

Marshall glanced at her with genuine surprise. "Why?"

"Preparing for what I thought was inevitable," Marta said, her eyes still fixed on the passing desert as it faded into nightfall. "I couldn't be so...invested in you. When you... left...I had to be able to continue. I had to protect myself from—"

"I still could die. Forget about time travel. I could get hit by a bus tomorrow."

"No, you couldn't. We don't have busses at the complex. You could only get hit by a golf cart, and I think you would survive that."

"You know what I mean. There are no guarantees."

"The thing is," Marta said as she turned and smiled at him, "I realize that now. I realize nothing comes without risk. Until I was able to see reality through the mind of my *Gunsmoke* counterpart, I didn't understand what I've missed. I've been pretty much willing to risk anything intellectually or physically to accomplish my goals. But not emotionally."

"And now?"

She took a deep breath.

"I want to take the risk. You have to understand, though, that this is all new for me. This is an aspect of myself I don't know very well . . ."

Her eyes and her smile left him with a hopefulness he hadn't dared feel for weeks.

". . . so, I'm warning you. This may end up being a bumpy ride. I really do want to try, though."

Marshall grinned and reached across the car seat to take her hand.

"I like your bumps," he said. "I'll do my best to hang on."

MARTA AND MARSHALL HAPPILY tucked themselves in for the evening, while in Phoenix, a ninety-three-year-old man named Sean Brady, six months removed from his home in a small town on the high plains of eastern New Mexico, undertook a lonely evening ritual.

He'd abandoned that town, the home of his childhood, at the age of eighteen. He'd never intended to live there again. A newspaper career took him on a geographical odyssey through the western United States. A divorce in his late thirties sent him on a journey of failed relationships, a few of the partings bitter, but most amiable.

Finally, he ended up where Marta Hamilton had begun—embracing his emotional solitude.

He'd returned to that hometown in his sixties to participate in a retirement business venture which, combined with social security and a pension from his last newspaper posting, made his financial life comfortable, if not spectacular. He'd agreed to the business proposal because his participation would afford him time to write.

It did, but the words wouldn't come. Half a dozen fits

and starts left his computer littered with the bones of manuscripts that never drew breath.

On his ninety-second birthday, he mistook forward for reverse and drove his car through the wall separating his garage and kitchen. The next week, he forgot to turn off the stove and a neighbor helped him use an extinguisher to put out the fire.

"He's still sharp," Sean's doctor told his three sons. "I see no signs of dementia. But he needs help with the day-to-day task of living. As you know, he's on a number of blood-pressure medications. I'm most concerned that he's not taking them regularly."

Liam, the son who lived in Phoenix, suggested Sean consider assisted living facilities there. His instinct was to say no. Trying something new would be difficult for anyone of his age. What swayed him, though, was the worry that he knew complicated his sons' and grandchildren's lives.

So, he moved to Arizona, and as always, found a way to make the most of it, maintaining a sense of humor, if not a sense of adventure.

Unlike some elderly people whose lives hadn't quite worked out the way they'd hoped, he didn't dwell on past mistakes. Except for a moment each evening, waiting for the sleep aid to kick in, when he thought of Maggie Stanfield and what might have been.

ACKNOWLEDGMENTS

As always, first and foremost, I thank Nancy for her patience and dedication to all my endeavors. Thanks to Laura Taylor, who has championed my work from the day we met at the Southern California Writers' Conference. Thanks to Shanna McNair, Scott Wolven and Elyssa East of The Writers' Hotel who have shaped my education. Thanks to Jessica Therrien and Holly Youmans of Acorn Publishing for the opportunity.

The three books that so far make up this series were written several years ago. During that time, my writing companion was Hef the Cat. She lived for twenty years but was not around to see this project through to completion. Her successor, Lumpy Cat, has bravely picked up the torch. (I would never have allowed either of them to be waxed.)

Mike Murphey Books

Tales of Physics, Lust and Greed

Taking Time
Wasting Time
Killing Time

www.mikemurpheybooks.com

AUTHOR'S NOTE

Thanks so much for reading *Wasting Time*, the second book in my Physics, Lust and Greed Series. Writers write for a lot of reasons, but one of the most important is to be read. With a couple million new titles to choose from, believe me, it's a tough market out there. If you enjoyed this book, or even if you didn't, you can do one more thing to help. Write a review and post it on Amazon here:

http://www.amazon.com/review/create-review?&asin=B08HSRDWX2

Thanks again for reading Wasting Time, and I hope you will be on the lookout for Killing Time, the third installment in the Physics, Lust and Greed series, appearing soon.